SPURIOUS

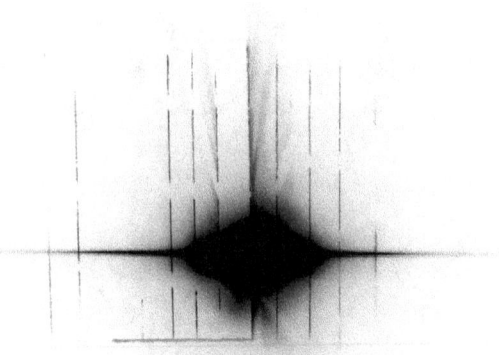

SPURIOUS

THE WORLD HE THOUGHT HE KNEW

RYAN HARTUNG

Published 2014 By Molecularly Primed Publishing

Spurious : The world he thought he knew
Copyright © 2014 Ryan Hartung
ISBN 978-1-942123-03-3 Paperback
ISBN 978-1-942123-04-0 Electronic
www.ryanhartung.com

Cover illustration and interior design by Raven Tree Design
www.raventreedesign.com

Contents

This book is dedicated to my beautiful wife Elizabeth.

PROLOGUE:

BACK TO THE PAST

John Coulter glared at Chet. His longtime friend and current roommate sat across a sea of beige shag carpet covering their rental house's living room floor. Chet tried not to notice the visual daggers being thrown his way, but instead focused on a trailer from a new movie called *Back to the Future* being broadcast on their small hazy color TV.

"That movie's going to be great!" Chet exclaimed with excitement in his voice once the preview was finished, "Michael J. Fox is hilarious. Don't you think?" Chet said turning his attention away from the TV and towards his annoyed friend. Chet had to dig his toes deep into the thick shag to swivel the chair containing his hefty two-hundred pound frame to face John. Chet's light brown unkempt stringy hair flowed in multiple directions due to the static electricity generated by turning his head against the chair's worn fabric.

John stood in the middle of the doorway adjacent to the house's kitchen. At just under six feet and built like a linebacker, John's muscular frame protruded from under his warm winter red knit sweater. His dark brown eyes and chiseled facial features gave Chet's disheveled appearance another once-over, but he still didn't speak. John was still struggling with what had gone wrong between him and his girlfriend, of less than a month, Lisa.

After a few moments of silence, save for the endless commercial blather emanating from their small TV, Chet knew John needed a slight push to call his latest girlfriend and talk out whatever issue they were having.

"Look, do you really want to have to explain to everyone you work with why this girl they've heard so much about didn't come with you to the Christmas party?" Chet questioned.

Chet waited a few seconds and after not getting a response, "well?"

"No, not really," John sullenly replied.

"And, do you really like this girl? Is she someone you want to continue to see? Or is she someone you just don't imagine yourself being with for the long term?" Chet questioned again.

"No, I could see myself dating her for quite a while actually," John replied even more sullenly this time than that last.

"Then push down your pride, give her a call and tell her you were wrong so you crazy kids can patch things up then. It's not too late. You've got at least three or four hours before your Christmas work party starts. That's more than enough time for you two to make up, get some dinner and vamoose to your company's party."

"Vamoose?" John thought, but he simply nodded in acceptance. He knew his TV loving friend was right and had given good advice; even if John couldn't remember the last time he had seen Chet alone with a girl, not to mention dating one.

John slowly walked to the back of the small rental house where the bedrooms were located and picked up the receiver of his beige corded phone. He could hear the dial tone's monotonous sound radiating from the earpiece, but he didn't raise it to his head. Was what he had said so bad? He had only told Lisa that he wasn't ready to get *that* serious yet and that it was fine with him if she wanted to date other guys for the time being. Of course dating other people would have applied to him too, but he didn't have any other prospects at the moment.

John took hold of the phone's beige spiraled knotted chord and dropped the receiver. He watched as the weight of the receiver, dangling like a perch on fishing line, spun out the kinks and knots in the coiled telephone wire. After a minute the receiver stopped spinning and hung motionless. John's momentary spurt of courage had melted away and John set the dangling receiver back onto its cradle.

"This is ridiculous," John muttered as he turned and stared out of his bedroom window. He tried to forget the phone call he knew he would eventually have to make. Outside, the New Jersey winter was in full swing. A white powdery snow had fallen the night before and had blanketed most of the surrounding areas in upwards of three inches of the frozen precipitation. Standing next to the window, John could feel the cold air sneaking in through the single pane of glass and around the rotting wood of the window's sill.

John turned from the window and walked back into the hallway, still not having made the call and stopped mid-stride when he looked up from the shag walkway and saw Chet standing in his path. Chet had a serious look plastered onto his normally jovial face, which John didn't appreciate one bit. Chet pointed John back towards his bedroom with a stern scowl and a quick flick of his wrist. John didn't utter a defense and admitted defeat. He would make the dreaded call.

As John disappeared through his open door Chet smiled at John's quickness to obey his command. From time to time Chet loved to mess with John in some way or another and from the limited interactions he had with Lisa Chet knew she was a keeper. Chet returned to his swivel chair opposite of the TV and turned the volume down just enough, hoping he might accidentally overhear John begging for forgiveness.

John sat on his aging bed and sunk deep into the fabric as the springs quickly flattened like they always did. John knew that eventually his engineering job at *Evergreen Resources* would pay off and purchasing a new bed was close to the top of his priority list when it did. Although *Evergreen Resources* was a relatively new company at only five years old, he understood its tremendous potential and he planned on being a major part of its upwards trajectory.

John reached over to his nightstand, picked up the beige receiver and quickly dialed Lisa's number before he lost his nerve.

"Hello?" Lisa's voice sweetly rang to John through the receiver.

"Hey, it's me," John said and stood as his nerves got the better of him.

"Make it quick, I'm getting ready for a date," Lisa quipped in return; the sweetness in her voice quickly disappearing.

"Come on, don't be like that. I'm sorry. What I said was stupid. I don't want you to date other guys. I only want you to be dating me."

"Well, why did you say that then?" Lisa asked. John could hear the hurt in her voice. Those stupid, stupid words. He had never meant to hurt her, just the opposite, he knew she could do so much better than him. What did she even see in him?

"I don't know," John lied, "it was stupid. I just thought that maybe weren't ready to be serious, you know?"

"Well, in my opinion you weren't thinking," she replied. "Did I ever give you even a hint of wanting to be with somebody else?"

John stopped pacing and dug his toes into the deep shag carpet. "You're right, I wasn't' thinking and no, you've never given me any indication you would rather be with somebody else." John allowed himself to become as submissive as a dog on its back and its tail between its legs. "Please, can we put this behind us and go to my work party tonight?" he gingerly pleaded.

Lisa paused before replying, hoping John would be squirming on the other end of the phone and finally returned, "Alright, I'll go with you to your party, but I've got to cancel my other date first and he's not going to be happy."

John, thinking she had to be joking, let a stressed chuckle escape, but was not greeted with a response on the end of the receiver. She was joking, wasn't she?

"Ahem," John cleared his throat, "well, how about I pick you up around five and we can go out to dinner before the party?" he meekly asked.

"That's not going to work John. These are the people you work with and I want to look nice at the party, so how about you pick me up at seven so I have enough time to get ready?" Lisa said.

"Okay, that sounds great too. I'll be by to pick you up at seven. See you then," John said while adding excitement about the evening into his voice. The phone clicked on the other end. John knew Lisa had hung up to start getting ready. John thought Lisa was beautiful even without make-up, but when she put in the extra time she could make herself appear absolutely stunning.

John let out a sigh as the tension of the conversation slowly escaped his body. Women can be exasperating he thought to himself. Even in his cold drafty bedroom, the uncomfortableness of the conversation had made John's forehead perspire. He wiped his brow with the back of his sleeve before returning to the living room and updating Chet on the situation. In the end John just hoped Chet could give him some solid advice on a flower arrangement she might like, but highly doubted it.

Lisa Paulus angrily tugged on her sleek black dress until her head and wet thick auburn hair emerged through the stretchy fabric and onto the other side. She let the black semi-sheer material flow down her athletic body until it stopped just short of her bare knees.

"Men!" she exclaimed to no one in particular. Lisa looked in the direction of her white and orange tabby cat Merlin resting on a pair of her light pink nursing scrubs, as if expecting him to offer some sort of feline support. Merlin gazed back at her, knowing she was talking to him, but quickly lost interest and resumed washing his feet with rhythmic laps of his rough pink tongue.

"Ha, what am I talking to you for, you're one of them aren't you," Lisa said to Merlin. This time; however, Merlin refused to acknowledge the voice and remained focused at his cleaning task at hand.

Lisa huffed into her small apartment bathroom. She flipped on the light switch and winced at the hideousness of the sky blue tile that covered the room's walls. What were the interior decorators in the 60's and 70's thinking she wondered? Even the toilet was colored a light porcelain blue. As atrocious as the bathroom was, it wasn't the true cause of her angst. John, that silly man, had waited until the last possible remaining seconds of the day to call and apologize. Now she only had about an hour and a half to get ready and even that was pushing it. She lived twenty miles away from him and another thirty miles from Hoboken, where the party was going to be held.

At the ripe old age of twenty-four Lisa had found good men hard to come by and John was a breath of fresh air. He was highly motivated, not much unlike her, very handsome and seemed to have a good heart buried under his somewhat intimidating muscular physique. He had studied hard enough to earn a degree in electrical engineering and from what he had told her *Evergreen Resources* was one of the most promising up and coming businesses in the area.

Lisa quickly began blow drying and then teasing her hair; creating more and more volume until the look she was going for was achieved. She could do her make-up in a flash; it was the current trend in women's hair styles that took forever.

"There's no way these hairdos are going to last," she muttered and she teased her long locks for a little more volume.

"You better be worth it Mr. Coulter," Lisa continued as she shifted gears and began applying her foundation.

Only a few minutes after Lisa had finished her makeup she heard the doorbell chime and hurried up to the peep-hole of her apartment's front door. There, standing in the apartment's dimly lit hallway, was John holding a dozen yellow roses.

Lisa smiled. Yeah, she could see herself ending up with him, but first, he needed to be trained. She didn't want somebody who wasn't going to be open and honest with here. This argument had been their first and this time John had passed with flying colors.

After waiting a few seconds for effect Lisa gently pulled the off-white apartment door open and motioned for John to come inside.

"You didn't need to bring me flowers," Lisa said, then added with a smile, 'but I'm glad you did." She gave John a hug and a quick peck on the cheek and taking the flowers into the kitchen.

"I'm glad you like them," John replied with a twinkle in his eye. Yep, I'm definitely glad Chet and I agreed that flowers were going to be necessary, John thought.

"Shall we go?" John asked after Lisa had exchanged the roses' crinkly cellophane wrapping with a more suitable clear reddish-pink glass vase along with some water.

"We shall," Lisa said with a smile.

As soon as they exited the warmth of Lisa's apartment building, the New Jersey winter wind hit them with its full force. The sky was black, as the sun had disappeared a few hours ago from the horizon and the evening temperatures were dropping rapidly.

Lisa and John hurried to his car and once inside, sat shivering in silence while the engine slowly warmed.

"This definitely seems like Christmas weather," Lisa mentioned after she had warmed enough and her teeth stopped chattering. As they began their drive, the flow of heated air became hotter and hotter, causing Lisa to sweat inside her warm winter court. Although the evening sky was devoid of any clouds, the wind was howling and blowing the previous night's snow. John grabbed the steering wheel with both hands as they hit another stretch of roadway completely engulfed in thick blowing waves of snow.

"Given our current weather conditions, I guess I'm not going to be drinking that much tonight," John quipped as he squinted, trying to see the road through the snowy haze.

"That's good since you know I'm a lush," Lisa said with a giggle. John briefly stole a glance in her direction and shot her a quick grin before returning his attention to snowy road that lay before them. On their first date Lisa had told John how alcohol had torn her family apart and because of that she rarely drank. Lisa refused to let herself fall into the same vice that had taken her father and ruined her childhood.

After an hour and twenty minute drive, that under normal conditions would have been completed in under forty-five minutes, Lisa and John arrived at their destination. Although it was now a little past eight o'clock on a Saturday night, the frigid temperatures and strong winds had left the normally bustling Hoboken streets fairly deserted.

John shifted the car into park and the turned off the engine. A flashing marque above the side walk in front of their parked vehicle read Burly Bar in bright pink neon with a single red neon cherry off to the right. Almost instantly after the car's engine had been silenced and the warmed air filling the car had ceased, the blistering wind outside began eating away at their steel and glass bubble of warmth.

With the wind whipping around and howling against the car windows, neither of the two was extremely anxious to leave the still slightly warm confines of the car.

"Alright, on the count of three get into the building as fast as we can, okay?" John asked Lisa smiling.

"If you say so," Lisa replied and pulled her thin winter dress coat around her even thinner semi-sheer black dress.

"One," John said and looked at his date.

"Two," Lisa added looking back at him and smiling.

"Three," they said in unison.

Simultaneously they threw open their respective car door and jumped out of the car. The force of the evening wind caught both of them by surprise, but it did nothing to deter their plan. They both forced their doors shut against wind and rushed over the curb and onto the sidewalk. Lisa was in the lead and almost to the door when one of her heels hit a patch of ice. Out of nowhere she was falling backwards and she knew the landing was going to be painful. Before she had even fallen halfway, John was at her back to catch her. His strong frame pushed her back upright and once she regained her footing she dashed through the bar's door with John right behind her.

"Wow, that was close!" she exclaimed once they were well inside the building.

"Yep, good thing I was there to catch you," John replied triumphantly and not pushing his chest out at all.

"Yes, you saved me," Lisa feigned and grabbed his arm faking the need for support. Inside the building, John and Lisa realized they weren't yet in the bar, but on a landing with stairs leading down. The stairs were wet with melting snow and Lisa knew her heels provided little traction. She carefully stepped down each concrete stair while clutching the hand rail with all of her strength. All was well until she slipped again on the last stair. John, watching her movements like a hawk, swooped in and stabilized her before she had a chance to fall.

"Now I've had to save you twice," he said, proud of his athleticism, to which he received a generous smile.

John stepped in front of Lisa and opened the thick black door at the bottom of the stairs. Immediately the smell of stale beer and musty water filled their nostrils.

"This place smells worse than my fraternity's bathroom," John commented.

Lisa laughed and replied, "I would have felt bad for you if it didn't!"

While they were laughing and enjoying each other's company, a tall broad shouldered man started walking towards them. John noticed the man out of the corner of his eye, but played it coy, as if he didn't see him coming. Once the man was within arm's length, John quickly rounded and threw a jab at the man's stomach. The m, however, had been expecting something of the type and daftly dogged to the side and caught John in a tight bear hug from the rear.

"Come on Hal, not in front of the lady," John pled knowing he was now completely helpless in front of his beautiful date. John had thought roughhousing with his friend and of course gaining the upper hand, could only add to his physical intrigue he knew Lisa felt. He had not counted on Hal being so quick though.

Harry "Hal" Roberts let him go at his request with a little shove. He then flipped his Miami Vice styled bangs out of his face with a flick of his wrist and approached Lisa.

"So, this is your new beauty I've been hearing so much about." Hal thrust out his large hand, which Lisa promptly took. Lisa noticed he was maybe an inch taller than John and probably a little wider in the shoulders too. Even if John hadn't told her about his gym regiment, she could tell just by looking at him he regularly worked out. Hal didn't have that same appearance, but Lisa judged from his body type that he could be quite muscular too if he put the time and effort into it. Hal did have a much thicker and longer head of hair than John. Although both of them had dark brown hair, it was apparent Hal put extensive time and effort into forming its look just right. Lisa instinctively wanted to run her hands through Hal's thick hair, but gripped his hand harder resisting the urge.

"I'm Lisa. It's nice to meet you Hal, John's told me a lot about you," Lisa replied as courteously as she could. John had really only mentioned Hal briefly and that meant she knew he was John's boss and was quite a lady's man. Now, meeting him in person, she could see why he was good with the ladies. Hal had a vibe, an aura about him. His demeanor said, "I'm confident and successful," but he didn't come off boastful or arrogant. With his confidence and good looks Lisa felt an immediate attraction.

"Only the good stuff I hope. You can't believe any of the bad that comes out of this guy's mouth." Hal said. He flashed a wide grin showing his pure white teeth and perfect smile. "Let's go get some drinks!" he added.

"Maybe later Hal, Lisa here…" John started but was cut off. He wanted to inform Hal that Lisa didn't drink and he would only be having a few himself.

"Come on man, this here's our Christmas party we've got to get a drink, right Lisa?" Hal insisted staring at Lisa for support.

"Why not," she replied feeling put on the spot. She saw John give her a questioning look and returned a reassuring smile. She hadn't had a drink in a long time, but she didn't want to spoil the mood either. In the end Lisa reassured herself that she wasn't her father and she would be okay.

Hal led them to the long mahogany bar a couple yards from the tavern's entrance. He leaned against a thick brass railing, where the finish had long since been rubbed off.

"Three boiler makers please," he directed to the bartender.

John heard the order and knew what was coming. Again he looked at Lisa and whispered, "We really don't have to have a drink Lisa."

"Relax, it'll be fine. It's just one drink," she replied.

With fewer than twenty people, all from Hal and John's company, in the bar the drinks were served up in short order. Three tall beers in ice chilled mugs and three shots of premium gold colored whisky. Lisa hadn't heard Hal's order and was surprised to see two drinks slid in front of her. After years of watching her father drink himself to death the beer before her was ridiculously obvious, but she was unsure what was in the shot. Lisa sniffed its contents and recoiled at its putrid smell.

Hal, oblivious to her displeasure in his choice of drink, pulled John to one side and Lisa to his other. "To a great Christmas and a great new year," Hal said as he raised his shot of whisky high into the air. John, unable to see Lisa around Hal, clinked with is friend. They dropped the whisky into the light yellow beer, which over flowed and spilled onto the bar's richly lacquered surface. Lisa, not wanting to be left out, quickly copied and followed suit. All three of them raised their glasses, toasted once more and drank their fill.

Hal finished first, with John only a hair behind. They slammed their drinks onto the bar pleased with their manliness. Lisa forced her throat to gulp down the vile mixture; ignoring her taste buds' complaints. Before she finished another beer had already been placed in front of her.

John walked around Hal over to Lisa's other side. "Don't drink that," he said about the second beer in front of her. "Let me finish this one and I'll take care of it for you."

"It's not going to kill me," Lisa snapped. "Seriously, everything is alright. It's only two drinks, I can handle it," she replied trying to soften her tone towards the end. Lisa wasn't sure why she had just snapped at John, he was only trying to watch out for her.

John slightly winced at the change in Lisa's behavior, but tried not to show it. He was worried for her. The combination of an empty stomach along with alcohol was a recipe for disaster. The stories she had told him of her father's metamorphosis from a gently loving father to a brutal savage when he drank was something he'd never forget. His family was a hodgepodge of casual drinkers, but rarely did anyone get too out of line. In fact, the worst John could remember was his grandpa stripping and wanting to give everyone in the family a giant bear hug after a few too many beers. This was different.

Hal, John and Lisa talked for fifteen minutes at the bar, exchanging pleasantries with newly arriving co-workers in between telling various stories. John and Hal slowly nursed their second beers and to John's relief Lisa hadn't touched hers.

The music had certainly grown louder over the last few minutes and John noticed a stage at the end of a large swath of tables towards the bar's furthest wall. Atop the stage were four microphone stands and to his dismay a large karaoke machine.

"Let's karaoke," Lisa exclaimed also noticing the lit up stage. She felt looser and freer than she had in years. Lisa grabbed her waiting beer, spilling a few drops with her jerky motion and pulled it off the bar. She drank a gulp and marveled at how much the taste of it had improved since the disgusting boilermaker.

"Come on John," she demanded pulling him towards the stage.

John recoiled from her vice-like-grip. "That's not really for me," he admitted wanting nothing to do with the beckoning microphones.

"Come on, don't be such a baby. It'll be fun," Lisa chided and took another swig of beer.

"Yeah, come on and show us your stuff," Hal joined in, making John feel even more uncomfortable.

"Really guys, I'm not going up there," John said with firm resolution.

"What about you Hal? Wanna sing with me?" Lisa asked. She turned away from John to Hal slightly swaying.

"Why not. I don't have any insecurities," he said and shot John a devious smile.

Hal and Lisa left John standing alone by the bar. With her drink in one hand and Hal's hand in the other, she rushed towards the back of the bar. The glittering lights and pulsing music seemed to call her by name to the stage. Lisa jumped onto the stage and started thumbing through the list of possible songs.

John watched with interest, wondering what song Lisa was going to choose. Normally, John wouldn't have liked seeing Hal alone with any girl he was dating, but this time karaoke was involved. John was happy just not being on stage.

After thumbing through the song choices available, Lisa finally settled on *Stand by Your Man*. John watched as Lisa and Hal whispered back and forth and at one point Hal put his large hand on her arm. But again his jealousy took a back seat to not wanting to be on stage. By the time their off-key rendition of the song was complete, Lisa's second glass of beer was empty. All one hundred and ten pounds of Lisa started stumbling off the stage, when she caught the tip of her foot on the protective side stripping. If not for Hal's quick reflexes she would have face planted into a basket of popcorn on the nearest table.

"Woo, thanks Hal," she gushed, "you're such a gentleman. Somebody must have just put that there, cause I know it wasn't there before," she slurred. John rushed to the stage to help Lisa out of Hal's strong arms.

"Thanks Hal, I've got her," John said asserting his boyfriend status.

Lisa pushed against John's chest, not wanting to be held. "You're no fun. Hal, now Hal's fun. He sang with me," she said. Hal smiled at John at the comment.

"Come on Lisa, I think maybe you've had enough to drink, maybe we should leave."

"I'm not going anywhere," Lisa stated in defiance. "Hal, let's go get another drink."

Before Hal could say yes or no to the drink, John intervened. "I'm not going to stay here watching you get drunk."

"Good, I don't want you here," she angrily spat. How dare he tell her if she could or couldn't drink. He wasn't her father. It wasn't his right. Deep down Lisa knew she was drunk, that she should stop drinking and that she should go home. But the alcohol easily masked her common sense. Right now all she wanted was another drink and to party.

"Please, let's just go home," John pleaded. He knew she wasn't used to drinking and only had her best interest at heart.

"You can leave! I'm staying," she retorted in defiance and walked to the bar.

"Don't worry about her buddy. I'll see that she gets home alright," Hal reassured, placing a reassuring hand on John's shoulder.

John was so mad at Lisa's demeanor and the way she'd been treating him, against his better judgment he agreed and left the bar in disgust.

With John now out of the picture, Hal strode to where the beautiful Lisa was seated at the bar nursing a fresh Long Island iced tea. "So what do you want to do now?" he asked.

"I want to sing," she replied, dramatically throwing her arms into the air. She hopped off the bar stool with her stiff drink in tow and headed back towards the stage. Hal followed like a leopard stalking its prey. "Like taking candy from a baby," he muttered with a sinister smile. Too bad John never specified *which* home he needed to get her back to.

The night's events blurred by Lisa like a blowing torrential sideways rain. She had difficulty keeping her balance, but continued to drink. By the end of the night, she hadn't a clue how many drink's she'd drank or how many songs she'd sung, but she was pretty sure it had been awesome.

"Take me home whatever your name is," she slurred to Hal as the evening came to a close. Only the two of them, a couple of bartenders and three other employees from Evergreen Resources, too plowed to drive were left in the beer-smelling bar.

"Do you mean your place or mine?" Hal asked. He might be the type of guy to take advantage of a beautiful inebriated woman, but he still knew no meant no.

"Yours you big hunk," Lisa slurred. Truthfully she didn't care where they went. Almost all of her brain power was currently being diverted to stopping the room from swaying. She was so drunk off Long Island iced teas the brief vision of her boyfriend John passing through her mind barely registered.

Hal grinned widely and quickly moved to the bar's cashier to pay his tab. At first glance he was shocked to see the sizable tab, but reasoned it would be worth it later. Hal paid the man in cash for the overpriced drinks and helped Lisa to his car.

The snow had tapered to light flurries during their time inside the bar, greatly increasing Hal's line of sight compared to earlier in the evening. Hal's American muscle car's V8 engine quickly warmed the cabin's air as they traveled to his condo.

Twenty minutes later and inside Hal's bachelor pad, he directed Lisa to his bedroom's bathroom. Lisa splashed water on her face in an attempt to revive her senses. Her eyes felt groggy and she was certain the room's spinning had only increased since the drive from the bar. She looked out the bathroom's door and saw Hal's King sized bed. The bed beckoned her to come to it. Lisa didn't have the energy to resist.

Lisa slid herself across the satin bedspread and onto what she could only describe as the best pillow she'd ever felt in her life. Before she had a chance to close her eyes, Hal appeared in the doorway.

"Are we comfortable?" she thought he asked, but wasn't sure. She mumbled something in reply and before she knew it he was lying next to her. Thirty minutes later Lisa was fast asleep. Hal lie next to her with his hands clasped behind his head and a wide smile on his face. Unable to sleep, he went into the kitchen and foraged for food. While eating a crudely made ham sandwich Hal reasoned his extracurricular activities with Lisa were through for the night and called her a cab.

Lisa barely remembered anything from the latest parts of the evening the next day. However she knew one thing for certain, Hal the magnificent had been nothing but a cheap parlor trick. She had been made a fool. There were a few things that Lisa was now certain of. The first was that hell would have to be more frozen than the current New Jersey turnpike before John would ever find about her one-time transgression. She knew she desperately needed to call him and apologize for her behavior the previous night. The third item Lisa was certain of was the need for aspirin, sleep and water; today she could not exist without any of them.

CHAPTER 1

A TIME TO KILL

O ver the past few weeks, Hal had been preoccupied with visions of Lisa more than usual. Over twenty years had passed since their one-time love affair, but time so far had not diluted his memory of that one night stand. He still remembered her horrid, but humorous karaoke singing and her complete lack of tolerance for alcohol. That intolerance however was partially responsible for their one night. Of course Hal knew his dashingly good looks and quick witted personality had also played a considerable role.

Each time Hal reminisced over that fantastic evening, he wished he had acted differently. If he was ever granted a do over, that cab would have never been called, Lisa would have never gone back to John and the rest would be history. But the past was the past as it had now been over twenty years ago.

Over the years he had seen less and less of Lisa and he guessed that could be partially responsible for still feeling her allure. Each time he saw her it appeared time had only added to her beauty. Now, happily married to John Coulter for most of those twenty years and with a college aged son, she rarely came around the office anymore. Maybe she didn't want to be reminded of that night now so long ago, or what could have been, or maybe she had told John about their one night together and he was keeping her at bay. Even though she was largely absent from his life, Hal knew what a great woman she had become and how lucky John was.

Regardless of the reason, Lisa had become Hal's primary obsession. Money, power, fame, he had all of those and in large supply. What he didn't have was a woman worthy of his stature to share it with. Lisa had everything, beauty, wits, the drive to succeed and she was gorgeous. For Hal, Lisa was the unobtainable object his heart desired. In Hal's mind he had waited in the shadows for Lisa long enough. As his dad had always said, "Either crap, or get off the pot," and for Hal it was time to get off the pot.

Hal reached for the sleek black office phone sitting off to the right on his massive reddish brown mahogany desk. Hal was still a somewhat taller man than normal at six foot even and had only recently started balding on the front of his head. At fifty nine years old, Hal was used to getting what he wanted. No was not an option. Anything or anyone that stood as an obstacle between him and his target was swiftly and methodically dealt with. Many people and corporations over the years had attempted to thwart his attempts at growing his ever rising empire to new heights and not one of them had succeeded.

Still holding the receiver and hearing the buzz of the beckoning dial tone over the sound of his computers cooling fan, Hal turned and stared out over the sprawling metropolis of the Dallas-Fort Worth area. Gazing through the thick glass panes that separated his gigantic CEO's office from the outside world, he remembered some of his greatest triumphs against those that had considered standing in his way.

There was Art Manchild who had dared to take Hal's burgeoning business at the time to court, now over a decade ago, over a land dispute in which the court had sided with Hal's company *Evergreen Resources*. Hal's lawyers had won that battle for him and later the court awarded him half of Art Manchild's net worth via a civil suit for punitive damages. The civil suit hadn't been necessary as Art Manchild's business had all but been destroyed by the first verdict. However, the civil suit sent a message to those that would stand in Hal's path. Think twice before you messed with Hal Roberts.

Years after his struggle with Art Manchild, there had been Peggy, one of Hal's many beautiful secretaries. She had foolishly threatened to expose his less than legal attempts at manipulating the Environmental Protection Agency for the rights to particular mining and drilling expeditions. Once she had threatened him, Hal had one of his many trusted private eyes dig up more dirt on Peggy than was probably necessary. In the end they came to terms where she received a hefty pay raise alongside a nice promotion in exchange for keeping her mouth shut. Of course her promotion including her position being transferred to one of *Evergreen Resources'* less desirable locations. Peggy had been a learning lesson for him. After Peggy, Hal still hired attractive secretaries, but only ones smart enough to plan his schedule, nothing more.

Most of Hal's petty skirmishes had been before *Evergreen Resources'* rise to international prominence and certainly before the corporate headquarters had been moved to the top floors of one of Dallas' tallest skyscrapers, where Hal was now standing.

Hal thought of John Coulter and what a brilliant designer in the company's energy division he had been and still was. Throughout the course of John's career Hal had steadily raised him amongst the ranks of his peers. Not only did John deserve his promotions, but it allowed Hal the opportunity to inch his way closer to Lisa without raising any red flags. Now, John was one of the top project leaders in the company and a brilliant inventor.

Hal's thoughts shifted back to Lisa. He was tired of attempting advances on her only to be shot down time after time. She was completely devoted to her husband and until he was out of the picture, Lisa would continue to be off limits.

Hal depressed the numbers on the stylish office phone and waited for his associate Mick to answer.

"Mr. Roberts, it's been a long time," Mick's gruff voice answered. In the background Hal heard what sounded like electric power tools.

"Where are you at?" Hal questioned out of curiosity.

"Better for both of us you don't know," he replied.

Hal understood and didn't ask again. Mick was one of Hal's sketchier acquaintances he'd known for years. Someone of Hal's stature rarely arrived at their position by one hundred percent hard work. For someone like Hal, situations were almost certainly to arise where less than legal means were needed, which was where Mick's useful services came into play.

"Can you talk or should I call you later?" Hal asked. He knew sometimes Mick's less than legal opportunities required the utmost concentration. Failure to concentrate could mean jail or worse.

"My guys have it under control," Mick replied. Hal heard a sharp scream in the background and shuddered to think what Mick might be up to. "What can I do for you?"

"I have a little problem I need taken care of, but I'd rather not talk about it over the phone."

"Not a problem," Mick replied fully understanding Hal's request. "Let's meet at Fred's diner for dinner."

"I haven't been to that place in years," Hal said as he remembered the sixty's styled eatery. "Say six o'clock?"

"I'll be there," Mick replied. Before Mick hung up his end of the phone, Hal heard the power tools running again and a quick yelp from someone in the background before the call was finally disconnected. Another shiver ran down his spine at Mick's clandestine activities.

Being a CEO of one of the world's fortune 500 companies, Hal had little difficulty in finding something to occupy his time before his meeting with Mick. After what had only seemed like minutes, Hal's leggy secretary popped her head into his spacious office and let him know she was leaving for the evening.

"Five o'clock already Pam?" Hal said as he noticed the time.

"Yep, sure is," she said with a spring in her step.

"Alright, see you tomorrow," he said. He watched her with hungry eyes as she turned and left for the evening. One of these days he'd have to find the time to make a move on her. Of course he wanted Lisa to be his wife, but Hal had no intention of also giving up the finer things in life. Like his father used to say, "Monogamy is a type of wood, not a way of life."

At five thirty Hal locked his computer and left his office for the night. Driving through the large metropolis and past the touristy stockyards, he wound his way to a portion of Fort Worth usually only visited by the locals. On the end of a long block of semi dilapidated structures was a bright red neon sign blinking *Fred's Diner*.

Hal surveyed the area after pulling his black Mercedes into a vacant spot. His upper class car was a stark contrast from the beat up and decades older cars that surrounded it. He didn't bother searching for Mick's car as he'd never seen him drive the same one twice. Hal was usually kept in the dark on Mick's activities, but he knew his colorful friend had a chop shop somewhere in the city. For him cars were like socks; you changed them once a day.

Hal pulled the restaurant's door open. Two brass bells bounced against the stickered glass signaling a new patron's arrival. He scanned the diner searching for his future accomplice and found him sitting in a far corner. One of the diner's waitresses in a light blue apron splattered with stains, which were probably permanently resistant to washing, was pouring Mick a cup of black coffee. Mick's large belly pushed against the side of the table, with his burly arms resting on its top. As usual he was decked out in a plaid cowboy shirt, jeans and dark brown boots Hal could see sticking out from underneath the table. He couldn't see Mick's belt, but he knew there was a massive buckle somewhere under his equally large stomach.

Hal slowed his gait, allowing the waitress time to leave and sat down across from Mick.

"It's been years huh," Mick said without emotion and added a spoonful of sugar to his coffee. He swirled it with the small spoon dissolving the sugar instantly into the hot brew.

"Yeah, it's been a while Mick; that's for sure." Hal was about to continue when the waitress from before returned and asked the two men for their orders. Both Mick and Hal ordered the same apple-wood bacon burger and fries. They looked at each other slightly amused as their order was exactly the same as the last time they had met at the diner years ago. Hal glanced over at Mick's cowboy hat off to his right on the table and wondered where Mick was carrying his gun. He knew Mick never left home without one.

"So, what can I do you for?" Mick questioned once the waitress was again out of earshot.

Hal stared at Mick's unshaven face and raggedy hair for a few seconds before speaking. "Well Mick, I have a problem that I need permanently taken care of," he said. Hal's previous undertakings with Mick had been highly illegal, but for some reason this time felt different. When they'd conspired on arson and theft, although people's lives were destroyed, no one was physically hurt. This time he was asking Mick to murder someone.

"Just come out with it man," Mick said, annoyed by the run-around. Mick always preferred to get straight down to business. If he liked the individual they could chew the fat later, but it was always business first.

"I need one of my employees to have an accident and it has to be fatal."

"What did you have in mind?" Mick replied.

"This employee comes to work alone every day at the same time. I was thinking maybe you could mess with his brakes or something on his car. You know something that wouldn't necessarily seem suspicious?"

"Now you're speaking my language. Break malfunctions are pretty nasty from what I've heard. Kills a fair amount of people every year too," Mick said with a sinister sneer.

"So it won't be a problem then?"

"Nope, can't see why it would. Just give me the poor sap's address and the day you want it done and I'll let you know when we're good to go."

"Here," Hal said and slid across a piece of paper with John Coulter's address written on it. "I want it done as soon as possible. Any day Monday through Friday will be fine, but it has to be a weekday. He takes the interstate to work just so you know and there's lots of stop and go traffic. An accident along that stretch wouldn't raise anyone's suspicions I wouldn't think."

"Consider it done. My fee's 20k now and 20k after," Mick said and licked his lips in anticipation.

Hal reached inside his pants pocket and pulled out two stacks of bills, each worth ten thousand dollars. Unbeknownst to Mick, Hal had been ready to offer forty thousand for the initial down payment, but kept the two remaining bundles of cash hidden in his trousers. Hal checked to make sure no one was looking and quickly handed the cash to Mick's hungry hand. Mick thumbed through each stack making sure they were indeed comprised of only one hundred dollar bills. He knew the tricks of the trade. Some people tried to get away with sheets of newspaper sandwiched between two hundred dollar bills. Those were easy to spot. When someone replaced the newspaper with ones or tens, then you really had to pay attention.

"Alright, we're finished here," Mick said after certifying his client's cash. He slid a small red disposable flip phone across the table to Hal. "I'll call you on that when it's done."

Mick grabbed the rest of his leftover hamburger and left the table without so much as a see you later. The bells jingled as he opened the diner's door and disappeared outside, leaving Hal with the bill. Hal paid well, but he and Mick were from two completely different worlds with almost nothing in common. Besides, Mick had a car crash to plan.

Hal took his time finishing the large burger the diner had nicknamed "The Heart Attack". He ordered one of the diner's famous strawberry milkshakes to go and paid for both of their meals. Outside the diner Hal was surprised to see his Mercedes wasn't already up on cinder blocks. He revved the engine and tapped his own brakes out of paranoia. It would be a long couple of days until the sinister deed was done.

John Coulter stared at a picture of his wife Lisa and their boy Jon. It was from a summer vacation they had taken the previous year in between two of Jon's summer internships. He thumbed over his son's infectious smile. Jon was as good of a son as any father could ever want. He was courteous, highly athletic and extremely studious. However there was more to it than that. Although Lisa had told John twenty years ago that she was pregnant with his son, he had never been fully convinced Jon was his.

John remembered back to *Evergreen Resource's* Christmas party two decades ago. In retrospect that was the first and only time he had ever seen Lisa completely smashed. He'd be surprised if she had taken ten drinks since in the following twenty years. John had never asked her what had transpired after he left, nor had she ever offered any information.

Something had definitely happened though. Ever since that evening when Hal's name was mentioned he could see the hate in her eyes. She also had more excuses than a cat has lives for reasons to get out of being somewhere Hal was also sure to be. Lisa's extreme repulsion of his boss Hal was only one piece of the puzzle though. The other piece was his son Jon, or was he really his son at all? John had wondered from the first day Lisa told him she was pregnant if the baby was really his. They'd only been together a few times and each time he'd been prepared.

"These things happen," she'd told him. "Ninety-nine percent effective means once and a while a defective one is going to make it through their Q.C."

John had just shrugged not knowing what to say. Regardless of the baby being his or not, he loved Lisa and she loved him. He decided the right thing to do was to marry her and raise the baby as his own and that's what he did.

John looked back down at the picture in his hands. He was as close to positive, as one could be without definitive proof, that Jon was almost certainly Hal's son. His eyes watered in their corners. He hadn't kept his unsaid promise that he would be a good father to Jon very well over the years. He knew why, it had just been too hard. Between knowing his son wasn't genetically his, the constant reminder that once upon a time Lisa had cheated on him and loving his son so much it hurt, John had always kept Jon at arm's length, not wanting to somehow get hurt. His treatment of his son wasn't fair, but it allowed him to keep his hurting soul at bay.

"It's time for a change," John muttered. A solitary tear fell from his watery eyes and splashed on the slick glass covering the picture. "I swear to you I'll be better," he said to the inanimate picture as though it was Jon himself. He loved his son and Jon was his son, biologically or not. He and Lisa had raised him for twenty years. Twenty years they had been the major investors in his life.

Jon was set to graduate from his undergraduate studies in a few weeks. As soon as that occurred, John was going to change their relationship. No longer would they be estranged father and son. John reasoned that twenty years should have been more than enough time to get over his wife's one time indiscretion. Jon was the priority now, not his father's silly feelings.

He rubbed the picture's plate glass covering against his shirt, clearing the smudge his tears had made. Gently he replaced the picture on one of his office's bookshelves and returned to his computer. Between burning the midnight oil at both his home and office, John had almost completed the specifications on a new type of solar cells. Super thin layers of graphene, so thin they were transparent, would serve as the medium where he would affix the solar cells. Since the cells were semitransparent, John could then layer them, letting the sun's rays through multiple levels of solar cells at a time. Even with the added layers they would still be the same thickness as the ones currently on the market today.

John had earlier tried his hand at cold fusion, using a hydrogen generation device activated by electromagnetic pulses, but had been met with spectacular failure. Each time he had started the cursed device; it had blown up or caught on fire. In his last attempt at cold fusion he had replaced the hydrogen generator with tritium, but had not yet had a chance to try the machine again for fear of an even larger explosion.

John double clicked on a large file and a window popped up with a diagram of the new solar cell array. "I'll never have to see that S.O.B. again," John said as he marveled at his handiwork and thinking of Hal. The spectral diagram of his new invention brought a smile to his face, as it was his opportunity to start a business for himself and his family. No longer would he have to work for that pompous, arrogant piece of crap he had been under for the past twenty years.

He had finally devised a way to turn the sun's rays into a wealth of renewable energy and with phenomenal efficiencies. Most of the solar cells on the market were lucky to achieve thirty percent efficiency. If his calculations were correct his new solar cell arrays would have an efficiency of over sixty percent. However, if he could manage to get his fusion reactor online, even for a few seconds, the scientific world would be his oyster.

Most of the schematic work John had been able to perform in his home's rudimentary office, but occasionally his project had called for higher computing powers than his personal computer could provide. The last few days, unbeknownst to Hal, *Evergreen Resource's* computers had been chewing on simulation after simulation for the final catalytic converter prototype. He had calculated sometime during tonight the simulations would be complete. Tomorrow he was going to pull the files and depending on their readings he was going to quit in spectacular fashion.

"Hal you pompous S. O. B. I know you slept with Lisa years ago. I thought back then we were friends, but now I realize how naive I truly was. You're a jerk and a horrible person. The only reason this company's grown to the size it has is from you stepping on the backs of talented people. I QUIT!" He had rehearsed his little speech more than a hundred times. Each time he wanted to add more, but short and sweet was better. Tomorrow; hopefully tomorrow would be the day.

"John, supper," he heard his wife yell down the hall.

"Coming," he replied and quickly exited out of the open files. Neither Lisa nor Jon had the slightest inkling of what he was planning to do. He wanted to surprise them each separately. Both his son and wife had mentioned to him on separate occasions they wished he had his own business. Now, that was about to become a reality. John smelled the scrumptious dinner on the opposite side of the house and his stomach growled. Tomorrow, tomorrow would be the day, John thought as he gave his home office one last look before shutting the door and heading to dinner.

A few days had passed since Mick's meeting with Hal. Mick would have liked to tackle Hal's problem little sooner, but a current job he was working on had taken more time than he was expecting. Running a chop shop in one of Dallas' back corner alleys was normally a pretty sweet gig. There were plenty of cars for his crews to choose from between the three cities and until a few months ago the competition had been close to zero. He wasn't exactly sure why the Russians had now decided to open a shop of their own in his city and to be honest he didn't care. What Mick cared about was that the Dallas area was his and his alone.

When Hal had called him the other day, Mick and his associate had just entered the Russian's chop shop unannounced. Mick had yet to decide if the Russians' deaths were a certainty, but he needed to send a clear message to the interlopers; they were not welcome in his town. Upon entering the shop there were only three of the Russians and seven of Mick's men, not including him. Outmanned and out gunned, the Russians had given up without a fight, knowing if they hadn't each of them would be dead in a blink of an eye.

Quickly Mick figured out which of the three was in control and went to work on him. That was the moment when Hal had called. Mick needed to send a message to the Russians and anyone else thinking of invading his turf, that his shop was the only game in town. Normally once Mick brought out the power drill, just the sight and fear of what was to come was enough to make his enemies change their mind. The Russian leader was however quite different from his normal prey. Mick had needed to drill through three of the man's fingernails before he agreed to take his cronies and leave the city forever.

Mick still wasn't sure if the pain had changed the Russian leader's mind or if after the third finger had been drilled clean through, he and Mick now saw eye to eye. Mick would not stop until the Russians were dead or gone and he guessed the Russian had figured that much out. Mick had to give it to this particular Russian though; he certainly had balls of steel. He was certainly one of the toughest people Mick had ever met.

Now that the major threat to his livelihood had been squashed, it was time to make good on his agreement with Hal. Mick pulled a black Escalade out of one of his shop's large bay doors and onto the gravel alley. On one side of the alley was a long section of rusty chain linked fencing belonging to his cousin's salvage yard. The other side of the alley was lined with a somewhat newer section of fencing belonging to a storage facility spanning the entire block. Both businesses were obviously aware of Mick's illegal dealings and in no small respect played an integral part in his success, as each had assisted in his clandestine affairs in some way or another over the years.

Mick reached the end of the alley and turned onto a beaten down road, where potholes seemed to cover more of the road's surface than the original paving once did. As he reached the Coulter's residence, Mick wasn't worried the least bit about his Cadillac being photographed or being called in for suspicious activity. This particular car, like most of his others, had a set of recently stolen license plates and all identifying V.I.N. numbers had been filed off; even the hidden ones.

Nonetheless, Mick was careful to obey the city's traffic laws. He was always careful. Why draw attention to yourself when you didn't need to, he always said. Early in his illicit career, Mick quickly learned one of the tricks to running an illegal business and not getting caught was never ever giving the police a reason to talk to you.

That meant no speeding, no drinking in excess and no fighting, an ideology he desperately tried to convey to his associates.

As Mick turned onto John Coulter's street he turned off the Escalade's powerful headlights and slowed his speed through the sleepy neighborhood. A few houses down the quiet street, Mick found the address he was searching for. As Hal had told him, there were two cars sitting idle in the driveway. The red two door coupe was supposedly John's wife's car, while the blue Ford F-150 was Mr. Coulter's. Mick continued past the house and parked his ride a few houses down. He turned off the cabin's light before opening the door and then slinked along a hedge of bushes to the edge of John's yard. Mick looked to his right and left making sure no nosy neighbors were watching his cat-like movements. Seeing no one observing his actions, Mick sprinted across John's lawn and knelt against his truck.

Mick rolled onto his back and quick as a cat he was under the front of John's truck. Twisting the mini-Maglite's top until the light turned on, he positioned the light in his mouth so it pointed up towards the truck's engine. He reached amongst the cables and wires, feeling around until he found the one he was searching for. Holding the cable with one hand, he pulled a sharp needle from his pocket and punctured the line. A few drops of the reddish fluid squirted out at the initial prick, but stopped immediately afterwards. Being this wasn't Mick's first trip to the rodeo and he knew the fluid bleed would be a slow one. The truck's brakes would slowly hemorrhage their fluid until eventually they would be unresponsive, no matter how hard someone pushed on the brake pedal.

Mick turned off his small flashlight and scooted out from under the truck. Before sprinting across the lawn he once again checked to make sure no eyes were following him. Again feeling well hidden, Mick raced back to his car and not wanting to attract attention slowly drove out of the neighborhood. Now all Mick needed to do was call Hal and wait.

CHAPTER 2

JON 2.0

Jon Coulter, John and Lisa Coulter's twenty-one year old son, was deep in thought; immersed in his upper level biochemistry text book. At six-foot even his knees were only an inch below the table's bottom. Unconsciously he was bumping the top of his knees against the bottom of the table as he listened to some classic *Metallica*, while reading the thick textbook. For some people, music, TV or any noise for that matter was a distraction, but for Jon it simply acted as white noise, which helped to enhance his concentration.

After two straight hours of continuous studying, Jon's large muscular frame was beginning to cramp and he knew an extended break to stretch and get some grub was quickly approaching. Lucky for him, the Ohio State union was just a few quick steps away from his fraternity house.

As Jon finished the last paragraph detailing the synthesis of mRNA ad nauseam, a set of feminine hands gently but tightly, clasped around his face, matting his dark brown hair against his eyes and forehead sealing him in complete darkness.

"Hey, who turned out the lights?" Jon jokingly asked, already knowing who the hidden culprit was.

"If you don't know, then I'm not going to tell you," a secretive female voice said from his rear.

"Sarah? Jessica? No, wait it has to be Amber. It's Amber, right?" Jon questioned with a devious smirk.

The hands blinding his vision were removed in an instant and he felt a quick slap against the back of his head. The slap wasn't hard enough to leave a welt, but definitely strong enough to let Jon know this was one girlfriend he shouldn't dare cheat on. Not that Jon had ever cheated on any of his girlfriends or had even been tempted to do so, but this one was feisty.

"Who's Amber?" Beth Carmichael said as she rounded the table and stared Jon eye to eye, while trying to suppress a smile. She gazed into Jon's dark brown eyes and flicked a strand of his equally brown hair off his forehead.

As usual Jon was mesmerized by Beth's beauty. Her long blonde hair hung down a few inches past her shoulders and onto her bright pink thinly knit tank top. Her bright blue eyes seemed to pierce straight through him. There was nothing he would ever do to hurt this girl. Was it love? Sure he loved her, he had told her so on numerous occasions and she him, but was this *true* love? The answer was a resounding yes.

As Jon peered back into those mesmerizing bright blue eyes he knew there was no doubt it was indeed true love. Three more weeks and he'd be graduating with his double major in biochemistry and electrical engineering. It had been a hard four years, full of studying and more studying, but college was almost at an end. With the never ending support of his parents, his Beta Theta Pi fraternity brothers and for the past two years his girlfriend Beth, the light at the end of the tunnel was ever increasing in intensity.

"Hey, earth to Jonny," Beth said and snapped her fingers in front of his face, "I said who's Amber?"

The sharp click of Beth's fingers pulled Jon out of her deep blue eyes and back to reality.

"Oh Amber, she's nobody. You don't know her," Jon said grinning wide. He stretched his long arms high into the air over his head, interlocked his fingers and cracked his knuckles. Jon's reflexes were fast, but this time not fast enough. While his arms were still in the air, Beth made a quick jab with her small hand balled into a fist and connected with the side of his ribs before he was able to lower his arms for protection.

Jon let out a gasp and smiled at the look of satisfaction on Beth's face. Even though Jon worked out with free weights almost daily and played numerous intramural sports when he found the time, Beth always seemed to get the drop on him. At 5' 5" and maybe a hundred and twenty pounds, Jon was constantly amazed at Beth's quickness and strength when she chose to use it.

"Oh come on you big baby, that didn't hurt. Plus it serves you right for making me think maybe there's someone else in your life beside me. That's not nice you know," Beth said pretending to pout.

"You know you're the only for me babe," Jon said standing up, using the back of his legs to push back his chair. Jon took a step towards Beth and grabbed her in a big hug. He immediately felt her arms wrap around his thick frame and hug him back. Wow he was hooked. Jon hadn't understood the extent of many of the idioms he'd heard throughout his life about couples, but he knew one of them definitely applied to him. Jon was definitely wrapped around Beth's little finger, as there was nothing he wouldn't do for her.

"I'm starved, want to get some food?" Jon asked while the perfect couple was still in a full embrace.

"I thought you'd never ask," Beth replied and let her arms drop to her side.

Jon began closing his open textbooks and stuffing them into his olive green backpack. Next he tossed his papers, pencils, calculator and anything else scattered over the table into his bag in no particular order. Finals were only three weeks away and Jon knew he still had another three or four hours of studying left in him for the night.

"So, where do you want to go?" Jon asked his girlfriend as he slung his heavy bag over his muscular shoulder.

"How about Chinese?" she quickly replied, knowing he always let her pick. "My dorm never has Chinese food."

"Sounds good to me. I'll buy you the best Chinese food the student union has to offer," he replied with a smile. He knew that somewhere, buried inside his book bag, was a wadded up ten dollar bill, which would more than suffice for the cheap Chinese-American fare. Jon and Beth marched up the fraternity's basement stairs to the main floor of the house. After rummaging through his bag and retrieving the ten dollar bill, Jon tossed his bag in a corner littered with those of his fraternity mates.

Out the door they went and into the warm evening air. The large meticulously trimmed campus trees rustled in the gentle spring breeze. Jon and Beth simultaneously reached for each other's hands like clockwork and smiled at their synchronicity. As the evening slowly passed, they took their time leisurely strolling to the union and eating their highly salted meal. Eventually Jon's studious mind reeled him back in from their overly casual date and he walked Beth back to her dorm.

"Aw, is our date over already? A cheap meal and a quick walk, you really shouldn't have Mr. Coulter," Beth teased and poked him in his side.

"Careful there, someday it'll be Dr. Coulter and you'll be sorry for making fun of me." In truth Jon hadn't decided if graduate school was in his future or not, but he did like the ring Dr. Coulter had when he said it.

Beth smiled and Jon forcefully pulled her in for a departing kiss. He loved her and from her outward actions he was fairly certain she felt the same. In a matter of weeks he'd be graduating and not long after that he planned on proposing.

"Anxious to get back studying?" Beth asked as they came up for air.

"Not as much as I was before," he smiled. Truthfully he didn't want to leave her, but his mind told him a few more hours of hitting the books still awaited him. Plus, he hadn't talked to his parents in a while and felt they deserved a phone call. After giving Beth a final departing kiss, he watched her disappear with a wave into the brightly lit halls of her dorm.

Jon typed the fraternity's pass code into the front door's number pad and entered inside. The entryway's dark wood interior greeted him, instantly evoking emotions of being home. Jon was sad graduation meant leaving the campus, his fraternity and most of his friends, but he understood it was part of life. He retrieved his backpack and decided against returning to the downstairs study room. Instead he headed up the dark blue carpeted stairs to his room.

On a normal evening such as this, his roommate would almost certainly be at the gym working on his summer muscles, as he called them. Sure enough, when he entered their joint room it was quite and empty. Jon cracked open his books and studied undisturbed another two hours before his mind was nothing but a ball of mush.

"Might as well call the parental units," he said and smiled at his witty wordplay. He dialed the phone and waited for his mom to answer as she always did. No matter how many times anyone called their house; his mom was almost always the one who answered, regardless of what she was doing. Maybe once or twice his dad had picked up the phone, but those times were far and in between the norm.

As he guessed, within a few seconds he was greeted with a, "Hi Jon, how's everything going?"

"Pretty good mom. Just been studying for my upcoming finals."

"Oh and how is that going?"

"Alright I guess. I think I've got a fairly strong grasp on most of the stuff. Studying three or four hours a day does have its benefits, regardless of how boring it gets." Jon knew, unlike most of his friends, that when it came to school he was a perfectionist. Whether he wanted to admit it or not, Jon would already be able to easily pass all five of his finals, but simply passing a professor's test wasn't enough. Jon wanted complete mastery of any subject he took and it showed. By the end of each semester Jon had yet to finish a class without at the very least being tied for the highest grade.

"I'm sure you'll do just fine son," his mom replied in a motherly tone. She knew of her son's overly studious habits and was not worried a bit. While other moms might have been hesitant to let their little boys join a fraternity in college, Lisa had been elated when Jon showed a keen interest in joining the Greek system. She hadn't been worried about Jon's over involvement in partying or hanging out with the guys, just the opposite. Lisa had been worried Jon would let the majority of his college years pass him by, while he was holed up in the bottom of one of the campus' many libraries.

"I just hope you're not neglecting that beautiful girlfriend of yours too much. It'd be a shame if she got away because your head was always stuck in a book."

"Actually I just dropped her off at her dorm a few minutes ago. But it's funny that you bring her up mom. I was calling because I wanted to tell you that I've decided to ask Beth to marry me after I graduate."

"Oh, that's so great!" his mom replied, clearly extremely pleased with his decision. She was happy to have had the pleasure of meeting Beth on several occasions and couldn't have picked a better match for her son if she tried herself.

"You think she'll say yes?" Jon asked, wanting a little motherly reassurance.

"Of course she will. She'd have to have her head examined if she said no," Lisa added, slightly incensed her son would ever think a girl might say no to his boyish charms and good looks. "If I was her it'd be a definite yes."

"Ah mom, come on," Jon quickly replied, slightly repulsed at the thought of marrying his mother.

"I'm guessing you haven't run this by your father yet?" Although her husband hadn't mentioned a conversation about Jon's future proposal, she wouldn't be surprised if he had simply neglected to bring it up. John and Jon had an interesting relationship. Their usual exchanges were more like two ships passing in the night rather than the normal strong bond between a father and son. Lisa knew her husband loved Jon, but she wished they could be closer.

"No, I haven't talked to dad yet. Do you mind getting him on the phone?" Jon asked. Almost everybody he had ever heard of loved his dad. They would say, "He's such a great guy," or "you're so lucky to have him as your dad," but truthfully Jon rarely felt a stronger connection to his father than he did to some of the other adults in his life.

"John, your son is on the phone," he heard his mom yell into the house. "Alright, here he comes. I'll let you men have some privacy. If we don't talk again before your finals good luck and I love you."

"Love you too mom," Jon replied and waited for his dad to answer. Jon started pacing his small fraternity room in anticipation of talking to his father.

"Hello son," Jon's dad said, though not unkindly through the receiver. "Do you need some money?"

"No dad, I don't need any money," Jon replied a little dejectedly. Most of the times he talked to his dad on the phone his dad skipped the chit chat and went straight to practical questions, like money, grades and clothes.

"Oh. Well are you prepared for your finals? You know when I went to college I aced most of my engineering classes."

"Yeah, I know dad." This wasn't the first time Jon had heard about his dad's college smarts and he knew it wouldn't be the last. Even though his dad had been close to the top of his class, Jon *was* at the top of his; a point he'd wanted to let his father know many times, but never had the courage to do so.

"I'm ready for the finals. There's still a few more weeks to go, but I think I could take them now if I had to. But that's not what I wanted to talk to you about."

"Okay, I'm listening," his father said matter-of-factly, definitely not out of the norm.

"I just told mom, but I wanted to tell you too that I've decided to ask Beth to marry me after school's out." Jon waited for an answer of any sort, but was only met with silence.

"Son," his father began. Son? His father rarely, if ever addressed him as anything other than Jon. In fact Jon couldn't actually recall ever hearing his dad refer to him as his son.

"I think that's fantastic. She's a lucky girl," his father finished. Fantastic? Lucky? Was this the same man he'd grown up with his entire life? Was he dying? Jon *knew* he'd never been complimented twice in the same sentence like that before.

"Is everything okay dad?" Jon asked genuinely concerned. Something had to be wrong for his dad to be so full of compliments.

"Everything is fine son. Actually I'm glad you called because I wanted to talk to you about something too. Do you have a few minutes or do you need to get back to your books?"

Curious at what his dad seemed to be yearning to discuss, Jon replied, "No, I'm fine. I've put away my books for the night. I studied most of the afternoon, so I'm not sure how much extra would still sink in right now anyway. What did you want to talk about?"

His father paused for a few seconds, searching for the right words to start with what he wanted to tell his son. "First of all, I just want you to know how proud I am of you and what a fine young man you've grown up to be. From the way you carry yourself in life to your studies, you've proven to me that you're a remarkable young man. I know you don't know where you'll be working or what you'll be doing in the future but I'm sure you'll be fantastic at it."

Jon's mouth hung wide open in astonishment. He wiped a few tears forming in the corner of his eyes with his free hand and continued listening in complete awe.

"I know that there's been many times when I've treated you more as a guest in our house than my son and I want to say I'm sorry for that. I've had my own issues to deal with and I realize now that I included our relationship as part of those issues and for that I again apologize."

What issues was his father talking about? As far as Jon knew, his dad had lived a pretty normal childhood and from what he could tell his dad and mom's marriage was close to perfect. He knew they loved each other very much and rarely if ever saw them fight. Of course they wore on each other's nerves from time to time, but nothing out of the ordinary for any normal married couple.

"Um, thanks dad. That really means a lot," Jon slowly replied, stumbling over his words as he tried to find the right thing to say. Usually Jon's words flowed like a cool stream, as he was very articulate, but this conversation had thrown him off his game.

"I know I can't make up for our lack of a real relationship in the past, but I'd very much like to try in the future if that's okay with you?"

"I'd like that a lot dad," Jon quickly replied.

"Great," his dad said sounding generally enthusiastic. "Maybe after your finals are finished we could go out to eat just the two of us and catch up on life and get to know each other a little better."

Well, that was it. His dad had become certifiably crazy. Father and son time? Jon had given up hoping that would ever happen and now his dad wanted just the two of them to get dinner together.

"I think that'd be awesome dad!" Jon exclaimed as his excitement from the conversation bubbled to the surface of his normally calm demeanor.

"Well until then good luck on your finals and I'll talk to you later. I love you son."

Jon heard his dad hang up the phone, but didn't set his down. For minutes he stood like a statue in the middle of his fraternity room processing and reprocessing the conversation with his dad. Although he couldn't have seen him, Jon swore it sounded like his dad had been smiling during the last portion of the conversation. Smiling? His dad had actually been smiling, about him?

Jon was absolutely floored. There would definitely be no more studying tonight, for he knew his concentration was shot. But what had his dad been talking about past issues he had to deal with? Although Jon was elated with his dad's apparent change of heart, his dad's past issues bothered him.

The entirety of Jon's instincts told him his dad's issues concerned him somehow, but how, he didn't know. Although, never enough to lose sleep over, his and his dad's names had always nagged at him. If he was named after his father, why was his first name spelled differently? And why hadn't he ever been called John Coulter the Second or John Junior. He had always thought something was weird that he and his father's names were spelled differently, but now he was fairly certain there was more to the story.

With his back to the door, Jon recalled and rehashed the conversation with his dad over and over searching for clues as to his father's apparent change of heart. All of a sudden Jon felt a bump against the door and heard an umph on its other side. Startled, he quickly moved out of the way and on a second attempt his roommate entered through the now unblocked doorway.

"Yo, what's the deal dude?" his somewhat perturbed roommate asked once in the room. "You trying to keep me out or something?"

Andre shut the door behind him and went straight to their shared closet. Dripping sweat and smelling like he had just come from the gym, he was in dire need of a shower. Andre's black gym shorts and Beta Theta Pi jersey stuck to his dark wet skin as he moved. Both of his parents were black and had been somewhat skeptical we he had told them he wanted to join a fraternity four years ago; especially one that was predominantly white. He understood where they were coming from, but the guys he knew at the time had not once treated him with anything other than respect. In fact over time his parents grew to believe the fraternity had probably kept him out of more trouble than if he hadn't joined.

"Sorry buddy," Jon replied. "I just had the strangest conversation with my dad."

"What'd that hard ass have to say?" Andre questioned as he pulled a small basket from their closet containing his shampoo, soap and a bright neon green loofah. Andre had met Jon's father a couple of times and had never been impressed.

He could see the way Mr. Coulter barely recognized his son's existence and it bothered him. Unlike his dad, Jon's seemed to see his son's life on this planet as an afterthought. It was funny though, everyone else thought Jon's dad was such a great guy. Maybe Andre didn't like him because he was looking at him through his friend's eyes and not those of a regular person. Andre took off and tossed his ripe clothing in a dirty clothes basket and shut the top, concealing the smell within.

"That's just it, he couldn't have been nicer," Jon confided in his friend.

"Huh, that's a rarity. Let me take a shower first and then we can talk." Andre said while opening the door.

"Yeah, a rarity," Jon mumbled as Andre left the room, closing the door behind him. A few moments later Andre returned smelling much better than before. Scrounging around in his dresser drawers, Andre pulled out a clean pair of neon yellow shorts and a plain white t-shirt.

"So, what'd your old man have to say?"

"He said he wants to get to know me better. I think he wants to try and make up for being a crappy dad."

"Whoa, that's huge man. What brought that on, he's not dying or anything is he?" Andre asked somewhat sarcastically.

"Andre I wondered the same thing, but I think he's okay."

"I'm sure he's got his reasons, but that's huge no matter what." Andre said, truly impressed Jon's dad might make a real effort to be a good father. "Love to talk more, but I've gotta get cramming. I can't believe I haven't started studying yet. Man I'm toast."

Jon watched the door shut behind his best friend and wasn't surprised in the least his loveable, but not entirely scholastic friend had neglected his studies. Jon would have loved to talk to Andre longer, but knew his friend desperately needed to study.

Jon opened the front cover of his senior physics book, but made it no further. His mind, a jumble of thoughts and emotions refused to concentrate. What had his father been trying to tell him? Something was different between the two of them; for some reason. Jon knew he hadn't changed so something with his dad must have.

Jon tried off and on for the better part of an hour to pull himself back into his studies. By the time he successfully stripped his mind of the evening's conversation, he was too tired to study any longer. Eventually Jon fell asleep on his room's futon with one of his large text books laying open on his chest.

Andre returned to their joint room a little after midnight and saw his friend asleep on the futon. Looking at the open book laying on his chest, Andre shook his head with a smile at what a bookworm his roommate and best friend was. *If only I had a brain like that I'd be studying all the time too,* he thought to himself. Andre passed one of their joint mirrors and caught a quick glance of his muscular frame.

"At least I've got you guys," he said while flexing a muscular pose in front of the mirror. Andre let out a deep yawn of his own. He turned off the light and crawled into his bed falling asleep almost instantly.

"Huh, that's odd," Lisa said putting her cell phone back into her purse.

"What's that?" John said as he tried unsuccessfully to suppress a grin.

"Well," Lisa started to say as she closed the distance between the two of them. "I've been working every Thursday for as long for as I can remember, but there was a message on my phone that says I've been granted my request for a day off."

"Well imagine that," John said. "So, do you have any plans for your special day off?"

"I don't know, do I?" she said. She stepped up to her husband's muscular flat chest to where they were touching each other.

John put his thick hands on the side of her shoulder and gave her a quick squeeze. He then dropped to a knee and took one of her smaller hands in his. "Lisa, would you do me the honor of marrying me again today?" John gazed up at her lovingly and waited for an answer.

Lisa had tears in her eyes at John's loving gesture. "Of course I will," she said without hesitation.

"Great! Okay, so here's what I've got planned. We'll hop into my car and stop by my work for a quick minute. I've just got to run in for a second to check on something and then we're off to a bed and breakfast where Pastor Phil is going to meet us."

"Oh my goodness, Pastor Phil?" she laughed. "I haven't thought about him in years. Do you think he still has those horrendous side burns he was growing the first time he married us?"

"Ha, ha, I don't know. But there's only one way to find out." John grabbed her hand and started leading her to the garage door.

"Wait, we can't go yet. I haven't even packed anything."

"Don't worry about that my dear. I've got a bag for you in the car and a few extras already at the B and B."

"Well I guess I'm all out of excuses then aren't I," she said and let him lead her to the car.

"Are you ready to marry me again my love?" John asked as he backed his large pickup out of the driveway. "Hmmm," he said before she had a chance to answer.

"What's wrong?"

"Oh it's probably nothing. The brakes just felt a little loose there, but they seem fine now."

John shrugged his shoulders thinking he was imagining things. They drove through their maze of winding neighborhood roads eventually popping out into a major intersection. A few more turns and John and Lisa had entered onto the interstate in the middle of the morning rush to work. As they merged into the congested traffic, cars and trucks were as usual zipping back and forth, jockeying for the choicest of lanes.

"Aren't you glad you're coming to work with me?" John joked in reference to the busy traffic. Lisa grinned and rested her hand on his, just happy to be enjoying his company on the impromptu date.

Up ahead in the distance John noticed the morning traffic was beginning to snarl to a halt and began applying his breaks. Almost immediately he noticed they felt even softer than he had noticed before. Both he and Lisa were oblivious to the small line of red brake fluid trailing their vehicle. Although the brakes were noticeably squishy, John easily brought the truck to a stop with plenty of time.

"I've definitely got to get this truck to the shop," he said after they were stopped for the moment. "These breaks just aren't as responsive as they were a few days ago."

"Do you want to stop now?" Lisa asked. She hoped John didn't think there was a serious problem with his truck. She was swept off her feet at his highly romantic gesture and wanted nothing more than to renew their vows at the bed and breakfast.

As fast as the traffic had stalled it was flowing again. Within a quarter of a mile they, along with every other commuter on the road, were averaging close to seventy miles an hour; free of congestion for the moment. John noticed Lisa staring and smiling at him out of the corner of his eye. He turned and returned a loving smile of his own.

"I love you John Coulter," she said. Lisa leaned over to give him a quick peck on the cheek, to which John leaned in to eagerly receive. Before either of them realized, the traffic had once again become gridlocked. John glanced back at the roadway as any descent driver would have and noticed a steady stream of brake lights directly ahead. Slamming on his own brakes, John tried to slow their truck down before they hit the halted traffic, but nothing happened. John raised his foot off the brake and slammed it down again, but like the time before the pedal depressed with ease all of the way to the truck's floorboard, without slowing the truck.

"Oh crap!" John yelled as he repeatedly slammed the truck's brake to the floor. Lisa realized he wasn't able to stop and covered her face with her small hands. John knew there was little chance of escaping the poor soul in the car stopped ahead of them at still over sixty miles an hour. John turned the truck towards the overpass's guard rail on their right to avoid the parked cars. John moved his foot to the left and slammed it down on the emergency brake as a last resort. The truck's tires squealed and laid down a solid line of fresh foul smelling black rubber before the truck itself smashed into the guard rail. Had they been driving a smaller car, the rail would have dramatically slowed the car's out of control motion.

However, John's truck was easily twice as tall as some cars and instead of being slowed by the guard rail, the truck flipped end over end and sailed twenty feet in the air. John and Lisa both screamed up until the point of impact. The truck's cabin hit the roadway below the interstate first. The cabin, not built to withstand the vehicle's full tonnage of force resting on top of it, collapsed as the truck's weight came crashing down upon it on the smaller roadway. John and Lisa were killed instantly without any pain or suffering as the truck compacted into a smaller, mangled version of itself.

Finally the truck finished sliding to a stop on its mangled roof, leaving sparks behind in its wake. Not long in the silence afterwards, sirens began to sound in the distance. When the ambulance and fire department finally arrived moments later, they found the truck laying wrecked and ruined on its top with all four tires slowly spinning in midair.

CHAPTER 3

AFTERMATH

"How was I supposed to know he wouldn't be alone?" Mick yelled into the phone. "You owe me the other twenty thousand. Don't make me tell you what'll happen if I don't get it," he openly threatened.

"You'll get your money!" Hal yelled back and slammed the phone down on his desk. What a mess. Mick's tampering with the break line had worked like a charm, but now Lisa was dead too. Hal felt horrible that she had been killed; though not that it had been his doing. Although he still desired that Lisa was his, Hal quickly realized his emotional attachment to her had begun to wane the instant he heard the news of her death.

Hal's waning desire of Lisa reminded him of wanting an item at auction so bad one time he'd briefly considered killing for it. However, as soon as someone else won the overpriced item, its lure was instantly forgotten. However, Lisa was a real person, not something that could be purchased. Luckily for Hal, he knew the change in his emotions would be the same this time and whatever guilt he was felling at their deaths would quickly dissipate.

As Hal stared out of his large office window towering over the Dallas-Fort Worth area, his receptionist buzzed him on the intercom.

"Mr. Roberts, there's a lawyer here to see you."

Hal's heart immediately thumped harder. A few beads of anxious sweat popped onto his forehead. He wasn't expecting a lawyer today. He tried to calm his nerves. John and Lisa had only been dead a little over seven hours. If the lawyer was here about their death, he'd have cops with him to make an arrest.

"I'm not expecting anybody right now, especially not one of those blood sucking leeches," he returned. Although Hal had many uses for lawyers, both personally and through Evergreen Resources, they were vermin. They always charged too much and billed him for more hours than were remotely possible. Scum.

"He says it's in regards to John and Lisa's death," she returned.

Hal gulped at the mention of their names. Who was this guy and what the heck did he want? "Alright send him in," Hal ordered, letting curiosity rule his decision.

Through his office doors strolled in a stocky short man dressed in a dark suit and carrying a professionally styled black suitcase. Definitely a lawyer, Hal thought as the man entered with an air of entitlement. His lawyers always carried that type of suitcase and held their noses in the air.

"It's a pleasure to meet you Mr. Roberts. My name is Sam Thomas," the stocky man said and reached to shake Hal's hand.

Hal reluctantly accepted the man's brief but sweaty handshake, after which he waved him to a chair on the opposite side of his overly large office desk.

"What can I do for you Mr. Thomas?" Hal questioned with an air of distrust. He eyeballed the lawyer distastefully, wondering what tricks he had up his sleeve.

"I've been told you learned of the death of one of your employees and his wife earlier this morning." The lawyer paused to make sure Hal had indeed been informed of his employee's death and then continued. "First of all, let me say that I'm sorry for your loss."

Hal mumbled a, "thank you," not interested in the man's condolences.

"I was Lisa's lawyer for a number of years and I was told to give you this in the event that both her and her husband John died." Out of the shiny leather briefcase the man withdrew a normal letter sized white envelope and handed it across the table.

The lawyer waited for Hal to open the enclosed letter.

"Do you need to be here for this?" Hal asked, wanting this particular lawyer out of his office as soon as possible.

"I guess not," the lawyer said and retrieved his suitcase from the richly carpeted office floor. "Good day Mr. Roberts." He tossed a business card on Hal's desk directly in front of him. "In case you need to get ahold of me here's my card."

Hal stared the lawyer down without saying a word until the lawyer shrugged his shoulders uncomfortably and quickly left Hal's office.

Once he was again alone, Hal stuck his thumb under the envelope's paper flap and slid it from side to side. Inside the envelope was a single sheet of folded paper. Pulling out and unfolding the sheet of paper, Hal realized it was a short hand-written letter addressed to him. The letter read:

> Dear Hal,
> If you're reading this then both John and I are now dead. Since my son is now alone in the world, it is time you know that you are his biological father. I never told you because quite frankly you're not a good role model for him. However, now that he's alone, you're all that he has left. I hope being a father will change who you are. Please take good care of our son.
> Lisa

Hal let his hands drop against the sides of his chair. The hand holding the letter retrained its grip, slightly crinkling the piece of paper as it rubbed against his seat's dark leather surface. A son? He had a son? Although Hal and John had drifted apart over the years, his somewhat twisted fascination of Lisa kept him up to date on the Coulter family. He knew their son Jon was quite book smart and working on a double major if he wasn't mistaken. Hal thought he was actually graduating in a few weeks, but wasn't certain. He'd have to check on that.

"Me, a father, that's a laugh," he chuckled in his empty office. Out of everything that had happened between him and Lisa, finding out he'd secretly been a father for the past twenty plus years was one surprise he was not expecting. At least Jon was old enough to have almost finished college. Hal lived a life only fit for a bachelor. Ladies, booze and then more ladies and more booze. This was his life and one of which he enjoyed immensely. There was no room for a snot-nosed kid.

Not only were there personal ramifications of finding out he had a son, but there were legal ones too. Hal hadn't yet contemplated about what would happen to *Evergreen Resources* when died. Currently his will had the company split in between his worthless brothers whom he never talked too. Hal just knew they were crossing their fingers and hoping that he'd meet an untimely death so they could reap the spoils of his hard work while they were still young. Now that he knew of Jon, things were different. Now he had an heir.

"Mr. Roberts?" his secretary said as she knocked on his open office door.

Hal halted his daydreaming and pulled himself to a more upright position in his chair. "Yes?" he questioned with an air of annoyance.

"Ryan Smith is outside and he thinks there's something on John's computer you should see."

"Send him in," Hal ordered. Once the secretary had left, Hal folded Lisa's letter and replaced it in the plain white envelope. He stood and walked over to a black safe in the corner of his office and placed the letter inside for safe keeping. As he did so, Ryan Smith entered and stood nervously in the door's entrance waiting to be addressed. Hal's reputation as a shrewd and many times hateful man was well known to his employees. Not many had the stones to request a meeting with the CEO unless it was absolutely necessary.

Hal eyeballed the systems analyst with a shrewdness reserved for anyone entering his office. Only through distrusting absolutely everyone, valid or not, had Hal achieved the highest level of success. The systems analyst in his daunting office doorway had been tasked to repurposing John's computer and technical systems once the company had been informed of his death.

"Well, what's so important you needed to come up here?" Hal asked letting his annoyance show. There had better be a good reason this low level worker was interrupting his busy schedule. Could this day get any worse? Lisa was dead and he had just found out he had a son he'd never met. What now?

"I've been searching through Mr. Coulter's computer and I've found a few irregularities." Ryan Smith meekly said.

"Irregularities? What do you mean irregularities?"

"There are some files on his computer that have specifications for systems that we don't currently work on. I've asked around his floor and no one knows anything about them. If I had a guess, I'd say he's been working on energy generation prototypes for himself," Ryan said, starting to gain confidence the longer he talked, while attempting to sound as professional as possible.

"That's it? There're a few files on a dead man's computer that may or may not be company files. That's what you came to bother me about?" Hal retorted, killing whatever confidence Ryan thought he had found.

"I… I'm sorry sir, bbbbut there's something else too," he started to stammer.

"Well, out with it son. Cat got your tongue?" Hal chided, cherishing the fear of him this young man felt.

"He's been using the supercomputer on the weekends and at night to run simulations on two of these files. But what caught my attention is he never logged in the time. It's as though he was doing it secretly. Honestly, if I hadn't been searching his computer I don't think anyone would have ever known," Ryan finished. He wanted nothing more than to get out of the CEO's office and back to his floor where life made sense. This was his first time meeting Mr. Roberts and he already wished it was over. From only his brief interaction with the company's CEO, Ryan now believed he was indeed as big of a dick as he had heard.

Hal took a moment pondering over the pathetic systems analyst's findings. He was sure the analyst was making a mountain out of a molehill, but what if there was some truth to what he had found?

"Here's what you're going to do. Don't tell anyone about what you've found. Go back to John's computer and send me the files in question. I also want the readouts for all of his supercomputer simulations that he didn't sign the log book for. Got it?"

"Yes sir," Ryan replied. He felt somewhat vindicated Mr. Roberts was taking his claims seriously, but still desperately wanted out of his office.

"After you do all of that, I want the hard drive from his computer and I want you to personally bring it to me."

Ryan gulped at the thought of returning to the lion's den, but nodded in acceptance just the same.

Hal watched the beaten down young man leave his office with satisfaction. He'd scared the crap out of that kid and in doing so ensured John's files would stay a secret. The kid had been quite resilient to find the files. "Maybe they're not all worms," Hal said to himself as he walked back to his desk, but not before retrieving Lisa's letter from the locked safe to read once again.

"Jon. Jon," Andre said. He gently rocked his friend, trying to wake him up.

"Huh?" Jon replied half asleep. He tried to open his sleepy eyes. Squinting through chunks of sleep, Jon checked his alarm clock. 4:42. His last class wasn't until 5:10 causing him to wonder why Andre was shaking him from his afternoon siesta.

"Your aunt is on the phone. She's crying buddy. I think something's wrong."

Jon sat up and took the phone from his roommate's outstretched hand. Andre listened in silence as Jon heard what his aunt had to say. Jon said few words and judging by his downcast facial expressions, Andre knew something seriously wrong had just happened. After only a couple of minutes Jon handed the phone back to his friend in stunned silence.

"What happened? Is everything alright?" Andre asked out of concern.

"My parents are dead," Jon mouthed slowly, one word at a time.

"Aw man, I'm so sorry. How'd it happen?"

"Car accident," Jon said, but did not elaborate further. Andre didn't ask for added details, knowing his friend would tell him when he was ready.

"When's the funeral going to be?" Andre knew how hard his buddy had been studying and hoped he could at least finish his finals without having to deal with a funeral being scheduled smack dab in the middle.

"It's in a couple of weeks. My aunt said they wanted to be cremated so her and my uncle are going to plan the funeral for after graduation.

"Man, I don't know what's worse. Having the funeral in the middle of finals or having to wait until afterwards. Both situations really suck," Andres said trying to support his friend.

"I don't know, probably after I guess," Jon replied, clearly not in the mood to talk. In actuality he barely noticed Andre was even in the room with him. Andre patted his forlorn friend on the shoulder and left the room for dinner. Jon sat in stunned silence on the edge of his mattress, trying to comprehend the afternoon's shocking news. His Aunt Jenny, who he had talked to on the phone, was his mom's older sister. His aunt and her husband Harold lived on a farm in the middle of Nebraska's farm belt.

Jon had vacationed at his aunt and uncle's Nebraska farmstead many summers growing up. He loved each of them almost as much as he had loved his parents. Their presence at his parent's funeral would be priceless. Thankfully, his aunt had offered to take care of all the funeral arrangements. Aunt Jenny hadn't mentioned a will, probably because both of them expected everything to be left to Jon, but a will was the last thing he wanted to think about. Although Aunt Jenny and his Uncle Harold were on his mom's side of the family, Jon knew his dad was actually quite close to them as well. Jon's dad had actually visited them numerous times over the past year, Jon remembered.

Although slightly comforted by the thought his relatives would be arriving in a couple of weeks, for the moment Jon didn't want to be alone. Uncharacteristically leaving his books and skipping class, Jon trekked across campus to Beth's dorm. Seeing Beth step off the dorm's elevator, Jon's emotions broke loose. Long sobs and crocodile tears flowed down his face. Beth's smile at first seeing her boyfriend turned from joy to empathetic concern in seconds.

"What's wrong?" she asked as Jon reached out for a hug.

"My parents are dead," he said between heaving sobs. Every so often other students walked by, gawking at the emotional outburst. Normally Jon was an emotionally reserved person and would have been horrified to be making such a scene, but today they could stare all the wanted.

"I'm so sorry Jon," she said. "I know how much you loved them and they loved you too."

"Yeah, I know," he sniffed.

"It's okay. Don't worry, I'll help you through this. This would be hard for anyone to hear so unexpectedly."

"I know, I know," Jon replied as his cascade of tears began to ebb. "I just need some time," he sniffed again.

"Well it's good that you're brilliant. I know you could already ace each of your finals even if you can't concentrate to study the next few weeks," Beth said trying to lighten the mood.

Jon formed a fake smile at Beth's attempt to cheer him up. He loved her with all his heart and didn't want her to leave his side. Beth, although smart herself, did need to study for her upcoming finals, but she knew there would be no studying today. She spent the rest of the day consoling Jon and he spent the rest of the day loving her for it.

One by one John's secret files began to populate Hal's inbox. When the last one finally arrived, Hal counted twenty-one files in all. His reading and deciphering of the new information was much slower than at the speed Ryan was sending them. By the time the final file arrived, Hal had barely finished reading through the second document. Even before John's death, Hal had known he was one of the company's best, now he was certain of it.

Hal wasn't the engineer John had been, but he was still quite competent. He marveled at John's ideas. Although some of his ideas were more realistic than others, each of them had to a degree at least some merit.

Opening up the fifth email, Hal studied John's designs for his cold fusion reactor. Scientists, mathematicians and engineers had been working on its design for decades. Each time however, they had been met with complete failure. Hal assumed John himself had given up on the idea as multiple flaws in his prototype were immediately apparent.

Hal closed the fifth email attachment and moved on to the next email and then to the next and then to the next. The electronic clock on his computer said the time was 7:08 in the evening. Hours of staring at the computer screen seemed to have flown by. Even the night's dinner had escaped Hal as he was too preoccupied with John's secret files to think of food.

Hal yawned and rapidly blinked his aching eyes. Staring at the computer screen for over four hours straight in a row was beginning to take a toll. He rubbed each of his closed eyes with his large hands and opened them, immediately seeing spots from rubbing too hard. Hal yawned again and clicked open the next file. For minutes he stared in disbelief at what he saw. John had actually done it!

Hal read and reread John's schematic on the cutting edge solar array. Using clear graphene sheets, only a few microns thick to attach the solar cells was sheer brilliance. However, graphene sheets were at the moment prohibitively expensive for the large scale production of John's fantastic design.

Pushing his chair out from under the desk, as Hal stood both knees popped. He saw the sun beginning to set in the distance as he gazed out of this panoramic office windows. If he could start producing graphene sheets himself that would bring the cost down substantially. First and foremost Hal needed proof John's hypothetical solar array actually worked. He went back to his computer and scrolled through Ryan Smith's pushed emails. Finally, scrolling to the last email, Hal noticed this email's attached file was many times larger than the rest. Hal opened the email before clicking on the attachment.

Mr. Roberts,
Here's the data from the last simulation Mr. Coulter ran. The simulation was only completed early this morning. I erased the data from the supercomputer.
Ryan Smith

"He's definitely not incompetent," Hal commented after reading the analyst's message. He opened the attachment and scoured through the data. As he had guessed, John's solar array hypothesis appeared to be accurate. Not only was it possible, but if the supercomputer's calculations were correct the solar panels could have close to seventy percent efficiency!

Hal picked up the office phone and dialed Mick's number. "Mick I've got another job for you."

"After the last fiasco you set me up for I'm not sure I want any more business form you," Mick responded, surprised at Hal's gal to ask for more work so soon after their last screw up.

"I'll pay you the same for this one. Forty G's and no one needs to get hurt. This job is strictly reconnaissance."

Mick was quiet on the phone for a brief while, considering Hal's offer. "Alright, but if this isn't as smooth as butter, I'm done." Mick still wondered if the Coulter's deaths could possibly be traced back to him. He knew his reservations were silly, he was a professional after all, but anytime someone died, there was always an investigation. When he had commented about their deaths to a friend of his in the police department, the officer had fortunately given him no indication they were suspecting foul play. Nonetheless, Mick would probably be wary of all police officers for the next few months until it all blew over.

"Great. Here's what I want you to find," Hal began. "John was apparently working on a secret prototype for a new type of solar cell. I know there's a prototype somewhere, but I don't know where it is. It might be pretty delicate as I'm guessing he made it himself, so I just want you to find it and call me."

"That's it, just find this thing and call you and you're going to pay me forty thousand?"

"That's it. I don't have a picture, but I can send you a diagram so you at least have an idea what you're searching for."

"Okay, send the diagram and we've got a deal. Same as before half the money now and half after it's completed," Mick finished and hung up the phone.

Hal smiled, thinking of the millions he could make with John's invention. He still felt bad Lisa had been killed in the car crash, but her memory was fading fast. For the moment Hal was preoccupied with visions of wealth and grandeur.

CHAPTER 4

GRADUATION AND A FUNERAL

Over the next few weeks Jon shared many of his wonderful memories of his parents with Beth and Andre. Both of them listened with sympathy to his stories even though he probably droned on more than they would have liked. Jon felt neither of them could have been more loving and supporting; helping him through one of the most difficult times of his life.

On days when he was able to hold his emotions in check, Jon studied as much as possible. The university offered him an extra semester to finish his coursework and graduate. However, Jon turned them down, wanting to graduate on time with everyone else. Even though his emotions were frayed, his command of the subject material remained intact.

Two and a half weeks after his parents died, Jon graduated college with his double major and with honors. As he stood with the rest of the graduates, he looked into the stands of thousands of family and friends. Although his parents weren't there, Jon saw his aunt and uncle cheering him on. After the ceremony he turned in his cap and gown for his hard earned diplomas. Waiting for him at the main entrance of the university's basketball arena, where the ceremony had been held, were his aunt and uncle. Beth and Andre had already turned in their gowns and were there waiting too.

"Congrats Jon. You've done well for yourself," Uncle Harry said and gave him an overly hard slap on the back.

"I'm just so proud of you," Aunt Jenny gushed. "You're so much like your father." She put a hand over her mouth the moment the words escaped her lips, sorry she had brought up his deceased father during such a happy occasion. Aunt Jenny tried unsuccessfully to stifle a tear behind a fake smile, as memories of her sister came flooding back.

Beth came alongside him and took his hand in hers and squeezed. He squeezed back in response and gave her a loving smile.

"I can't believe I graduated!" Andre said.

"Yeah, me neither," Jon said with a smirk. Although he said it jokingly he really was surprised his friend was graduating. Jon scanned the people standing next to him. Although his parents were dead, he was still extremely lucky to have such loving friends and family in his life. An extremely supportive girlfriend, a goofy but completely loyal best friend and his aunt and uncle were more than he could ask for.

The two weeks after his parent's death had been harder than Jon would have imagined. He guessed some of it was due to the funeral being postponed until after his graduation. If he were asked again what he would prefer; the funeral would have been as soon after their cremation as possible. Although he hadn't seen their matching urns, without them being buried their presence still seemed to linger on.

Jon looked around the crowd of graduates and their families, knowing almost all of them would be celebrating in one way or another. He assumed he was the only individual that would be planning a funeral instead.

Mick waited until dark to return to the Coulter's residence. As he always did, Mick drove a different car each time he performed an illegal task. There was just no sense in looking suspicious, trolling the same neighborhood in the same car; that was just plain stupid. Today's car was a nice Buick. Nothing special, but he could see why older people enjoyed driving it. There was plenty of power in the engine and the car's interior was more comfortable than most.

Unlike the last time he had ventured into their quiet neighborhood, this time Mick parked over a block away. The death of both

Mr. and Mrs. Coulter had been a shock to their neighbors, most of whom had known them for years. The last thing Mick needed was to be seen sneaking around the neighborhood, especially if someone remembered him from before.

Mick idled and then killed the engine in front of a house whose backyard butted up against the Coulter's. The night was still warm, as a clouded sky kept the day's heat trapped against the earth. Careful to shut the car's door as quietly as possible, Mick dashed into the neighbor's backyard. A new wooden fence, where each slat of wood had a triangular spike at the top separated the two yards.

Surveying the fence, Mike didn't see a gate. He grunted in frustration and scanned the area. Almost every house was darkened except the occasional flashing light from a lone T.V. Mick grabbed hold of the triangular spike and heaved his not so light frame over the wooden divider. Long gone were the days of his youth, where volleying over the wooden fence would have been done with ease.

Mick's ample frame was almost over until the end of his foot caught on one of the triangular cut pieces of wood causing him to flip end over end and land on the mushy ground with a thud. Apparently the Coulter's sprinkler system was on a timer as the grass surrounding him was soaked with water. Recoiling in disgust at the mud, blades of grass and dirty water now stuck to him, Mick crouched against the concealing wooden structure and wiped himself off.

Again he searched for signs of life and observing none, he sprinted to the Coulter's rear sliding glass door. Of course it was locked, but Mick being a thief among other things, was prepared for just an occasion. He pulled out his small set of lock picks and within seconds the solid glass door was sliding open.

Inside the house, Mick flipped on his trusty Maglite. This not being his first rodeo, Mick instantly searched throughout the house for an office. Finding John's office with relative ease, Mick sat in his office chair and began riffling through the contents on the top and inside of his desk. If the current circumstances weren't that he was in a dead man's house, one in fact he was responsible for the death of, Mick would have stolen the computer's hard drive to take a crack at later. However, this time Mick didn't want the smallest of possible traces to be present of his incursion into the locked home.

Taking his time, Mick searched diligently through each folder and file he came across. After half an hour of searching, Mick came up empty handed. The only interesting piece of information he had found was an old ticket stub to Lincoln, Nebraska. Mick made a mental note of John's past destination and returned the piece of paper to where it had lain.

Next he turned on the computer and was less than surprised to see it was password protected. This John guy had been an engineer after all, he thought. Mick returned the computer to its hibernating state and left the office. He continued searching the house, but still came up empty. Lastly, Mick ducked into the house's garage. With no windows he didn't need his flashlight for the moment and flipped on the overhead lights.

The garage's painted white sheet rock radiated the overhead lights to the extent Mick needed to cover his eyes until they adjusted to the brightened surroundings. With only Lisa's red little sports car left in the garage, he had ample room to move around.

BAM!

Mick jumped three feet off the ground and whirled around. His heart was beating over one hundred beats a minute and adrenaline pumped through his veins. He hadn't noticed entering the garage that the door leading into the house had security spring-loaded hinges, which closed it automatically with a bang. Mick wiped the nervous sweat from his perspiring head. The garage of course was not air-conditioned. Between the day's heat, persistent humidity and the palpable tension of breaking and entering, Mick's heart continued beating much faster than normal.

"If this guy's got a working prototype, he'd need somewhere to build it," he thought out loud, while trying to relieve some of the tension. Early on in Mick's unsavory career, he learned that talking out loud to someone or no one in particular had a calming effect on his demeanor. He was used to having his lackeys take care of the break-ins these days and was feeling a little out of his element.

Still feeling jumpy, but once again in control of his emotions, Mick walked over to the large wooden workbench situated along the wall joining the house to the garage. Immediately he noticed John's meticulous nature as each individual tool had its own designated place for storage. Some tools were displayed on hooks, where others were neatly placed in drawers and cabinets.

Upon further examination, Mick noticed quite a few of the tools appeared to be missing. He checked the workbench's surface and the surrounding area, curious if they had just not been stowed in their designated locations. Eventually he gave up and came to the conclusion that the tools were simply missing.

To the right of the workbench hung a cheap, large golden-yellow corkboard with in a light yellow wooden frame. The board was full of stick pins and a random assortment of colored pieces of paper. Mick meticulously read each scrap of paper, hoping to find a clue to where the mysterious prototype might be held. Same as the office though, nothing stood out to him.

The last slip of paper Mick found, which was stuck behind a large pizza flyer, was another airplane ticket stub for a round trip to Lincoln, Nebraska. Mick removed the ticket stub and shoved it into his pocket.

He pulled out his cell phone and dialed Hal's number.

"Did you find it?" Hal greedily asked as soon as he heard Mick's breathing.

"No. There's nothing here. I've searched the entire house and there's no prototype. I'm in the garage now and there's a few tools missing. I don't know, maybe he took them somewhere to work on what you're looking for."

"Well did you find anything even remotely useful? Anything at all?"

"Not really, but this guy does fly back and forth from Nebraska of all places for some reason."

Nebraska? Hal wondered why the state of Nebraska seemed to ring a bell. "Wait a minute. If I remember correctly Lisa's sister and husband live on a farm somewhere in Nebraska. Maybe he's building the prototype there."

Mick sighed, he hated flying. Whether he liked it or not, he knew he was headed to the Cornhusker state.

Jon's flight back to Dallas was a depressing one. Although surrounded by Beth, Andre and his aunt and uncle, hardly a word was spoken between them. After a three hour plane ride, accompanied by another half hour in the car, each of the five crashed when they rolled into his parent's empty house later that night.

The next morning, Jon took his time dressing in his old room. Every single item reminded him in some way or another of his parents. On a corner of his bed were a stack of legal documents he'd received from his parent's lawyer Sam Thomas. Jon had never met the man, but had heard his parents speak highly of him. "One of the most trustworthy men I know," he had once heard his mom say.

Being an only child, his parents had left everything they owned to him. Although not rich by any means, while alive his parents were making relatively decent salaries; they had been upper middle class for sure. With their insurance policies, savings and assets, Jon was instantly worth north of three million dollars; a sum he would have gladly paid just to have them back.

Dressed in a dark blue suit his mom had bought ahead of time for graduation, Jon wiped a single tear from his eye as he walked through his house in silence. The others were already in the car waiting for him to leave together for the dual funeral. Jon stepped into his parents' bedroom and then into his dad's office. He missed them so much it was overwhelming.

Jon dashed out of the house and into the day's sunny morning. He felt if he stayed in his house of memories any longer he'd break down into sobs and never be able to get back up. He needed to get away from everything and everyone once the funeral was over. No college, no Dallas and no friends, he just wanted to be alone.

"Come on Jon, we're going to be late," Aunt Jenny said. She had gotten out of the car and was on her way to find him when he had burst out the front door.

"Sorry, just took me longer than I guessed," he mumbled. Three weeks of exams, then finals and then graduation had left Jon basically no time to come to terms with his parent's death. Even now he felt as though he was operating in a haze. I just have to get through the funeral and then my life can get back to normal, he thought.

On the way to the funeral his uncle and Andre made idle chit chat, while Beth held tightly onto his hand. No one talked directly to Jon. They all hoped he'd join into the light conversations, but understood when he didn't.

The memorial service took place at the cemetery where his parents' ashes were to be held. After forty five minutes of Bible verses and short comments on his parents' lives finally came to a close, a reception and a casual brunch in their remembrance was held. This was the time Jon was dreading the most.

Friends of his parents, childhood acquaintances now forgotten and strangers he had never met, lined up to give him their condolences. Jon politely nodded as each guest eventually made their way to his table, telling him how sorry they were for his loss.

As Jon relished a moment of alone time while waiting in the serving line for seconds, a hefty rounded individual made his way towards him. Jon would have recognized the heavily weighted fellow anywhere. His dad's best friend Chet smiled as he caught Jon's attention and waved.

"Hey there Jonny boy, how's my favorite God-son?" *In lieu* of reaching out to shake Jon's hand, Chet was instead preoccupied with pulling up his elastic banded trousers. Although not easy on the eyes, Chet had been one of Jon's favorite friends of his father's from since he could remember.

"Okay I guess," Jon replied, already feeling slightly more upbeat with Chet around.

"Good to hear my boy. Don't let all these old farts get you down. Plus I lost my dad when I was around your age and look how I turned out!" Chet said, slapping his protruding belly. He smiled a wide grin at Jon. Jon couldn't help but smile back. Years of sitting in a swivel chair as a computer programmer had wreaked havoc on what Chet had said used to be a muscular frame. However, Jon had yet to see a picture where Chet was even close to being considered thin.

"You know your parents and I go way back, right?"

Jon nodded solemnly in return.

"I was there when your dad got his job and when he met you mom and even when you were born. Well, I wasn't actually in the room when you were delivered or anything like that, but you know what I mean. That would have been weird."

Jon smiled again at Chet's lack of social awareness. Even the death of his best friend couldn't curtail Chet's love of life. Still cracking jokes and punch lines, Jon knew Chet as well as most of his family members and this was the saddest he'd ever seen him.

"Look son, just know that if there's *anything* at all you need ever and I mean ever, I'm going to be really pissed if I found out that you didn't call me."

"I know Uncle Chet. And thanks, it means a lot."

Chet smiled back at him and tussled his hair. Jon always hated when Chet did that, but this time it couldn't have been more comforting. Why didn't he just give him a hug?

"Alright, I can tell you're having a ton of fun, so I won't keep holding you back from it." Chet said sarcastically as they neared the end of the lunch line. Lingering at the end of the food line, both Chet and Jon saw a few individuals milling around, waiting for the opportunity to talk to him. Jon said goodbye to Chet and sighed as the individuals began their approach, like vultures circling rotting meat.

Towards the end of the reception, when the guests had already begun starting to leave, Jon sat unbothered at a round table with Beth, Andre and his aunt and uncle. A tall man on the far side of the room caught Jon's attention as he walked towards him. Jon knew the man was Hal Roberts, his dad's boss. He'd only seen the man a few times in his life, but each time Jon felt an overwhelming dislike for him. Maybe it was the way Mr. Roberts leered at his mom when she wasn't looking and even sometimes when she was. Or maybe it was the air of arrogance that surrounded him; like he was better than everybody else. Whatever the reason, Jon's mouth filled with a foul distaste as the man approached him.

As Mr. Roberts neared his table, Jon stood to cordially shake his hand, but not before catching the faces of his aunt and uncle. Their pure hatred of the man was painted on their faces plain as day. He wondered why even his aunt and uncle, who lived four states away, despised him so much. So, I guess I'm not the only one that doesn't like this guy, Jon thought as he turned to greet the approaching millionaire.

"It's Jon right?" Mr. Roberts asked. He studied the young man before him. He noticed Jon's muscular frame was not much different than his own and that many of their facial features were close to identical. Although he believed the snake-like lawyer, seeing Jon face to face convinced Hal that Jon was indeed his son.

"Yeah, that's right," Jon rudely replied. There would be no "sir" used to address this man. After hearing condolences and being forced into idle chit chat with strangers for the better part of an hour, Jon's normally gracious social interaction had taken a break.

The kid's got backbone, Hal thought. Not letting Jon's curt reply interrupt his flow, he continued, "I knew both of your parents for many years Jon. They were good people and the world's worse without them in it. Also your dad was one of the best engineers we had at *Evergreen Resources*."

"Thanks," Jon muttered. He just wanted the man to go away so he could go back to sitting down. In the distance, over Mr. Robert's shoulder, Jon saw Chet leaving the reception. Chet gave him a hearty wave goodbye, but then curiously pointed to Mr. Roberts. At least Jon thought he was pointing to Mr. Roberts. Chet then pointed to both of his eyes and then with an outstretched thumb pointed to Mr. Roberts again, just to make sure Jon understood who he was talking about. He was warning Jon to watch the arrogant CEO. Before disappearing through the reception room's double white doors, Chet mouthed the words, "be careful," and then he was gone.

Jon turned his attention from the empty doorway back to Mr. Roberts. What was it about this man that made everyone hate him so much?

"I said, do you have a job lined up?" Hal questioned for the second time. The boy might be smart, but his attention span needed a little work. Hal caught the disapproving looks from Jon's Aunt Jenny and Uncle Harry, but they rolled off him like grease on a pig. Lisa's older sister Jenny was pretty, but in Hal's opinion she never came close to her sister. Lisa had contained a fire at her core and eyes that could have melted a man's heart. Hal felt her sister was plain by comparison.

Jon jerked back to reality, not having heard the question the first time while lost in thought. "Uh, no," he replied. "I've been pretty busy the last few weeks." Not that it was any of Mr. Robert's business.

"Well, we have some openings at my company. I think there's a chance you'd be a great fit, just like your dad was."

"Really?" Jon replied, his interest in the conversation slightly percolating.

"Yeah, of course. It's the least I could do for you. From what I hear you were an even brighter student than your old man. I think *Evergreen Resources* would be lucky to have you. How about this, take as much time as you need to work through everything going on in your life and then come and check out our offices sometime. I'll even give you the tour myself."

Hal pulled out his wallet and fished out a glossy jet black business card with his contact information printed in brilliant gold lettering. Before giving the card to Jon, he wrote his personal cell number on the back.

"Here," he said handing him the card. "My personal number and email are on the back. You don't even have to make an appointment, just stop by and I'll personally give you a tour of the facility."

"Well, thanks," Jon said a little shocked. A conversation he had expected to be a complete waste of time had turned out to be quite interesting.

"Oh, and if for some reason you aren't interested in *Evergreen Resources*, come by anyway. I want to discuss something else with you not job related."

Jon politely said, "Thank you" once again before he and Mr. Roberts parted ways. Jon watched as Mr. Roberts left the dining hall and wondered what else they had to talk about. It was probably nothing. Maybe Mr. Roberts just wanted him to stop by and pick up his dad's belongings. Whatever it was, Jon doubted their meeting had much importance to his life.

Jon turned and sat back down at the white linen covered table. As the day's events progressed he had started feeling a sense of relief and closure concerning his parents' deaths. Having a ceremony to remember them and knowing that was the last piece of their puzzle in his life had calming effect on him. There was still of course all of the legal mumbo jumbo he needed to deal with, but those were all *things* and they could wait.

"Jon," his A bunt Jenny said from across the table.

"Yeah?"

"You need to stay away from that man, he's a horrible person. He might own one of the top energy firms and wear the best suits and drive the most expensive cars, but he's hurt so many people along the way, including your parents."

"I know you say that Aunt Jenny," Jon replied. "But what's he done that's so bad?" It was an honest question, wasn't it?

"You know what, after this is all over today, why don't you come to the farm for a few days. We can talk about it then."

Jon paused a moment and then said, "I'll think about it, okay?" Maybe spending a few days at his aunt and uncle's farm would do him some good. Leaving Dallas for the Midwest would be an easy way to get away from it all. Before the early afternoon's lunch came to an end, Jon had decided Nebraska was exactly what he needed.

"No, you have things to do. Go ahead and go. I'll be fine," Jon reassured Beth. Beth arched a questioning eyebrow but agreed nonetheless.

Andre had already left the car and was waiting for Beth at the airline terminal's front door. Over the past four years at college and in their fraternity, Andre had easily become Jon's best friend. He knew his friend was hurting, but figured Jon could handle it better on his own. Plus, Andre hadn't spent the past few months buffing up his physique for nothing. Back in New Jersey, his group of fifteen friends had already rented their house on the shore for the summer. Bikinis, beer and countless late nights were waiting for him there. He sighed as Beth and Jon said their cute goodbyes, knowing this would be his last summer at the shore. Come fall, he'd be finding a job and entering the workforce. Andre shuddered at the thought.

"You better call me every day," Beth said. She wrapped her thin arms around Jon's muscular frame and squeezed tight. "I'm going to miss you," she whispered.

"I'm going to miss you to. I'll call you tonight after you get in." Jon smiled a reassuring smile and kissed her goodbye.

Seeing they were finished, Andre grabbed one of Beth's bags and disappeared inside the terminal; his figure quickly obscured by the darkly tinted plate glass walls. Jon followed Beth with his eyes as she too was swallowed inside the enormous building. She gave him one last quick smile and a wink before the doors shut behind her.

Jon slowly got back into his mom's car and left the airport. He still intended to ask Beth to marry him, but now was definitely not the best time. He thought maybe later in the summer would be better, once everything from his parent's death was squared away for good.

Jon's aunt and uncle had left for the farm a few days ago. In truth, they were itching to return to the quiet surroundings of their farm. The corn was growing fast during this part of the summer and his Uncle

Harold needed to be there to make sure there was adequate water, pesticides and fertilizer if needed. Jon had one last item in town he wanted to address before he too would meet his relatives in Nebraska.

Jon pulled his mom's red car into an open space directly in front of the police station handling his parent's death. He had never been inside a police station before and wasn't sure what to expect. Were there going to be criminals chained to benches like in the movies or had Hollywood led him astray?

He pushed open the heavy glass door and was immediately greeted by the building's cool air. Before approaching the clerk directly in front of him, he noticed how brightly lit and clean the building was. Thinking back to the movies again, it seemed as though the police departments were always portrayed as either decaying spaces of lackadaisical human interests or so futuristic the technology present alone would have bankrupted the city. This police department was neither of those, but more like a normal office building.

Jon continued scanning the cubicle farm and offices along the building's outer walls as the department clerk drummed his fingers in anticipation of Jon's arrival.

"Can I help you young man?" the clerk asked, somewhat annoyed at Jon's apparent aloofness and at having to wait.

"Yeah, I'm looking for Officer Ryan or Detective Briggs," Jon replied. He had briefly talked to both on the phone a couple of times about their investigation into his parents' deaths. Officer Ryan had been the first responder to the accident, while Detective Briggs was the person handling the investigation. After speaking on the phone with each of them, their positions were clear, in that although what had happened to his parents was a tragedy, there was nothing to lead either of them to believe the crash was anything more than an unfortunate accident, but Jon wasn't convinced.

As long as he'd known his dad, which was all of his life, his father kept both of their vehicles in pristine condition. If so much as a single drop of oil was seen on the garage floor from either vehicle, his dad would have spent numerous hours isolating the problem. Jon just couldn't believe that his dad had been driving the truck for weeks or months while the brakes slowly got worse. It just didn't make any sense.

After a few minutes Officer Ryan emerged from the back of the office and found Jon waiting for him on a bench off to the left of the clerk's front desk.

"Hi Jon, I'm Bob," Officer Bob Ryan introduced himself. "I know I said so on the phone but again, I just want to tell you personally how sorry I am about your parents. This probably won't help, but if it's any consolation their truck hit the ground so hard I don't think either of the felt any pain. They probably both died on impact."

"At least they didn't suffer," Jon replied, depressed at the visual his mind conjured.

"So, last time we talked you said you wanted to have a look at your dad's truck?"

"If you don't mind, I really would appreciate it," Jon responded.

Officer Ryan scratched his head and shrugged his shoulders. "I'm not sure what you expect to find that we didn't, but suit yourself. Detective Briggs is giving the truck one final onceover and then we're done with it. After you have a look and give us the okay we'll have it taken to the scrap yard." Officer Ryan waited for Jon to tell him otherwise, but when he didn't he shrugged his shoulders and said, "Well, follow me then."

Jon walked alongside Officer Ryan and out of the precinct's main doors. Once outside Officer Ryan asked, "Do you want to ride with me or follow behind?"

"It's not here at the station?" Jon asked.

"No, we don't have room for it here. We have an impound lot where all of our wrecks are towed to. You can ride with me if you want. I'm coming right back to the station after we're done."

"Sure, sounds good," Jon replied. At the beginning of the day he'd never been in a police station or in a police car, now he was getting the opportunity to do both; too bad it wasn't under different circumstances. Jon followed Officer Ryan to his patrol car and rode with him to the impound lot. The lot's entrance was sealed with a razor wire topped chain linked fence, which they had to wait to open before entering the semi-secure area.

Officer Ryan pulled his patrol car to the front of a brick building on the lot's left side. Several large bay doors were open, revealing the wreckages of numerous cars. Jon saw people inside walking around the extremely damaged vehicles and taking notes.

"That's Detective Briggs over there," Officer Ryan said as they walked inside the wide open structure. He pointed to a stocky man bent over a crumpled heap of metal that now barely resembled Jon's father's truck.

"Detective Briggs," Officer Ryan yelled across the open building.

The detective looked up, seeing Officer Ryan and his guest. Detective Briggs hurried the last few scribbles of writing on his yellow legal pad and walked briskly to meet the two guests. The detective was a thin man with almost no hair at all atop his bald head. What greying hair he did have along the sides of his scalp was kept short and neat and reminded Jon of a somewhat younger Patrick Stewart. If the detective had been clothed in a dark red and black skin-tight shirt along with a signature Star Trek communication pin, Jon would have sworn the man had just left the Enterprise; him and the actor were dead ringers.

"My condolences," Detective Briggs said as he took Jon's hand and shook it.

"Thanks," Jon replied. Man this was getting old.

"Are you sure you want to look at this?" Detective Briggs asked in reference to the wreck. "There's some blood in there and it's not very pretty. I just want you to know what you're going to see."

Jon gulped. His stomach churned slightly, but he ignored the discomforting feeling and pressed on. He had to see the wreck for himself. "I'll be okay sir," he said, although not entirely sure his insides agreed.

The three men walked over to the vehicle. Officer Ryan and Detective Briggs stayed a few steps behind, allowing Jon some space.

"I've just finished my inspection of the vehicle, so you're free to touch anything or fish anything out of the cab that might have personal significance or anything like that. Take your time," the detective said. When Jon wasn't looking the detective gave Officer Ryan a gesture that said, "Hey, whatever floats this kid's boat."

Jon circled the mangled heap of metal and fiberglass, not exactly sure what he was looking for; closure maybe or was there something else? Jon stopped in front of the passenger window or where a window used to be and took a peek inside. Dark brownish red stains covered the seats and the carpeted ceiling above where his parents would have been sitting.

Again a wave of nausea swept over him. Immediately he took a step back and inhaled a deep breath of fresh air mixed with a hint of gasoline and oil. The smell faintly tasted like chemicals causing him to quickly exhale.

"What did you say the cause of the wreck was?" Jon asked over the truck bed.

"When we found the vehicle the brake fluid was virtually empty," the detective replied.

"Was there brake fluid found at the scene of the wreck?" Jon replied.

"Nope, none at the scene or in the reservoir," Jon heard the detective reply with a slight hint of annoyance in his tone. Jon understood. He wouldn't want someone questioning his work either, but this accident was about *his* family.

Jon rounded the front of the truck and lay on his back and disappeared underneath. "So I can pull parts off?" he questioned under the two tons of smashed wreckage.

"Sure, knock yourself out," he heard the detective reply.

Jon's father, although not the most loving that a father could be toward him, had at least taken the time to teach Jon the ins and outs of how vehicles work. Actually working on the family cars with his dad was one of the reasons Jon had followed in his father's footsteps in engineering.

Jon scoured the maze of wires, metal and tubes under the truck's engine. Quickly he found the one he was looking for and pulled hard. The line supposed to be full of brake fluid snapped at its connection and fell towards the floor. Jon pulled his body and the limp tube out from underneath the truck.

"What are you going to do with that son?" Detective Briggs asked. "We already eyeballed it for leaks."

"Just a hunch," Jon said. There's no way his father wouldn't have kept the brake fluid in check. Jon found a sink to the rear of the massive garage and pushed the end of the hose tight against the spout. Both Detective Briggs and Officer Ryan followed behind and watched as he turned on the faucet. Once water began pouring out of the opposite end of the hose, Jon plugged its opening with a finger from his other hand. A few seconds later, as the pressure built within the hose, a small pinpoint spray of water erupted at the hose's halfway point.

"Well I'll be darned," Detective Briggs whistled. "We were only looking for a hole big enough to see. While Jon continued letting the water spray, the detective took a step forward and examined the small opening. "Folks, we've got a problem here."

"What do you mean?" Officer Ryan asked.

"Look at the shape of the hole under pressure. It's almost a perfect circle. No rock or accidental piece of metal is going to ever create a hole that perfect. It looks like to me someone deliberately punched a hole in this tubing just small enough they hoped we'd miss it. And we would have if it weren't for you," the detective replied and slapped Jon on the back.

"It, it was just a guess," Jon stammered. Jon dropped the hose from his hands and grabbed the sink basin with both hands. His parents were... murdered? But, why? Who could have ever hated either of them that much?

"Take a deep breath there son," said the detective. "It's only a hunch. I'll get one of the guys in the lab to take a look at this hole under one of their microscopes to make certain. Right now it's just a guess, so I could be wrong. How'd you know to look there?" he curiously asked.

"I didn't. My dad was a nut about his cars. I just knew he'd never have been driving with any of his fluids that low. It was just a hunch."

"That's sure one hell of a hunch," Officer Ryan chimed in.

"You've done good son. I guess I've got some more work to do here. You go on with Officer Ryan here and know that rest assured we'll find out what happened to your parents."

Jon nodded, still in shock and followed the officer back to his patrol car. Jon was silent on the trip back, while Officer Ryan marveled at Jon's find. "Wait till I tell the guys back at HQ," he said. "They're never going to believe it. Detective Briggs is one of the best. Man, you should have seen the look on his face when that hose started spurting water," he laughed.

Back at the station Jon informed the officer he'd be leaving for Nebraska for a few days and gave him his aunt and uncle's contact information. Officer Ryan thanked him again for the miraculous find and shook his hand goodbye. Jon watched the officer disappear inside the police station before heading back to his car. "I guess

Nebraska's not going to be all that relaxing anymore," he muttered, alone on the road. Well, so much using his aunt and uncle's farm in the middle of nowhere to clear his mind. Instead of relaxing, he knew he'd be anxiously waiting by the phone to find out what really happened to his parents.

CHAPTER 5

NEBRASKA

"Hello?" Jon asked as he picked up his parents' telephone. He anxiously gazed at the living room sofa, where his suitcase sat fully packed and ready for the trip to the Cornhusker state. Lying on top of the suitcase was his plane ticket and I.D., also ready for traveling.

"Ahh, Jon, is that you?" a deep voice rumbled.

Jon wasn't sure which Jon the man on the phone was referring to, him or his dad. "This is him," he replied, not wanting to waste the time he needed to hurry to the airport.

"Great. This is Detective Briggs. I'm glad I caught you before you headed to Nebraska. Do you have a few seconds to talk?"

Jon's heart thumped at hearing it was the detective on the phone. Only a day had passed since their meeting at the impound lot. Had he found something new?

"You just caught me heading for the airport, but I have a few minutes," Jon said, trying to calm his nerves. "Did you find anything out about the puncture?"

"That's exactly what I wanted to tell you. After our lab took a closer look at the hole we're almost positive the break didn't occur naturally. I'd bet money that someone deliberately poked a hole in your dad's truck's brake line. We don't have any leads right now, but I did want to let you know that we're reopening your parent's case not as an accident anymore, but as a murder investigation."

Jon gulped again at the word murder. Again, who would have ever wanted to murder his parents?

"Jon, I need to ask you if you know of anyone that might have wanted to harm your parents. I've been on the phone the entire morning talking to people who knew your parents and everyone that I've talked to so far has had nothing but nice things to say about them. Right now I'm up against a brick wall and could use your help son."

Jon thought for a few moments concerning the detective's question. He was instantly reminded of his dad, when the detective had called him son and was having trouble focusing on the task at hand.

Finally he replied, "I can only think of two people you should maybe talk too. The first is my dad's old friend Chet; if you haven't talked to him already. He's a great guy and I know they were really close. Maybe he'll know of someone who my dad didn't get along with."

"Alright and the other?" Detective Briggs asked.

"The other guy is Hal Roberts."

"That's the CEO of *Evergreen Resources*, right?"

"Yeah, that's the one. He was my father's boss and for some reason, unknown to me, my parents didn't like him. I don't have any reason to believe he murdered my parents, but I know there was bad blood between the three of them." Not that they ever talked to me about it, he thought, but didn't say.

"Well, that's more than I had to go on before I talked to you, so thanks," the detective said. "Oh, by the way, I just wanted to let you know that was some fine investigative work you did with your dad's truck. If you even think about joining the force, we'd be lucky to have you."

Jon blushed at the compliment and was unsure what to say. "Thank you sir. I think I just got lucky on that one though. It's kind of hard not to be motivated when something like this involves your parents."

"I understand son, but don't ever discredit luck. If I could only tell you how many cases I needed a lucky break before solving them. Luck is something you make for yourself and you made it for us yesterday. Anyway, I've got to get back to these phone calls. Thanks for the leads and I'll get a hold of you the minute I find something. Have a good trip to Nebraska." The detective said good bye and hung up the phone. Jon had barely a moment to reflect on the conversation before he noticed the time and shot out the door.

Five hours later, Jon was aboard his Boeing 787 watching corn-fields whiz by as the plane slowly descended into Lincoln, Nebraska. Most of the flight had been over a mixture of brown and green semi-arid landscapes he had grown accustomed to throughout the years, which now seemed quite drab by comparison to the bright green fields. Jon stared out his window on the right side of the plane. He saw the university's football stadium proudly standing at the edge of the city and the gold covered dome atop the state's capitol.

The landing was quick and uneventful. Once the cabin door was finally opened, rays of bright sunshine filled its interior along with a healthy dose of strong humidity. Within a few seconds Jon felt his shirt and skin begin sticking together and heard the other passengers begin to complain. After Jon grabbed his carry-on and marched in line along with the other passengers towards the exit, he passed a hefty man with burly arms and a cowboy hat covering his face. Jon noticed the individual appeared to still be asleep in his airplane seat, but forgot him soon after.

As the steady stream of passengers ambled by, Mick watched from a small slit under his cowboy hat. What were the odds the Coulter's kid would have been on the same flight to Nebraska? Mick had been one of the first boarding groups on the plane and hadn't noticed Jon until he passed him by on his way to the back of the plane before takeoff. Mick had expected to get a good long nap in during the flight from Texas to Nebraska, but seeing the kid had derailed his plans. His presence had weighed on Mick's mind to the point he was unable to sleep.

After Jon passed by him on his way off the plane, Mick quickly gathered his belongings and deftly merged into the moving line, only a few passengers behind Jon. Although not part of his original plan, Mick thought he might use Jon's presence to his advantage. The local time was just shy of six in the evening and Mick's stomach growled. He ignored the urge to eat, as his mouth watered at passing two food stocked kiosks and continued following the boy.

Hal had sent Mick pictures of both Jon and his aunt and uncle along with the address of their farm. Those items, accompanied by a Google map, rested in the bottom of his pants pocket. Trying to keep his distance, but careful not to lag too far behind, Mick trailed the lad from the plane to the luggage carousel. As soon as Jon left the secured area of the terminal, Mick watched as he was happily greeted by his Aunt Jenny and Uncle Harold. Still careful not to be seen, he cleverly maneuvered into a position where he could hear what they were saying.

"Good to see you Jon," Uncle Harold said. "Did you have a good flight?"

Mick watched Jon nod his head and give his aunt and uncle a series of quick hugs. They started talking and continued walking to the carousel, which had yet to start turning and was currently devoid of luggage.

"Are you hungry?" Mick heard Jon's Aunt Jenny ask.

Say yes kid, Mick only thought but wanted to shout.

"Sure," Jon replied. "Anyplace you guys want to go is fine with me. Maybe a place we can sit? I've been stuck in a car or airplane all day. It'd be nice to have a break before we get on the road."

Mick smiled, displaying a row of yellowing teeth from too much coffee and coke. Perfect. While they sat and chewed the fat he could get himself to their farm and be undisturbed in his search for the other John's prototype. Mick's Google search had traced their farm to only about an hour's drive from the airport; close to the town of Grand Island.

Mick left the terminal, while Jon and his aunt and uncle were waiting for Jon's solitary bag and hurried over to the rental car counter. Twenty minutes later he was in a new Dodge Charger and speeding over seventy-five miles an hour on his way to the aunt and uncle's farm. Daylight's saving time had changed a few months prior and even at 6:45 in the evening the sun was still far from setting, providing his drive with plenty of light. A little over an hour on the road, Mick turned off the interstate and onto a small highway. Between large swaths of farmland filled with corn, alfalfa and soybeans, the highway was periodically lined with tall trees, swaying in the wind.

Mick rolled down all four of the car's windows and breathed in deeply the fresh countryside air. The smells of nature flooded his senses, helping to relax an otherwise tense situation.

"One hour. I've got one hour," he muttered to himself. If he stayed longer than that, Mick risked running into Jon's family and if that happened there wasn't an easy way he could think of to explain why he was there. That particular situation would no doubt end up being injurious to both parties involved. Mick's friend on the Dallas police force had already informed him the Coulter's case was being reopened as a homicide. If Jon or his family caught him snooping around their house his detection would only bring unwanted attention to him and possibly Hal.

Mick pulled off the highway and this time onto a gravel road. Just like Texas, he thought as the gravel crunched and spun under the car's tires. Another ten minutes and he turned the car into the aunt and uncle's graveled drive. At the approach of the car, two large raggedy dogs came tearing out from behind the garage, barking at the unknown vehicle.

Mick turned off the car and looked down at the dogs circling his vehicle. He didn't think they were mean, but he'd been in similar situations to many times to take the chance. Digging in his lone bag, Mick withdrew two dried pigs' ears from a plastic baggie.

"Here you go boys," he said and tossed the pieces of chewy flesh into the dirt a few yards away. The dogs instantly forgot the alien vehicle and began voraciously devouring the delicious treats. "That'll keep you boys busy for a while."

Mick carefully stepped out of the car, while keeping one eye on his canine companions; neither of which now seemed to care he was there. Grabbing a bag of randomly assorted tools, Mick trotted to the main house. He turned the front door's handle and smiled as the door opened freely. "Gotta love the farm," he said, figuring there were probably not many burglars around. He knew that might not necessarily be true, but any burglar dumb enough to be caught breaking into a farm was likely to meet the front end of a shotgun, which usually kept the crime rate down. Unlike the east coast, almost everyone on a secluded farm owned at least one firearm.

He searched the house room to room as quickly as possible. Finding nothing, Mick headed back outside. Both dogs paused from their meal, taking in the returning stranger in their midst. Only a couple seconds of uncertainty passed before each returned to ignoring him and gnawing on their leftover pieces of ears.

Mick briefly scanned the farmstead, searching for other possible prototype hiding spots. Three long rows of tall trees formed shelter belts around the farm keeping all of the buildings tightly shielded from the plain's high winds. Mick was certain from the height of the trees that they were probably planted sometime in the late 30s or early 40s. Ever since the decade long dust bowl in the 1930s, farmers were now much more aware of proper soil conservation, plus it kept the farmstead more protected from the Midwest winds.

Off to Mick's left was a small two car garage and across the gravel drive sat an enormous barn. Mick eyed his surroundings once more, this time searching for livestock. Besides the two dogs the farm appeared to be devoid of animals, making the barn a perfect place to house John Coulter's energy prototypes.

Mick didn't run, but briskly walked, crunching gavel under his feet towards the barn. Although the dogs were busy with their meal, Mick worried any sudden movements on his part might send them into a bit of a tizzy, which he dearly wanted to avoid. The barn's massive wooden front door was suspended on two rollers along a metal track at least fifteen feet above the ground. Mick pulled as hard as he could on the door's metal handle as beads of sweat immediately began collecting on his forehead.

SCREECH. SCREECH.

Slowly, inch by inch, the door's rollers began screeching and hollering as they slid along the weathered rail.

As the day's remaining rays of light flew through the door's opening into the barn, dissipating the shadows, Mick saw covered tables at the far end. Using his hand to mitigate the setting sun's glare, the large tables appeared to be covered with hefty canvas tarps, which kept the objects underneath hidden from view. Obviously needing a closer look, Mick stepped through the open door and into the barn. On both his right and left sides were empty animal stalls, more than certainly once used, but now vacant. Rusty tools and out of date machinery was now residing in the stalls gathering thick layers of dust.

Mick continued on into the barn's open middle, crunching old brown hay and fallen twigs from swallow's nests in the rafters under his feet. Lofts of browning unused hay rested above him on all sides. A ladder to one of the lofts sat in a far corner along with a dangling rope attached to a solid wooden beam on the barn's high ceiling. The thick rope reminded Mick of a similar one in gym class from when he was a kid. Having almost always been at least slightly overweight, Mick had hated the rope climb, always failing to reach the top. Before peeking under the closest large canvas tarp, Mick noticed three long sections of peg board nailed to the side of one of the empty stalls. Hanging in precarious positions and littered across the board, Mick spied many of the tools missing from John Coulter's garage.

His heartbeat quickened seeing the tools. All that was left was to remove the protective canvas tarps and take pictures of what most certainly lay underneath. Carefully he lifted the first tarp up and gently pulled it off the table. Tiny little solar cells littered the table's surface along with varying lengths of small plastic-coated copper wire.

Towards the end of the table sat five of the solar cells interconnected and attached to an incandescent light bulb. He knew the bulb had been dark under the tarp, but now it was providing a bright yellowish light even though only a limited amount of sunlight was making its way into the barn's recesses. Mick pulled out his cell phone and quickly snapped a couple of pictures and sent them to Hal. As carefully as he had removed the tarp, using equal care Mick recovered the delicate instruments as they had been before.

Although Mick had found what he was searching for and time was of the essence, his curiosity got the better of him. A much larger canvas covered hump beckoned at the far side of the open space. He moved towards the hump and grabbed hold of the canvas tarp. A small step ladder was sitting nearby, which Mick needed to get high enough to lift the tarp up and over the unseen device. He pulled the tarp off and was amazed at what lie underneath.

The object was larger than a double doored refrigerator lying on its side. Stainless steel piping ran in all directions, brightly gleaming in the evening sun. Mick felt as if he was in a sci-fi movie staring at the futuristic device.

Red, Blue and green wires were strung about the contraption, connecting one section to another. The maze of steel piping and colored wires crisscrossed in between larger sections of electronics and pieces Mick hadn't a clue what they were for. In the middle of the futuristic assembly was affixed a giant green button marked

"ON". Mick marveled in amazement at the contraption's beauty even though he hadn't the foggiest idea what it could be used for.

Like the solar panels, Mick whipped out his cell phone and snapped a few pictures for Hal. The contraption looked quite interesting to him; maybe Hal would feel the same way. Plus, forty thousand dollars was quite the payday in Mick's opinion for simply breaking into two different homes and taking a few pictures, quite a payday indeed. He might as well add a few extra snapshots for that amount of cash. After sending the pictures on their digital way, Mick climbed back up the step ladder and tossed the heavy canvas tarp up and over the strange device.

He turned to leave the barn and gulped as both of the farm's two large dogs were standing in the entrance, watching him. Mick still had a few extra pigs' ears stowed in his luggage. Unfortunately, the bag holding the ears was resting on the passenger seat of his rental car, opposite of the dogs. Slowly and methodically, Mick took one careful step after another towards the waiting dogs. Neither of the canines moved as he approached, causing beads of sweat to form on his brow. Three yards from the exit, Mick grabbed an old rusty shovel from one of the vacant stalls, gripping it tightly with both hands just in case.

Mick lowered the shovel at the dogs, forcing them to give him their ground. The dogs didn't turn away, but instead began walking backwards, never taking their eyes off the intruder. Mick continued towards the car, while the unrelenting dogs kept stepping backwards. Their tails were all the way to the ground and their ears were flat against their thick skulls. Mick understood the signs and knew the dogs would eventually attack in a blink of an eye.

He repeatedly thrust the rusty shovel's edge at the dogs, driving them backwards until he reached the passenger side of the car. The dogs, knowing their prey was close to vanishing, began snarling and ever brazenly taunting the shovel and redoubled their attempts at attacking the intruder. Mick opened the passenger door, his heart beating over a hundred beats a minute. He thrust the shovel one last time at the dogs, driving each backwards a few additional steps, then dropped the shovel and jumped into the car.

As if the dogs had sensed Mick was going to toss the shovel, as soon as the object left his hand, they leapt at him. As Mick landed on his bag on the passenger seat of the car, the larger of the two dogs made it around the passenger door. Mick kicked the mutt in the face, stunning its attack. Mick frantically scooted over the stick shift and into the driver's seat. For a split second his hand went towards the open door, but too soon one of the mutts was there trying to bite it off. Before he had a chance to turn the ignition, the second dog leapt into the passenger seat next to him. The dog's heavily foamed and snarling mouth repeatedly snapped for flesh while Mick wildly kicked with his cowboy booted foot.

By now the second dog was back on its feet and was also wanting inside of the car. Still flailing his one leg at the closest attacking mutt, Mick fumbled the ignition to on and slammed his left foot into the accelerator pedal. The car sprayed dirt and gravel as it tried to find traction against the unsecured surface. The car jerked forward leaving the second dog in its dust. The car's movement had only increased the first dog's violent frenzy and voracious appetite for Mick's flesh. Mick sped the car into a large graveled area in the middle of the farmstead and whipped the car in a counterclockwise three hundred and sixty degree circle. The dog's four legs were no match against the car's building momentum. The dog's footing eventually gave way as it slipped out the open door, but not before its teeth had taken a few bites out of Mick's unprotected calf.

Once the dog was out of the car, Mick was finally able to reach over and yank the passenger door shut. He straightened the car's direction and sped towards the farm's entrance. Although Mick knew leaving any evidence of his presence on the farm wasn't wise, he'd had it with the dogs and didn't try to avoid the snarling beasts. Luckily for the dogs, they were each quick on their feet and leapt out of the way before being hit. Out of the rear view mirror Mick could see both dogs were circling behind the car to give chase, but were already quickly losing ground. On the main road with one hand on the wheel, Mick felt along his bloodied calf. The smaller dog had gotten in a few good bites and Mick winced as his fingers touched the open wound.

"Damn dogs," he said, knowing he'd need to stich his torn flesh at the closest stop. As Mick flew along the graveled road another car appeared in the distance. Mick pulled his hand back from his ravaged leg and steered to the right, leaving enough room for the other car to pass. As the other car zipped by, Mick recognized all three of its passengers. "I guess that couldn't have been much closer," he muttered. Except for one brief medical stop a few minutes later, Mick sped his rental car all the way back to the airport, hoping to catch the next flight home.

Jon's Uncle Harold cordially waved at the stranger as their two cars passed, which was second nature when driving on the state's lesser maintained back roads. The other driver however ceased to return the cordial greeting and zoomed past.

"Jerk," Uncle Harold muttered, but loud enough for Jon and his wife to hear. "Those city people just have no manners sometimes."

"Settle down Harry," Aunt Jenny said. "I'm sure he didn't mean to be rude. They just don't understand the way things work out here; that's all." Although the lack of the other driver's returning wave didn't bother her, she understood where her husband was coming from. Jon's uncle was a fourth generation farmer from his family. His family had farmed in Kansas, Iowa and Nebraska. Farming was in his blood. To Harold someone not returning a wave was as rude as if they had refused to shake his hand.

"Well, he sure was getting somewhere in a hurry. He'd better be careful driving on gravel like that. You try and turn to fast and that car's gonna slide like you're on ice." Uncle Harold fumed.

As the dust kicked up from Mick's car dissipated in the distance, Jon could finally make out the square block of trees that hid his aunt and uncle's farm. Although many years had passed since he was last at the farm, memories of his childhood came flooding back. Jon had spent many summers at their farm and loved every minute of it. From whipping kiddies on a go-cart his uncle had bought to more juvenile activities like throwing dirt clods at a neighboring bull, those summers were some of the best he'd ever had.

Uncle Harold began slowing the car as they reached the farm's entrance. The tops of their two grain silos towered above the line of mature trees causing the trees to appear small in comparison. Eventually Jon was able to start seeing bits of the house, garage and barn peeking through the trees as well. His uncle slowed the car even more to turn onto the graveled drive.

"What in the world do those mutts think they're doing?" Uncle Harold complained. As he pulled the car off the gravel road and into their driveway both dogs were standing directly in the car's path as if they were waiting for something or someone.

"Get out of the way," Jon's uncle yelled through the car's open window, while honking his horn. At the sound of their master's annoyed tone and the shrill honking of the car, the dogs scattered left and right of their owner's sedan as his uncle inched forward.

"Your dogs always greet you like that?" Jon asked, not remembering if they always needed shooing away.

"Nope. I don't know what got into them. Normally they're lying under a tree or something. Who knows, maybe there was a cat around that got them all riled up. Generally they're good dogs. They must have been after something though, cause they know not to leave the farm. Did you notice how they were standing at the very edge of the property?"

"Yeah," Jon replied.

"Pretty impressive, huh? I trained them with shock collars and now there's nothing but maybe a giant clap of thunder that'll make them do otherwise. Alright Jonny boy, grab your bag and let's head inside," his uncle ordered after pulling and parking the car in its garage.

Jon opened his door and pulled out his suitcase, immediately smelling the fresh country air. The smells of corn, irrigation and country weeds flooded his senses. He was so glad he decided to come to the farm; the relaxed country atmosphere was exactly what he needed.

Jon hefted his overly stuffed suitcase behind him, following his aunt and uncle into their home. Even inside the house he still smelled the corn and other odors he associated with the country. Although Aunt Jenny tried her best to keep their quaint farmhouse clean, the country dust inevitably found its way into every crack and crevice.

As Jon reacquainted himself with the house's familiar surroundings, his aunt and uncle exchanged glances. The time they had agreed upon to tell Jon about his family's dirty little secret was now at hand. It was like a Band-Aid, it didn't hurt so bad if you just ripped it off and got it over with.

"Jon, have a seat. We need to talk to you about something," Uncle Harold said. Jon heard the darker tone in his uncle's voice and wondered what could be so dire. What could be more devastating than the death of both of his parents?

Aunt Jenny was already seated at the kitchen table and wringing her hands. Uncle Harold waited to sit until Jon joined her.

"Come on guys, what's wrong? You're kind of freaking me out," Jon nervously chuckled. He could tell they had something important to tell him as he caught the nervous glances they were exchanging.

"Harry, just tell him," Aunt Jenny pleaded.

"Alright, alright," he said and turned to his nephew. "I'm not sure how to make it any simpler so I'm just going to say it. Your dad John Coulter, wasn't your biological father. I'm sorry. I know you've been through hell the past month, but we felt you needed to know. We knew there wasn't ever going to be a good time to tell you; so there it is."

"I'm so sorry Jon. You've been through so much. It isn't right that you have to handle knowing this too, but we thought it would be better hearing it from us than finding out by accident from some stranger," Aunt Jenny added, somewhat filling the role as Jon's new mom.

"What do you mean my dad wasn't my real father?" he asked in disbelief. "If dad wasn't really my dad, then who is? Do you guys even know?" Jon's head was flooded with questions and emotions, while at the same time revelations into his dad's past actions were now more clearly realized. Assuming his father knew, him being another man's kid would definitely explain his dad's distance towards him.

"Yes, we know who your father is Jon," Uncle Harold said. "Your biological father is Hal Roberts." His uncle paused, letting Jon process the information.

Hal Robert's face immediately popped into Jon's mind. The business card with his phone number and personal email address felt like it was burning a hole in his wallet. Jon still hadn't much of a clue of what had happened in the past, but he now realized why everyone seemed to hate the man so much.

"You're talking about the millionaire or billionaire or whatever he is?" Jon asked. "Does he know?" A questioner by nature, Jon was barely able to contain the bevy of uncertainties he now faced.

"Yeah, that's the one," Uncle Harold confirmed. "Your mom never liked to talk about it, but from your aunt and I's perspective, he never knew about you. He's not a good man and your mom never wanted him or you for that matter to know. She didn't want him in your life, but now that she's gone I'm guessing that he's been informed that you're his son."

"Is that why he came up to me at the funeral?"

"Couldn't tell you Jon. You'll have to ask him that yourself." Uncle Harold paused. "But if you do seek him out just be careful. He wasn't nice to your mom and men like him don't get to the top without being a real son of a..."

"Harry, language!" Aunt Jenny butted in. If the conversation had been on any other topic, Jon would have cracked a smile at his barely a hundred and ten pound aunt putting Uncle Harold in his place, but this time her scolding barely registered on his radar. "We're really sorry you had to find this out," she added after glaring at her husband.

"It, it's fine. I guess I needed to know. And you're right, it's a lot better to hear it from you guys than someone else." Jon along with his aunt and uncle sat in silence for a few minutes. Both Aunt Jenny and Uncle Harold wanted to talk to their nephew, but they kept silent knowing he probably needed some time to reflect.

The sun had almost set on the horizon, causing most of the farm's night activated lights to flip on. Some nights they worked and some nights they didn't. Jon's Uncle Harold swore it had something to do with the humidity, but whatever the reason, tonight they were on. Jon watched fireflies fly past the kitchen window, while moths bee-lined for the artificial light and felt exhausted.

"If you guys don't mind I'm going to hit the hay," he said. "It's been a long day."

His aunt and uncle exchanged saddened gazes with each other and nodded in agreement.

"There'll be plenty of time to talk more tomorrow," his uncle confirmed.

Jon nodded stoically and without emotion marched his suitcase up the set of deserted wooden stairs up to their unused second floor. He dropped the suitcase at the room's entrance and flopped down on the country themed bed. Alone and in pure silence, his mind raced between his parent's death and his new father. He wasn't sure whether to cry over the loss of his parents or rejoice at finding out he had a second dad.

Well over three hours passed before Jon's mind finally allowed him to fall asleep. Even when he had fallen into a deep R.E.M. sleep pattern, he still dreamt of his forever changed family tree.

CHAPTER 6

HELLO DAD

Hal Roberts paced back and forth in the middle of Dallas-Fort Worth's International Airport's D terminal. After receiving Mick's pictures of the prototype the previous night, Hal had called his secretary at home, having her book the earliest flight to Lincoln, Nebraska. He couldn't believe now, of all times, that his company's personal jet was in the repair shop. After a few moments however, he supposed that maybe flying on his personal jet might not be that good of an idea anyway. If he got caught breaking and entering on the company dime, there'd be hell to pay. Now at the airport, Hal anxiously waited for the plane for his flight, which was *en route* from Atlanta, Georgia, to arrive.

For the first time in years he wasn't flying first class, but that was the price to pay for quick travel. Hal thumbed a manila envelope containing the pages of a crudely drawn legal document stating his right to the prototype and any technology related to it. John Coulter had used his company's computers, energy and other services to further his intricate device. With John now deceased and his son hopefully unaware of the prototype, Hal figured he'd easily be able to wrestle it from Jon's uncle's grasp with the documents in hand. Of course, the situation would be even easier if no one was home and Hal could just take what was rightfully his.

Finally Hal heard the plane's arrival announced over the loud speaker. A few minutes later he stood by the wall of large plate glass windows and watched the plane maneuver to the waiting jet way.

Assuming his flight was uneventful, Hal figured he'd be in Lincoln sometime around 10:00 a.m. that morning and be at the farm around noon at the latest. Although the plane's current passengers hadn't yet deboarded, Hal stood as close to the gate as possible ready for his trip.

His mind raced between the new solar prototype and if he'd see his son Jon. Mick had positively identified Jon at the Nebraska airport and in the back of his aunt and uncle's car. On one hand, John's prototype could make Hal millions, if not billions if it worked, but on the other hand there was his son Jon. Hal wasn't sure if he even cared he had a son, but all of that would be moot if they gave him any trouble with the prototype. No son would ever forgive a man who stole his late father's invention for personal gain. Maybe he could offer Jon ten percent of the profits or maybe five? There would be more research needed on the device. Maybe he could convince Jon it was in both of their best interest to have both the device and Jon working at *Evergreen Resources*? Whatever Hal eventually decided, his long flight and hour car ride afterwards would provide him ample time to think it over.

The upstairs floor quietly creaked as the new morning's breeze hit the aging farmhouse. Jon rolled from his stomach onto his back and stretched with a long yawn. The night's dreams had been varied and rather unpleasant. Luckily for Jon, he rarely recalled any of his full dreams, usually just bits and pieces.

Still not fully awake, he strolled across the old shag carpet and to the bedroom's large window. He slid it up as high as its wooden framing would allow and was greeted by birds singing and a warm summer breeze. Jon inhaled deeply, smelling the odor of freshly cut grass. Somewhere on the other side of his farm either his aunt or uncle was mowing the lawn. The gentle hum of the mower only added to the tranquility of the moment.

Jon lingered at the open window, enjoying the relaxing minute until he was fully awake. By the time his senses were fully alert; his mind began flowing with new questions about what he and his aunt and uncle had discussed the previous night. After shutting the window, Jon shaved and showered and headed downstairs.

In the kitchen Aunt Jenny was boiling some potatoes, while shucking some corn for lunch. At seeing her nephew enter the kitchen, she put down the ear of corn and held her arms outstretched for a hug. Even though Jon wasn't really in a hugging mood, he made the effort, which brought a smile to his aunt's face.

"How did you sleep last night Jon?" she asked as she picked up an ear of corn.

"Well it took me a long time to go to sleep, but I think I slept pretty well, all things considering."

"I'm sure that's to be expected. Unfortunately there'll probably be a few more nights that'll be tough as well. You've had to deal with more lately and at one time than most people ever have to," she commented while shucking the ear of corn.

"Looks like a nice day outside," Jon said, trying to change the subject. Although he had many questions to ask, he wasn't in the mood to start hashing through his new-found family history at the moment.

"Sure is. Your uncle is out mowing that back part of the lot. After you've had some breakfast I'm sure he wouldn't mind some help. That riding lawnmower is great for the open areas, but around the trees and bushes I'm sure he'd appreciate it if you wouldn't mind using the push mower to do some edging."

Jon happily agreed to lend a hand and after a quick breakfast hustled outside. His aunt and uncle's land surrounding their house was littered with large oak trees and flowering bushes. An old building which used to house chickens and was starting to lean to one side, was where Jon knew he'd find the outdated push mower. After pulling out the rusty faded mower from the aging dilapidated structure he pulled on the chord no less than ten times before its worn engine revved to life. Once the mower was running, Jon began pushing the smaller lawn mower around the trees and bushes his uncle's larger riding mower would have trouble with.

For the better part of two hours, Jon mowed in silence. Every so often he and his uncle's paths would cross as they each worked a certain portion of the lawn. They would briefly meet each other's gaze, then continue on their way. Around 11:00 in the morning, Jon had finally finished his edging and was stowing the push mower back

into the old chicken coop. As he shut the coop's door, Jon heard his
uncle approaching with the riding mower, also ready to put it away.

Jon reopened the door as wide as the hinges would allow, giving
Uncle Harold as much space to drive his mower through as possible.

"Getting kind of warm out here isn't it?" Uncle Harold commented after he had killed the mower's engine. "I think I'm in the
mood for a nice tall glass of iced tea," he said. Uncle Harold removed
his white and green Pioneer cap and wiped a line of ample sweat
off his brow.

"I'm not sure if it's the heat or the humidity," Jon responded. He
wasn't nearly as hot as his uncle was, which was surprising since his
uncle had been sitting on the mower while Jon was walking. With
both of the mowers' engines off, the trees blowing in the wind seemed
louder than ever. The warm breeze felt good, blowing through Jon's
hair and against the back of his neck.

"Do you want to go inside and get that tea?" Jon questioned
after a few seconds.

"You know what; my tea can wait a spell. I want to show you
something your dad was working on in the barn."

Scratching his head, Jon followed his uncle out from the shaded
lawn and into the glaring midday sun as it beamed down on the
graveled center of the farmstead. Small puffs of dust followed their
footsteps as they walked to the barn. His Uncle Harold's two devoted
dogs, which had taken a liking to Jon, followed close by out of curiosity.

Uncle Harold grabbed hold of the barn door handle and pulled.
The massive door slid to the side and three barn swallows shot out.
Jon marveled at the small birds as they took to the sky. Within
seconds the birds had turned and began dive bombing him and
his uncle. Jon knew the birds were only protecting their young
inside the barn. The swallows were too scared of the humans to
actually attack them, but he'd seen the birds get in a few pecks at
unwanted cats before.

Uncle Harold flipped a switch once inside the cooler barn and
four powerful spotlights attached to the rafters blinked on. Although
the large opening, from where the door was hung, provided more
than enough light for their immediate path, the spotlights painted
a warm yellowish glow across the aging wood throughout the struc-

ture. The barn seemed younger than its years as the synthetic light bathed its insides.

Jon had been inside the barn many times before; most of them while under strict orders not to. The barn was full of rusty metal, aging timber and a loft fifteen feet off the floor, all of which were accidents waiting to happen to a young rambunctious boy. Now older and a little wiser, Jon understood why the barn had been off limits.

"Dang bees," his Uncle Harold cussed.

Every so often Jon and his uncle would have to swat at the flying insects when they flew too close to their faces. Just to the left of entering the barn, a colony of bees had been living for years in a crack in the wall. Deep in the middle of each winter Jon's Uncle Harold would dress in heavy clothing and armed with nothing but a smoking branch and a thick rubber glove thrust his hand into the subdued colony. When he pulled his hand out of the barn's crack there was always a gigantic piece of honeycomb dripping with honey.

Jon swatted another of the annoying insects as he followed his uncle into the center of the barn's main room. Three large tables sat in the middle of the space, covered with equally large drab olive canvas tarps.

"You're dad, umm I mean your actual dad John Coulter, had been regularly visiting, oh I don't know, maybe once a month to work on these." Jon's uncle flapped the canvas tarp on each bench, filling its underneath with air. He then pulled and flawlessly removed their protective layers without so much as rattling any of the delicate items on the benches underneath.

Jon stared in awe at the delicate inventions laid out before him. He studied the intricacies of the individual wires and components that formed the alien devices.

"Uncle Harold, did my dad know I wasn't his biological son?" Jon asked while gazing at his father's inventions.

"Well, umm, that's a good question," his uncle stuttered, caught off guard. "I know your mom never told him, but your dad was a pretty smart guy. If I had to guess I'd say he knew and I'm pretty sure your aunt agrees. That's why we think he spelled your name different than his. He wanted people to know you were his son, but at the same time biologically you weren't. I don't know if that makes any sense or not or if it's even true, but that's my and your aunt's opinion anyway."

Jon continued looking at the gadgets, not wanting to look his uncle in the face. "Yeah, that's kind of what I thought too," he said sorrowfully. "You know the night before he died I talked to him about life and stuff. He said he wanted to work on our relationship and that he was proud of me. I'd never heard him talk like that before. It was almost like he knew he was going to die," Jon said teary eyed.

Uncle Harold cleared his throat a little emotional himself. "Son, he was always proud of you. He might not have known how to show it, but I can tell you for certain you were more important to him than any of these little gizmos."

At that moment, Jon's stomach let out a long rumbling gurgle. "How about we go and get some lunch and we can talk more okay?" his uncle suggested, to which Jon whole-heartedly agreed. By the time Jon finished walking with his uncle to the house, his appetite for sorrowful conversation had abated, while his hunger was only increasing.

"Are my two men hungry," Aunt Jenny asked as they came in from the heat.

"Yes ma'am," Uncle Harold dutifully replied. "The lawn's been mowed and now it's time for some chow." Jon waited in the entryway of the house's side door while his uncle washed his hands.

"All yours," Uncle Harold said to him as he left the bathroom.

Jon stepped inside for his turn and was completely unsurprised to the see the sink covered in wet black filth. When Uncle Harold wasn't performing a task for his aunt or working the farm, he could almost always be found in a large corrugated metal garage at the northwest corner of the property. His true love, even more than farming was working with metal. Over the years Uncle Harold had perfected his craft to where many of his neighbors brought him broken shafts, discs and anything else they needed to have repaired. Uncle Harold rarely charged any of them even close to what the going rate for labor was. In his mind, the farm provided the money, while welding and working with metal was a hobby.

Jon starred at the blackened white porcelain sink. Before wash-ing his hands, he rinsed the sink's basing with a few handfuls of water to wash away the remnants of oil and fine metal shavings from his uncle's hands.

After he too was cleaned and ready for lunch, Jon made his way into the kitchen and sat at the table. Laid before him was a plate of ham, a bowl of mashed potatoes and five ears of corn on the cob. Jon's stomach rumbled again as the sight and smell of the wholesome foods reached his senses. Jon reached for an ear of corn but was quickly shooed away by his aunt's flailing hand.

"Ah, ah ahhh," she said. "No food until your uncle has said grace."

"Oops, sorry," Jon replied. "I always forget about that when I'm here." Every time he visited his aunt and uncle's farm, there were always a few awkward moments at various meal times until he committed to memory their pre-meal prayer ritual.

It wasn't that church was completely foreign to Jon; his parents had just never made it and prayer a staple at their house. With everything that had happened over the past month, Jon wondered if religion had been more a part of his life if the trials he'd been facing would have been easier.

Jon bowed his head and folded his hands together. He listened to his uncle's words about blessing the meal and asking for the forgiveness of their sins. Being scientifically minded like his dad, Jon had in the past thought of religion as a way for people to cope with trouble in their lives. Not that religion was bad, but it was probably just a coping mechanism, nothing more.

Now older, Jon listened to the words and tone as his uncle prayed. The sincerity of his uncle's voice, as if he truly believed he was talking to God spoke to Jon. For the first time Jon could ever remember in his life, he felt connected in that moment to his uncle and to God in a way he had never felt before.

After Uncle Harold finished his prayer, Jon took a deep breath. When he breathed the stale warm air out of his lungs, the sensation of years of apathy from his dad seemed to flow away too. Lost in a pool of cool calmness, Jon didn't realize both his aunt and uncle were starring him down.

"What's the matter Jon, aren't you hungry anymore?" Uncle Harold asked, already slapping a gigantic mound of mashed potatoes on his plate.

"Maybe he got heat stroke outside," Aunt Jenny offered as an explanation.

"What? Don't be silly. He wasn't out there more than a few hours. If anyone got heat stroke it was me. I was the one cutting the grass out in the open. Jon was only taking the push mower around the trees and bushes. He was in the shade all morning for Pete's sake!" Uncle Harold replied, incensed at his wife implying Jon could possibly be that weak. "Look at him Jenny; he's as healthy as a horse. The poor kid's just got a lot on his mind that's all."

At that moment Jon's stomach let out another loud rumble, breaking his sense of tranquility. Brought back to reality, Jon realized he'd been daydreaming. He couldn't remember what he had been thinking about, but he could feel Aunt Jenny and Uncle Harold curiously looking him up and down.

"Um, can you pass the potatoes Uncle Harold?" he asked, ignoring the awkwardness in the room. Like his uncle, Jon slapped down a fair sized pile of the pasty yellow-white potatoes, followed by a generous slab of real butter, which garnered a "See he's fine," from Uncle Harold.

Jon and his adoptive nuclear family ate their fill of mashed potatoes, meat and milk; taking their time until almost an hour had passed. Usually his uncle would then take a quick nap in his favorite brown leather upholstered recliner. However today was going to be a hot one and his irrigation pipes had been plagued with problems all summer long.

"Jon, if you're done eating do you mind helping me lay out some irrigation pipe this afternoon?" his uncle asked. On any normal day it would only be his aunt and uncle on the farm, which meant his aunt would have to help with the irrigation piping. The pipes weren't all that heavy, more awkward than anything. Almost a foot in diameter and made of aluminum the pipes had a series of small plastic outlets for the water spanning each ten foot section of tubing.

Aunt Jenny smiled to herself, knowing for at least today she was going to get a pass on laying the pipe. Even if Jon said no, she knew her Harry would take him along for the ride regardless and get a little work out of the city boy.

"Sure thing Uncle Harold," Jon replied. Aunt Jenny's smile widened a little but she didn't say a word. "Can I spend some time in the barn afterwards when we're done? I'd like to get a closer look at what my dad was working on if it's okay with you."

"Of course. As far as I'm concerned all of those contraptions are now yours anyway." Uncle Harold recapped his head of thinning hair and headed for his trusty pickup truck with Jon not far behind.

Fuming and almost ready to throw a huge hissy fit, Hal stormed off the large airplane and into the Omaha, Nebraska airport. "Omaha? What the heck am I doing in Omaha!" he seethed in not so quiet a fashion.

The original plane Hal was to take from Dallas to Lincoln had developed some type of a leak in its engine, where the pilots never said and ended up delaying their flight over an hour. The airline had then frantically searched for a replacement plane, changing his gate number no less than three times in the process, making Hal run like an idiot back and forth throughout the Dallas airport. In the end, while his original flight was to have left from gate D33, the replacement flight ended up departing from gate D31 only a few feet from his original exit.

Once in the air, Hal had thought for sure the worst of the trouble was behind him until the pilot and co-pilot came on over the loud-speaker saying their new plane had also developed a mechanical issue and would need to land in Omaha rather than Lincoln. In the end a trip that should have taken Hal four hours at the most was now going to be eight or nine.

A little after three o'clock in the afternoon, Hal pulled his red Mustang rental car into his son's relative's graveled drive. He shifted the car into park and killed the engine. A few minutes passed as he waited to see if anyone had noticed his arrival. Unbeknownst to him, Jon and his uncle, along with their two dogs, were laying irrigation pipe, while Aunt Jenny was taking a well-deserved nap.

Realizing he was indeed alone for the moment, Hal grabbed two large empty duffle bags and began walking towards the barn. The day was hot and muggy. Mosquitoes swarmed his face as he strode through the uncut grass, disturbing them at rest. His face and body was oozing sweat as he reached the barn's wide wooden door.

Hal tossed the empty duffle bags off to the side and pulled on the door's handle with all of his weight. The door roughly rolled along its aging metal track to where an opening large enough for Hal's frame had appeared. Grabbing the duffle bags, Hal stepped through the opening and into the barn's cool recesses. Almost instantly the day's heat and humidity seemed to vanish as he was greeted with a cool, stale air smelling of old hay and dust.

With a flick of his finger he flipped on the light switch exactly where Mick had told him it would be. Sure enough at the other end of the small corridor lined with empty pens and stalls sat a cluster of tables.

Hal made his way to the tables and carefully uncovered them one at a time. He marveled at the solar cells, which had lit the incandescent light bulb the moment its cover was removed. Hal smiled at the crudely soldered mess of wires and solar cells as he held them in his hands. Carefully, one by one, he began stowing his precious cargo inside of the empty bag.

After filling the first bag with all of the solar cell components, leftover electronics and schematics he saw lying around, Hal zipped it shut and laid it carefully to the side. He then approached the largest of John Coulter's prototypes and began carefully visually dissecting its pieces one by one. Although still crude and lacking obvious pieces of equipment, John's cold fusion reactor wasn't too shabby.

Hal very much wanted to take the primitive reactor with him along with the solar array filled duffle bag, but it was much too large. He'd need at least another four bags to haul away the giant reactor after it was broken down, which he clearly didn't have time or room for in the small Mustang.

Out of the corner of his ear, Hal heard what sounded like a large vehicle pulling into Jon's relative's lot. Leaving the bags lying at the rear of the barn, Hal dashed to the barn's door and carefully peered around its side. Sure enough, there in the middle of the graveled drive was a large truck with what appeared to be long cylindrical tubes of aluminum in its bed. Inside the truck Hal recognized Jon and his Uncle Harold.

Unsure what to do, Hal rushed back to the one full bag and grabbed it by the handle. Through the barn's corridor he could now hear dogs barking and Jon and Harold's voices.

"Whose car is that Uncle Harold?" Jon asked, admiring the bright red paintjob.

"I haven't a clue," his uncle replied. "I don't have any friends that rich that I know of," he nervously joked. Uncle Harold was about to step inside the house to check on his wife, but noticed the barn's main door standing ajar.

"Stay here and don't move," Uncle Harold ordered his nephew and ran inside the house. Puzzled by his uncle's odd reaction, Jon looked in the direction Uncle Harold had just before scurrying away. He saw the barn's door wide open. His father's inventions were in there! Jon wanted with all of his soul to rush into the barn and protect what little was left of his dead father, but his uncle's words held him fast.

With a couple of seconds, while Jon was still debating whether to obey his uncle or not, Uncle Harold reappeared from inside his house carrying a shotgun in one hand and a handful of shells in the other.

"Stay behind me Jon," his uncle pointedly said. Jon let his uncle lead while watching him carefully add the shotgun shells into the gun. Carefully his uncle peered around the open door and into the barn. His two dogs whined incessantly, knowing someone was inside the aging structure, but remembering their training to follow their master's commands stayed behind their owner until said otherwise.

Sure enough, deep inside the barn's dim coolness Harold saw movement. He then abruptly and unafraid stepped into the barn in clear view of the trespasser and cocked the shotgun loudly.

Hal whirled to face the all too recognizable sound and saw Jon's Uncle Harold standing in his path. Between the loaded shotgun, Jon peering over his uncle's shoulder and the two hounds tensely pacing in the rear, Hal knew he had to think quickly.

"This is my property!" he yelled as Uncle Harold began walking towards him. "*Evergreen Resources'* equipment and technology were used to create these prototypes so legally they belong to me!"

Harold lowered the shotgun in line with Hal's chest and stopped ten feet away from him. "You've ten seconds to either show me some sort of court order proving what you say is true or to get off my property you piece of dirt. Nine, eight, seven," Harold began counting down.

Hal mustered what little courage he could find. "You wouldn't, we're family. Not in front of Jon," he said figuring by now they were all on the same page.

Uncle Harold didn't take the bait and moved a step closer. "Six, five, four. Just so you know, after I shoot you at this range I'm going to see right through your insides before you hit the ground. Three, two…"

Beads of sweat poured off Hal's forehead. He'd never known Harold, only seeing his pictures a few times over the years, but he believed his words to be true. This Midwestern farmer was just crazy enough to shoot him. He'd probably bury him in a pasture somewhere or feed his body to his mangy dogs. Anyway Hal dissected the situation, it was going to turn out badly for him. He had thought about showing the papers his lawyer had crudely prepared, but didn't think Harold would go for it.

In a split second Hal made a choice. He dropped the duffle bag full of the deceased John Coulter's solar prototypes and was about to split for the door before out of nowhere Jon jumped in front of Harold's shotgun. Jon had hoped cooler heads would prevail, but now he realized they wouldn't.

"Don't do it Uncle Harold!" he yelled.

"Get out of the way Jon. This man's a lying cheat and I can finally drop him like a sack of potatoes and not get in trouble for it."

"Please Uncle Harold, just listen to what he has to say," Jon pleaded.

Frustrated and obviously unwilling to shoot through his nephew to get to Hal, Harold reluctantly lowered his shotgun.

"Alright, you've got two minutes. This better be good or you'll be going home with lead poisoning," Uncle Harold menacingly threatened.

Jon took a step backwards from his uncle's loaded shotgun and removed himself from in between the two adults. Jon shuffled backwards a few more feet, while Hal and his uncle starred daggers at each other, until his back was touching the front of the table holding the dormant cold fusion reactor.

"Come on, you've got two minutes so spill it slime ball," Uncle Harold said impatiently.

"Look, I'm sorry your sister-in-law is dead and her husband too, but I didn't have anything to do with it. I know you're mad, but don't blame me," Hal said and regretted the words the second they left his mouth.

"Who said you did?" Uncle Harold demanded, growing hot under the collar. As each second passed he grew more furious at being forced to be in the company of one of the people he despised most in the world. Although twenty years had passed since Hal had treated his sister-in-law like garbage, old wounds took longer than that to heal.

"Nnn, nobody. I'm just saying I know your family's had a rough time lately and I think you're taking out some of your aggression on me. I'm just here to get what's rightfully mine. John Coulter used *Evergreen Resources'* computers and internal resources to come up with the designs for these prototypes. That makes everything on these tables property of my company," Hal said, pleading his case.

"That very well may be true, but you're not walking out of here, unless over my dead body, without the police or else a court order proving what you say is true," Jon's uncle said defiantly.

Hal starred into Uncle Harold's darkened eyes and a moment of clarity washed over him; whatever he did, this psycho with a loaded shotgun was probably going to try and kill him. Whether his thought was a rational one or not, Hal felt he had to act.

Hal looked to his left, as though something in the distance had caught his attention. Keeping his head turned, Hal rolled his eyes back towards Uncle Harold to see if he'd bite. Sure enough, Harold looked towards the unseen object and the second he did Hal jumped him.

The men struggled back and forth with all four hands on the shotgun in the middle of the fight. Hal pulled the shotgun closer to him, only to have Uncle Harold yank it right back. Jon initially not wanting to get involved, stayed off to the side hoping they'd realize the ridiculousness of their fighting and call it a draw. As the tug of war over the shotgun dragged on, Jon became increasingly worried their brawl would result in one of them being shot or worse.

"Stop it both of you," Jon yelled. He received no response as if he wasn't even there. "This is madness," he yelled again and jumped into the fray. Jon managed to lay one hand onto the prized weapon when both Hal and Uncle Harold swung their closest elbows at him not wanting the interference.

Jon took one of the elbows to the face and stumped backwards towards the table holding the unfinished cold fusion reactor. Just as he almost regained his balance, his left foot caught the edge of Hal's full duffle bag causing him to fall over backwards and lose all hope of regaining his balance.

Gravity took hold of his flaying body and he fell hard against the table holding the cold fusion reactor. In a split second, while trying to grab anything that could help to slow his fall, Jon reached out and hit the green ON button attached to the inactive device.

Instantly the machine roared to life. Bubbles formed around the ball of tritium as the electrical current surrounded the small elemental sphere. The seemingly innocent bubbles quickly turned to a violent froth as the core temperature and electricity output tripled nanosecond after nanosecond.

Between the half second from when Jon had struck the ON switch to his body almost hitting the ground, the machine was pumping out power faster than it could dissipate. Each light in the decaying barn burst in order from the closest to the device to the furthest. Sparks and shards of glass rained down in torrents as each bulb disintegrated into nothingness. Lucky for the barn, a burst of wind blew through, putting out the sparks before they hit the dry hay.

Hal and Uncle Harold, although both still tightly clutching the shotgun, stopped wrestling for the moment as their world seemed to be exploding around them. Jon grabbed a piece of the fusion reactor's bright chromed metal tubing and began pulling himself up.

By now the reactor was violently shaking on the long table and emitting high pitched squeals from pockets of boiling water vapors trying to escape. The tritium sphere was now glowing a brighter blue than any of them had ever seen before.

"Get away!" Uncle Harold yelled at the exact moment the device's structural integrity could finally bear no more.

A massive surge of energy, nothing Jon had ever felt before, radiated through his unwilling body as parts of the reactor exploded in massive succession. Wires, gadgets and piping sprayed the area in one violent convulsion. As the device exploded it sent a ring of brilliant blue and white light emanating from its core parallel to the ground. The ring of pure unexplainable energy pulsed first through Jon then passed through Hal and Uncle Harold. The blue-white aura then continued bursting through the barn's walls and disappeared to the outside leaving the barn devoid of artificial light. Only the warm summer day's high afternoon sun, shining in through the open door, illuminated the barn's inner surroundings. Hal and Harold stared down at Jon's limp body strung out on the hay covered floor.

CHAPTER 7

CHANGE

"Let go!" Uncle Harold yelled after the dust had settled and ripped the shotgun out of Hal's hands before he could react. He quickly rotated the gun and delivered a lightning fast blow of the gun's butt into Hal's unsuspecting chest. The blow to Hal's stomach forced almost all of the air out of his lungs, dropping him to his knees. Hal gasped for breath and looked up at his assailant to see a wicked grin painted on his face.

Uncle Harold was about to take a step closer to Hal and finish him off when Jon started stirring off to the side. Jon clawed in the ground in pain as his senses slowly returned. He remembered being shocked and seeing some sort of bright blue light and then everything had gone black.

Slowly and with aching muscles, Jon pushed himself up off the floor and onto all fours. Even moving just a small amount and at a turtle's pace, caused the room to swirl. He stayed on all fours for a few seconds hoping the room's rotation would eventually cease.

"Jon, are you okay son?" he heard a voice ask. With his head still hanging to the ground, as the spinning only increased when he looked up, Jon assumed the voice had come from his uncle.

Still stunned and groggy he only mumbled, "Uhuh," or at least that's what he thought he said.

A warm hand rested on his shoulder and the owner said, "That was a nasty shock you took; let me help you up Jon."

Jon turned his head to the side and looked Hal straight in the face.
As Hal helped him to his feet, as they both stood, Jon glanced up at his
uncle who was still holding his shotgun and pointing it at them both.

"Uncle Harold, can't you point that thing somewhere else? He's
just helping me up," Jon tried speaking clearly. As he continued to
rise the spinning slowed and his senses began returning to normal.
The smell of hay and burnt plastic reached his nostrils and the limited
sunlight that had at first been too bright, now appeared dimmed
to a reasonable light.

"Did I say you could talk to me you worthless turd?" Uncle
Harold snarled back.

"What?" Jon replied, completely taken aback. He was sure he
must have heard his uncle wrong.

"You heard me boy. I said shut up. I should shoot the both of
you right here and now for trespassing on my property," Uncle
Harold snarled again.

"Uncle Harold, are you feeling okay?' Jon asked with concern in
his voice. Maybe one of the flying metal tubes had hit his uncle in
the head or maybe Hal had when Jon was lying on the floor. Either
way, his uncle was not acting like himself.

"I'm be more fine when you two ingrates get off my property."

"Now, that's no way to talk to you nephew," Hal said and took a step
forward, while at the same time moving Jon behind his hefty frame.

Jon was completely dumbfounded. What was going on? His
uncle wanted to shoot him and the biological father he'd never
known was standing up for him? Maybe it wasn't Jon's uncle that
had been hit on the head, maybe it was him.

Jon felt along his scalp, but only found hair. There wasn't a scratch
or bump anywhere to be found. He peered over Hal's tall soldier at
his uncle's eyes. What he saw sent a shiver down his spine. There
was no love or even apathy, only pure hatred staring back at him.

"Uncle Harold please, it's me," Jon pleaded.

His uncle furrowed his brow at the remark and cocked the
shotgun. "You've both got two choices. Either taken one in the front
like a man or in the back like a little girl."

Even though it was crazy, Jon was about to run before Hal
jumped quick as lightning for the gun. Uncle Harold wasn't ready

for his antagonist's cat-like reflexes and tumbled to the ground with Hal on top of him. They wrestled for control of the gun while rolling around on the dusty, hay covered barn's wood slatted floor.

"Jon, get out of here, I'll hold him off," Hal yelled while rolling over and over. Jon was too stunned to move. Again he tried to reason why his estranged dad wanted to save him and his beloved Uncle Harold was ready to shoot him in the face. What was he missing?

Jon slowly started backing towards the barn's open door, when Hal found an opening and punched Uncle Harold as hard as he could. Just as surprisingly quick as before, Hal grabbed the duffle bag full of experimental solar cells was on his feet in a flash and yanking Jon out of the barn by his arm. The afternoon sun temporarily blinded them as they exited the barn's dimly lit surroundings. Nevertheless Hal continued dragging Jon towards his Mustang in a frantic effort to escape.

From inside the barn they could hear Uncle Harold cursing as he regained his senses. Almost at the car, a shotgun blast erupted from inside the barn and part of the large wooden door disintegrated into sawdust and splinters. Uncle Harold appeared in the entrance and cocked the gun again, ejecting the previous shell as he did so.

"Get'em boys," Uncle Harold yelled at the pacing dogs. Without even looking back at their master to make sure his command was true, the dogs tore into a sprint after their allowed prey.

"Get in the car Jon!" Hal yelled, not sure at the moment what was worse; the dogs or the psycho with the shotgun. Both were equally troublesome and he ran as fast as he could.

This time Jon didn't try to reason out what was happening. He had no doubt in his mind that for whatever reason his uncle was absolutely trying to kill him. Jon tripped over himself on the slick gravel in his haste and scurried the rest of the way to the waiting Mustang. He pulled on the door's handle as he picked himself off the dirt, but the door was locked.

"It's locked!" Jon yelled as the dogs closed the gap.

Rounding the car, Hal dug into his pocket, searching for the rental's keys. Frantically he pressed the unlock button until he saw Jon opening his door. Jon swung the door open then jumped inside. He slammed the red door shut just before the dogs reached his side of the car. Through the closed window he could hear the dogs jumping and barking at their escaped prey. Every so often they'd jump high enough to see him through the window, leaving trails of smeared drool on the window. As the dogs continued biting at the painted metal surface, Hal tossed the duffle bag of solar cells, rougher than he wanted to, into the tiny back seat before starting the car.

Jon looked past the dogs towards Uncle Harold who'd stopped halfway to the car and was lowering his shotgun.

"Duck!" Jon yelled right before his uncle squeezed the trigger.

BOOM!

Uncle Harold took a step backwards as the gun's recoil caused him to slightly lose his balance. The passenger window behind Jon fractured into a thousand small shards of glass, spraying Jon and Hal in the process.

"Time to jet," Hal said and shifted the car into drive. The car's sports tires spun gravel and lose yellow dirt in its rear as the muscular engine propelled the car forward towards Uncle Harold who was attempting to quickly reload his empty shotgun. A few feet in front of Uncle Harold the car had enough room to turn around and Hal pulled a one-eighty, spraying the farmer with a cloud of dust.

With the car now facing the direction of the road, Hal slammed the pedal to the floor board, covering Uncle Harold with another coat of the light dust, while pelting him with pebbles. Jon whipped his head around to see his uncle who, undeterred from the dusty haze, was loading the final shell into the gun's chamber.

Almost to the road, Jon saw his uncle lower the shotgun one last time. "He's going to shoot again!" he yelled and crouched low in his seat. Just before the car turned onto the main gravel road Uncle Harold's shotgun pellets tore through the car's rear window.

Hal spun the car to the right, leaving what used to be Jon's home away from home in a cloud of dust in the rear view mirror. His uncle and his two hounds were at the edge of their property yelling obscenities and barking at the escaped trespassers.

"Man Jon, that was intense," Hal finally said after a mile of silence. Both of their heart rates were finally descending back to their normal range, while the car's cool air conditioning dried away their nervous sweat.

"Are you okay son?" Hal asked as he looked over to see Jon picking bits of the shattered glass of his shirt and pants.

"That's the second time you've called me son. What gives you the right?" Jon incredulously asked. How could this man he'd known only in passing think he was anything other to him than someone he vaguely knew?

"I know I haven't been there for you in the past, but quite frankly I never even knew you existed. It wasn't until your mom died that a lawyer came to my office and gave me a hand written note from your mom telling me that I had a son. I can understand you're angry, but it shouldn't be with me. Had I known you were my son, things would have been much different," Hal replied looking Jon directly in his eyes. He could tell Jon needed time to process the day's events, heck all of the past month's events and was content to drive in silence while he did so.

After a few minutes of meditative silence Jon finally responded. "I don't understand, why didn't my mom ever tell me that you were my biological father? I could have handled it." Maybe knowing what I know now, my relationship with my real dad would have been a lot better; he thought but didn't say aloud.

"I don't think it was you that she was worried about Jon. I'm not a good person and she probably didn't want you to have anything to do with me," Hal responded. What the hell? Why did I just say that he wondered? It was like his mouth was moving, but his brain had ceased to function. Ever since the explosion in the barn, he'd felt uncontrollable love for the kid; where it came from he hadn't a clue. He tried to bury the feelings and the disgusting honesty that came with them deep inside him, but it was like trying to catch the wind; futile.

"Yeah, I've been able to tell over the years that my family didn't like you very much. As long as we're being honest, I saw the way you looked at my mom when she was around. You loved her didn't you?" Jon stared at the complete stranger, now his father, in the seat next to him, waiting for an answer.

"Well, I wish I could say it was love, but lust is probably a better word Jon. I wish I could tell you differently, but that's probably the truth." DANG IT! What the heck is going on? Can I stop telling this kid the truth to every stupid question he asks, Hal raged in his mind. But he couldn't. Something had changed in him during that blast. Maybe that bright blue ring of light had something to do with it. At the moment Hal wished he knew Jon better, not just because of his newfound love for his son, but so he could tell if something had changed in Jon too.

Finally off the dirt road on onto the main highway leading to the interstate, Jon and Hal's nervous energy had returned to normal. The way Uncle Harold had come at them, blasting away with his shotgun and sicking his dogs, neither of them would have been surprised to see him come tearing out of his drive, whooping and hollering in his big pickup. However as Hal's Mustang put more and more miles in between them and the farmstead, the likelihood that Uncle Harold was still out to get them was dropping precipitously.

Once they turned onto the interstate towards Lincoln, Jon decided he wanted to continue their conversation. Even though towards the end of their last talk he had started to become slightly annoyed.

"So what happens between the two of us now?" Jon asked genuinely curious. He still hadn't a clue why his uncle had snapped, but his logical mind was telling him to tackle one problem at a time and at the moment, that was his estranged father.

"I hadn't thought that far ahead my boy. But like I told you before at your parents' funeral, there's always a place for you at *Evergreen Resources*. I mean, before I just wanted to meet you, but now I feel close enough to you that I'd actually like you to come work for me. It'd be up to you. I could start you out in one of our top corner offices, since you're my son and all, or if you prefer you can start as an entry level engineer and work your way up the ladder on your own. Whichever path you choose would be fine with me."

Hal shook his head after speaking, disgusted with the raw emotions spilling out of his mouth. Yes, he really did love the boy and yes, he truly did want to work alongside him, but Hal was still positive those feelings hadn't existed before the odd blue-white ring of light had passed through his body.

Finally he couldn't take second guessing himself any longer and blurted out, "Jon, I'm going to be frank with you. When your parents died and the lawyer told me about you, I was intrigued I had a son, but truthfully I couldn't have cared less. I didn't come to Nebraska for you; I came to retrieve what is rightfully the property of my company. However, that being said, ever since that explosion and the weird ring of light, everything seems to have changed.

Now, I want to spend time with you. I want to get to know who you are, but these aren't normal feelings for me. I guess what I'm getting at is did anything change for you in the barn? You know, like in your head?"

Jon stared at Hal, unsure what he was exactly getting at. "I'm not sure what you're asking," he finally said after being unable to come up with an intelligent answer.

Hal took a deep humbling breath. "Flat out I think that colored disc of light changed me somehow. Right now I love you more than I do myself and that's just not who I am. I feel weird even saying it, but that's the God honest truth. I know I sound crazy, but something has changed in me and it doesn't feel natural."

Jon turned forward and gazed through the Mustang's clear windshield. Miles and miles of five foot high stalks of corn lined the interstate on both sides. The mass of dark green was beautiful and was part of the reason why Jon had decided to come to Nebraska in the first place. But even this refuge, his home away from home, was now in shambles. His uncle trying to kill him and the seemingly real possibility his biological father sitting next to him was nuts was almost more than he could handle.

Jon meditated on Hal's confession for over half an hour before speaking again. Nothing he'd seen in the twenty one years he'd been alive had ever sold him on some sort of odd blue light that could changes people's emotions or feelings. But on the other hand he was reminded of the theory of Occam's razor he had learned at the university, which stated that the simplest solution was often the correct one.

"I'm not saying I believe you, but your theory does account for my uncle trying to kill us. I mean, with your history with my mom and my aunt and uncle I can understand why he hates you, but he's always been like a second father to me. None of this makes any sense." Then an idea occurred to him. What did you do when you had an hypothesis, but nothing more? You tested it.

Jon dug into his left pants pocket and pulled out his cell phone. "Who are you calling?" Hal asked.

"I'm going to call Aunt Jenny and see what she has to say. I've been so wound up in being shot at I completely forgot about her. I hope my uncle hasn't gone nuts on her too," Jon said with concern.

He found her number in his list of contacts and pushed the little green phone icon on his smart phone. Through the phone's speaker he heard the number dialing then ringing and waited.

"Hello," came his sweet aunt's reply. Just like at his home in Dallas, here in Nebraska his aunt, not his uncle almost always answered the phone.

"Aunt Jenny are you alright?"

"Of course I am. Why wouldn't I be? You're lucky Harold didn't put a bullet in your back for coming out here. You're not welcome on our farm. Ever."

"I don't understand, what did I do?" he asked, flabbergasted at her response.

"What did you do? Nothing but be the pompous, higher than thou, snot nosed brat you've always been," Aunt Jenny returned, not pulling any punches.

Jon didn't know what to say. Losing his parents and now his beloved aunt and uncle hating him was almost more than he could bear.

"Have you always felt this way?" he asked afraid of the answer.

"I've been wondering that myself. For some reason my feelings concerning you became clear as day this afternoon. I can't understand why, but for all these years I've thought you were a good kid, then it hit me out of the blue."

"What hit you Aunt Jenny?"

"That I hate your guts," she said and hung up the phone on him. Jon was shocked and slowly allowed his hand holding the phone to come to a rest in his lap. Jon couldn't even process the strange conversation. He just stared forward as Hal continued towards Lincoln.

"I take your conversation didn't go well?" Hal asked after a few moments of silence.

"Hardly," Jon replied. "She said he hates my guts. I've never heard her talk like that about anybody in my life, not even you," he added straight faced.

"What did she say when you asked her how long she's felt this way?" Hal asked, digging for answers concerning his own change of heart too.

"Same as you and Uncle Harold. She said her feelings changed this afternoon."

"I knew it!" Hal exclaimed. "Don't you see Jon? Something about that blast or that weird ring of light changed our feelings about you. Don't ask me how, but it did."

"But why about me? Why didn't anything happen to me?" Jon questioned aloud.

"I don't know. Maybe nothing happened to you because you were right next to the device when it exploded or perhaps because you were holding onto it when it blew up. Maybe you're holding on to it grounded your body in some way from its shockwave. Just think of a loose wire. If you're holding onto it when a current passes through it you're going to get shocked something fierce, but if you're grounded, nothing happens to you. I'm just speculating here mind you, but maybe that odd ring of blue and white light worked in the same way."

"Do you think it's permanent?" Jon asked as he started to buy into Hal's idea.

"Couldn't tell you kid. It's just a theory that's all. Let's just hope whatever happened was confined to just your aunt and uncle and myself, otherwise I'm guessing there's going to be a lot of people that have changed their opinion about you and not in a good way."

Hal turned the car off the interstate and into Lincoln's small airport. After managing to get Jon a first class seat next to his own, they boarded the plane for Dallas-Fort Worth. Unlike the initial trip, which was plagued by delays, this once clicked along in perfect fashion. During the flight, Jon was relatively quiet, lost in his own thoughts about the day's events. Only a few days ago he couldn't wait to arrive in Nebraska to clear his head, now he couldn't wait to leave.

"Well I guess it's goodbye," Hal said with a hint of sadness as they reached his car in the DFW's parking garage. Regardless of what or how his feelings had been changed, Jon was his son and he loved him.

"Yep," Jon replied. "Maybe we can meet up some time later this week?"

"Sure. We could go out to eat or you could come meet me at work. I could give you a tour of the place. Maybe show you a few offices," Hal hopefully added. In actuality seeing Jon later in the week could prove beneficial for them both. If they put their minds together maybe they could come up with some answers for what had just happened back in Nebraska.

"That would be great Hal."

"Alright, well, until later this week then," Hal replied. He wanted to give Jon a hug, but wasn't sure if that would be okay with his son he'd only known for a few days. Instead of hugging, Hal reached out his hand for a noncommittal handshake.

Jon smiled and shook Hal's hand. "I'll give you a call in a few days to plan something," Jon finished. He left Hal alone watching him walk away. Even as Jon made his way to the opposite end of the parking garage where his car was waiting for him, he glanced over his shoulder for a quick second and still saw Hal watching in the distance.

Knowing that there was still someone, at least one person in the world, watching him and caring what happened to him, filled Jon with a sense of meaning. A sense of meaning that had been at all-time highs and lows during the last month.

After arriving home from the drive from the airport, Jon chucked his few personal belongings by the front door and headed for the kitchen. Unfortunately most of his items were still in his aunt and uncle's upstairs spare bedroom. The blinking red light of his parents' answering machine immediately caught his eye, causing him to veer from his beeline to the fridge. For the moment Jon ignored his growing hunger and approached the waiting machine.

Next to the blinking light was the number two, showing there were two unheard messages waiting to be played. Jon pushed play wondering who had called.

BEEP.

"Hey there good looking. It's me," Beth said. "I know you're in Nebraska but I just wanted you to know that I was thinking of you and wished you were here. Maybe you can come out to see me after you get back? Anyway, I just wanted to say that I love you and I can't wait to see you. Talk to you soon. Love you Jon."

The machine informed Jon the first message had ended and then beeped again before the second and final message began playing.

"Yeah, Jon Coulter, this is Detective Briggs. I'm calling about the investigation into your parents' death. I need to ask you some questions about your whereabouts the night before your parents were killed and during that day. I've seen the paperwork that shows you're in line to inherit a sizable amount of money from the death of your parents, which for me is always red flag. Well, I guess you're out of town, which is also somewhat suspicious under the circumstances. Anyway it's in your best interest to give me a call so we can straighten all of this out. Call me," the detective said ending the conversation.

"Well, that's a little odd," Jon pondered aloud. For a brief second Jon thought maybe whatever had happened in Nebraska was also effecting people as far away as Dallas, but shook his head thinking that was ridiculous and quickly ruled out the thought. He did think Detective Briggs' last words of "call me," sounded more like a command then a suggestion, but figured the detective wouldn't mind if he took a quick unplanned trip to see his girlfriend first.

Although Jon had never been much of a fan of the dreaded *pop in*, his and Beth's relationship was well past where that was an issue. He thought surprising her out of the blue was just what the doctor had ordered. Jon plopped down in front of his computer and began searching for the earliest available flights to Columbus, Ohio.

He was surprised to see a few tickets were still available for that evening's flight, but exhausted from the day's traumatic event and excessive traveling, he decided to pass. The earliest flight the next day was at 9:00 in the morning, which suited him just fine. The midmorning flight would give him a chance to catch a full night of sleep, pack another carryon of clothes and whatnots, since he'd abandoned his on his aunt and uncle's farm and still be able to make it to the airport on time.

Jon bought the round trip tickets, grabbed a quick bite to eat and then retired to his bedroom. Leaning backwards, he let gravity take control, dropping him onto his comfortable padded bed. Rolling his head to one side he saw a picture of his parents hanging on the wall. He longed to see them again. They'd know what to do about his aunt and uncle. His thoughts drifted to Hal and he wondered if the tradeoff had been worth it. Hal did seem to truly care about him, but was it all an act or had the explosion been the real reason for his new feelings?

Jon rolled his head back to where he was staring at the ceiling. So many questions and so few answers. Eventually sleep overtook his worn out mind and body as the day's light slowly ebbed to darkness.

CHAPTER 8

DISGUST

In his dream Jon was back in Nebraska at his aunt and uncle's farm. He was asleep in their upstairs spare bedroom where the walls creaked and the windows whistled. All of a sudden lightning struck somewhere close by, followed by an immediate thundery response. The loud KA-BOOM woke him from his restful slumber and sent his heart racing.

He pulled himself out of the bed in the farm house's upper room and walked towards the window. Outside it was raining and lightning filled the sky. As each burst of lightning lit the blackness he could see a tornado in the distance moving towards the farm.

"Uncle Harold, Aunt Jenny," he yelled. "There's a tornado coming, there's a tornado coming!"

Without hesitation or knocking, he burst into their bedroom, only to find it was empty. Frantically Jon searched the house, but they were nowhere to be found. He ran to the window again just as another flash of lightning lit the late night sky to see the tornado was even closer that it had been before.

Jon sprinted outside into the pouring rain, fully clothed. He knew he hadn't been in his clothes when the storm first hit, but it didn't matter; it was a dream after all. All that mattered was finding his relatives. Jon whirled his head about searching for signs of life, all the while the winds were increasing as the tornado approached.

Finally he saw a flicker of light in the barn. They must be in there, he thought to himself. Jon raced over to the barn's open door and entered. Inside the large structure there was only one dim light shining towards the other end. Jon could smell the wet hay and hear the rain beating on the old structure's wood slatted roof. His steps slowed as he walked towards the center of the barn. Something wasn't right, but he wasn't quite sure what it was.

As he came out from in between the empty stalls his uncle was standing in the middle open area waiting for him.

"There's a tornado coming," Jon said in a monotone, still stuck on warning his uncle even though something was *very* wrong. Jon looked down and saw Aunt Jenny dead on the floor, while smoke poured out of the barrel of his uncle's gun.

"Uncle Harold what have you done?" he said in shock.

"The same thing I'm going to do to you!" his uncle yelled back, lowering the larger than normal shotgun at Jon's face.

Without wasting a second more inside the barn, Jon was outside in an instant and running through the torrential downpour. No matter how hard he ran, each time he looked back his uncle was behind him blasting his gun. Jon ran through his aunt and uncle's property and into the corn field. The soaking wet leaves ripped against his skin, stinging him as he touched each one. Eventually Jon looked back again, but this time his uncle was nowhere to be found.

Out of breath and exhausted, Jon rested his hands on his thighs to catch his breath when out of nowhere the tornado was on top of him. The rush of wind threw him up into the air, tossing him around like a rag doll. Jon looked towards the ground while spinning and again saw his uncle aiming his shotgun in his direction. The twister spun him around and around then finally spit him out. Jon was falling faster and faster. He closed his eyes just before he hit the ground in the middle of the cornfield.

THUMP!

Jon landed on the light blue carpet covering his bedroom floor with a grunt. A few seconds passed while he awoke and remembered where he actually was. His forehead and right arm ached from taking the brunt of the impact after he had fallen out of his bed. As he lay on the floor, he could hear the summer rainstorm beating against his room's outside window. Peals of thunder mixed with bright flashes of lightning added an occasional flash of light to his otherwise dark room.

After minutes of laying on the floor and trying to erase the horrible dream from his mind he sat up. Jon dipped his head backwards to check the time on his now upside down clock. He sighed as his mind flipped the upside down numbers and letters to read 5:24 a.m. Sure enough after another splash of lighting burst through the windows and in its aftermath he could see the faintest glimmer of light on the easterly horizon.

Knowing he was up for good, Jon slowly stood and cracked his aching neck. He flipped on his room's light switch and tossed the empty carryon bag onto his messy bed. Letting out a long yawn, he began throwing in a few shirts and pairs of shorts into the open bag.

Still yawning and noticing the lighting was gradually decreasing its intensity, he lumbered into the bathroom and started drawing a warm shower. The shower's soothing water gradually revived his senses and although still early in the morning, he felt ready to go.

After he finished the rest of his light packing and brewing a single cup of black coffee, Jon was out the door. As he drove back to the airport the night's rain slowly transformed into a slow drizzle, to where by the time he reached DFW's covered parking the morning sun was already beginning to break through the dark grey clouds. As the first rays of sun hit him and his surroundings, Jon felt the temperature and humidity begin to spike. Quickly he rolled his suitcase into the cool air conditioned airport and let out an "ahh," as his stickiness faded away.

Five hours later, Jon had picked up the keys to his rental car and was outside of the Columbus airport ready to drive to Beth's house. He had thought of calling her to let her know he was coming or to even ask her to pick him up, but each time he thought surprising her would be more fun.

Turning onto the highway for ten miles or so until he reached the exit for Upper Arlington, Jon listened to music on the radio, trying not to let his lack of sleep and hours of traveling catch up to him. Finally in Beth's neighborhood, Jon slowed the car as he approached her block of houses. Each house he passed had a well groomed front lawn, where the grass was always a deep healthy green and flowering plants and bushes were placed in just the right spots around the yard.

The neighborhood was an older one, with many of the houses over fifty years old and some many years older. However the neighborhood was also one of the more wealthy areas of Columbus, similar to Bexley, Dublin or German Village. Some people had even originally wanted the small suburb to be named the Country Club District in the early nineteen hundreds, but Upper Arlington eventually stuck.

As Jon passed the wood and stone fronted houses, his excitement grew to see the one he loved. Although he knew he'd have to face his aunt and uncle again sometime, just one hug from Beth could help set the world straight. Slowly he turned the last corner with her house being the fourth on his right.

Driving past the first two stone houses, nothing at first seemed out of the ordinary. However as he approached her house he saw a book flying out of her bedroom window. The pages separated from the spine in midflight and covered her parent's lawn in a sea of white. He pulled the rental car alongside her curb. His mouth was agape at what he saw. On her parent's lawn, covering almost every square inch from the driveway to where the neighbor's lawn started was everything he had ever given her. Anything that could remind her of him littered the once green landscape.

"Oh crap," Jon exclaimed alone in his car. He was sure only Hal and his aunt and uncle were acting weird, but now his girlfriend too? She had left that message just yesterday afternoon saying she missed him. Then it hit him; he had forgotten the time difference. When the flash of blue-white light had changed everything in the midafternoon in Nebraska, it had been the early evening in Columbus, Ohio. She had left her phone message at 4:45 p.m. her time, which was still at least an hour before the strange blast had actually occurred.

While still working the time differences between the two states in his head, Jon heard a thump on the car's rooftop.

"What the heck?" he questioned in its quiet confines. Not soon after a bottle of bright pink fingernail polish came rolling down the car's front windshield, finally stopping against the rubber windshield wiper.

Jon got out of the car and looked up towards Beth's bedroom window. A second later she appeared, even more beautiful than he had remembered from just a few days ago.

At seeing him standing by his car she yelled, "I hate you!" with a ferociousness he'd never heard in her voice before and threw another glass bottle of fingernail polish towards his direction. This time the bottle fell short and burst on the light grey cemented sidewalk, covering it in a bright sparkly purple.

"Beth, take it easy," Jon yelled up towards the window. "Just come down so I can talk to you." Jon watched her flip him the bird before disappearing into her room again. Almost a minute passed before he saw any movement in the house. Finally he saw her through the house's dining room window stomping from room to room on her cell phone as she approached the front door.

The small tanned blonde beauty threw open the house's front door and tossed the phone behind her. She glared at Jon as though he'd killed her favorite pet and charged out the door.

Jon, unsure what to do in regards to his normally calm girlfriend, stepped forward to meet her thinking she would stop. However as she raced towards him, it became apparent she wouldn't. Running full speed she hit him with her head and shoulders right in his chest. If not for Jon's large muscular size and having planted one of his feet behind him, she would have leveled him to the ground.

"Whoa, settle down. Just take it easy," he said pushing her off of him. As he did so she took a swing at his face with her fist, missing by only an inch.

"I hate you Jon Coulter!" she screamed and took a step back.

"But you just called my house yesterday wanting to see me," Jon plead. He knew it was a losing battle, but he was determined to not simply let her go.

"Yeah, that was minutes before I realized that I don't love you, I hate you!" she yelled, more furious than he'd ever seen her before.

"Okay, you hate me," he said as calmly as he could muster. "Why do you hate me? What have I done to make you dislike me so much?" Jon stared into her deep blue eyes and truly did see nothing but hate. Even though he was standing in the middle of Ohio with the woman he loved hating him to death, he didn't feel overwhelmed by the situation. He guessed that somewhere, deep in the recesses of his mind, he had known this was going to happen.

"I... I...," she stammered. "I just do!" she yelled and took another swing at his face. This time Jon was ready and pulled his head back in time. As the momentum of her swing swung her around, Jon grabbed her from behind in a big bear hug.

"Let go of me!" she screamed.

"Not until you tell me why you hate me," he said a little breathlessly.

"I don't know why, I just do!" she said and stomped on his foot as hard as she could, causing it to go numb.

Jon released her and backed away. He shook his foot, trying to get some of the feeling to come back. Across from him she was standing with both hands on her hips and smiling at his discomfort.

"That wasn't very nice," he said, starting to get a little annoyed with her. "But see, you don't even know why you hate me. Can you just stop and think for a minute what I've done to you? If you really do hate me as much as you say you do then there should be a pretty good reason why."

Jon stared at her and her back at him. He could see the wheels turning in her mind as she pondered his question; searching for an answer.

"I don't know why. I just know that I hate your guts more than any person I've never known," she seethed a few seconds later. She glared at him again and then did something he didn't see coming. She stuck out her tongue at him and snarled.

"Well, that's very mature," Jon said as he tried to suppress a grin. "So you still haven't answered my question. What changed between yesterday and today that made you love me one minute and then hate me the next?" Jon asked, thinking it was time to try a new tactic. If he couldn't reason with her and she couldn't tell him what he had done wrong, then maybe it was time for a different approach.

"I said I don't know. All I know was yesterday I thought that I was missing you and then it hit me," she said with her arms folded in defiance.

"What hit you?" Jon asked.

"That I've wasted over two years with you. Two years that should have been the best of my life, in college, with my friends and hanging out. I'm never going to get those years back and it's all your fault. I hate you for *that*! And I'm never going to give you a moment's peace until your world falls apart like mine has," she said, her mood turning from anger to rage to an even more threatening tone. That tone sent a shiver down Jon's spine. She was the same as Uncle Harold. She just didn't hate him; she wanted to see him physically harmed.

"Alright, I can see you're really upset, so I'm just going to leave. If you change your mind just pick up the phone and call me. Regardless of how you feel about me right now, just know that I still love you very much," he said and took a step backwards towards his car. He didn't want to leave, but what other choice did he have? For the moment she was blinded by rage and there was nothing he could do.

By now numerous cars had driven by their squabble with some starting to stop. Of course Jon being a man with a large muscular build, most of the people were presumably worried about the pretty, angry little blonde who was yelling at him.

For the first time Jon began noticing people in their cars and on the sidewalk staring at them and knew it was time to leave. As he started walking backwards, not daring to take his eye of his completely irrational girlfriend, he heard a large throttling noise growing louder.

Jon recognized the sound of Andre's car almost immediately and sighed knowing the situation was about to get much worse.

Sure enough, within seconds Andre' orange 1969 mustang came barreling around the corner, leaving a double line of black rubber on the otherwise clean suburban roadway as his car skidded through its turn. Andre revved the engine one final time on his approach then slammed on the brakes a few feet from Jon's rental car.

The orange mustang came to a screeching halt only inches from the car's rear bumper. Andre shoved open is car's door and rose up as menacing as he could muster. He puffed out his chest and flexed his muscles as Jon stared at him across the lawn.

"Get him Andre!" Beth yelled. "You're going to be sorry now Jonny. I called Andre before coming outside. And now you're going to get what you deserve."

Jon wanted to argue, he wanted to try and talk some sense into her, but he knew that whatever he would say would be worthless. Jon turned to the side, not completely letting Beth out of his field of vision, to face Andre as he came storming up the lawn's sloped edge. He wondered what is friend was still doing in Columbus after working so hard on his physique for the Jersey shore, but now was definitely not the time to ask.

"You're dead meat Jon," Andre growled at him.

"Alright, I can see you're upset for some ridiculous reason, but just settle down. Can't we talk about this?"

"Nope, not this time brainiac," Andre said and shoved Jon hard in the chest. Andre's hard shove knocked a little of the air out of Jon's lungs, but not enough he couldn't quickly recuperate in a few breaths. Although Andre was a health nut and worked out a minimum of six days a week lifting weights and doing cardio, Jon's genes were good ones. On a normal week Jon would hit the gym three to four times himself with only doing cardio workouts intermittently at best.

The difference between the two was Andre worked out to improve his highly toned physique, while Jon used his workout sessions as a way to reduce stress in his life. However, seeing that Andre wanted to pound him into the dirt, Jon wondered if maybe he shouldn't have spent just a little more time working out and a little less time studying.

Jon regained his footing just as Andre stepped forward and shoved him again. Jon tried to absorb the strong push, but as his legs were pushed backwards to the point where he fell over one of the five pillows Beth had thrown out of her window.

"You better stay down if you know what's good for you," Andre said as he stood over him. Jon looked up at his friend, wanting to reason with him, but knowing it was futile.

As much as Jon wanted to stay on the ground, he knew he couldn't lay there forever. Eventually he was going to have to get up and leave. Jon looked between Beth and Andre's faces and only saw hate. Not a glimmer of love existed between the two of them. He guessed if either had a gun on them at that moment, he would have been dead in seconds.

Jon rolled onto his side and started to push himself off the lawn's wet grass. Within an instant Andre was at his side, kicking his arm out from underneath him. Jon fell back onto the ground as the arm supporting his weight disappeared.

"I said stay down," Andre growled.

"So you want me to just stay here and not move?"

"Yep," Andre said sounding sure of himself.

"Hmmm, that doesn't sound like much of a plan to me," Jon replied starting to grow annoyed. "You just want me to lay here all day? That's it?"

"That's right," Andre agreed.

"So I'm going to lay here all day and you're just going to stand here and watch me? That sounds a little weird doesn't it?" Jon scoffed, trying to draw Andre's anger.

"Just shut up!" he yelled.

"Beat the crap out of him!" Beth yelled at Andre, getting worked up herself.

Andre turned towards Beth after her remark and told her to mind her own business. As he did so, Jon hopped up, hoping he could get to his car before Andre noticed. However Beth only had part of Andre's attention and he whirled around to face his enemy.

"Did I tell you it was okay to get off that ground?" Andre questioned like a school yard bully. He took a step towards Jon and took a swing. Jon moved just in time to where Andre's hand sailed harmlessly past his face. Before Jon was ready to dodge another blow from Andre's muscular core, Andre's other hand connected with the side of his face.

Jon flew backwards and to the side as the momentum from Andre's fist smashed against his face, causing his body to instinctively jump away from the pain. Again, Jon hit the ground. He raised a hand to his throbbing face, feeling for damage, while he spit out a small stream of blood from where one of his teeth had cut the inside of his cheek.

"Ouch man," he cried. "What's your problem?" he yelled at his friend.

"My problem is you!" Andre yelled back.

"You're crazy, both of you," he said looking at Beth and Andre. Why were they acting so nuts? Something must have happened. There was no way that weird blue and white disc of light could have changed the minds of everyone in the world, could it?

"Dude, just let me up and I'll leave," Jon said in a calm tone.

"I don't believe you. You're never going to leave. That's why I'm here. Beth called me and said you wouldn't leave her alone and now I'm going to make you," Andre said and took a step closer to where Jon had fallen. Jon felt with his tongue across the inside of his cheek, which still tasted like blood. Again he spit out a small bit of blood, but thankfully there was more saliva this time than there had been before. His jaw ached and he could tell a welt was beginning to form on the outside of his cheek.

"You can't hurt me," Jon taunted Andre, trying to draw him closer. Andre took the bait and puffed out his chest like a peacock spreading its tail feathers. Andre stepped a menacing stomp forwards. As he did so Jon lashed out with one of his hands and pulled Andre's foot out from underneath him, sending his muscular friend to the ground with an "umph."

As Andre hit the ground, Jon bounced back up and start walking backwards.

"I don't want to fight you Andre. Just let me leave and I'll be gone," Jon said. Unfortunately he sighed as Andre angrily picked himself off the ground.

"You're dead meat!" Andre yelled as he started to run at Jon. Although Jon was smarter, he knew that physically Andre was bigger and stronger than he was. As Andre started sprinting towards him, Jon turned and ran towards his rental car. He no longer wanted to try and talk sense into his girlfriend or his best friend. At the moment they both hated him and there was nothing he could say or do to change that. No matter how much he wanted to use his brain to reason with each of them, neither one was listening to his rational thoughts.

Jon ran to his rental car, hoping to get to the driver's side door before Andre was able to catch him. As Jon pulled out his keys he glanced over his shoulder just in time to see Andre jumping over the car's hood. Jon kept the keys in his hand, but didn't stop running. He ran past his rental car and to the rear of Andre's mustang, which was parked right behind his car. As fast as he could, Jon ran around the rear of Andre's muscle car to where he could face his attacker over the car's bumper and figure out his next move.

Once Jon was on the opposite side of the car from Andre, he stopped and stared at his friend over the car. At that moment, Jon knew that if Andre caught him what would happen to him wouldn't be pretty, but Andre was still his friend. Although Jon still couldn't fathom why an explosion from over a thousand miles away would cause his friends to hate him, those were the facts. Jon didn't want to hurt his friend, because Andre *was* still his friend, whether he knew it at that moment or not.

Jon stood motionless as Andre glared at him over the Mustang's orange trunk. Jon let his body lean over the trunk just close enough he hoped Andre would think if he lunged at him he could catch at least a part of Jon's body. An evil look of pure enjoyment spread across Andre's face as he dove across the orange surface and took a grabbing swipe towards Jon's free hanging shirt.

Although Andre's reflexes were quicker than he had expected, at the last second Jon jumped backwards avoiding his friend's long muscular arm. As soon as Jon's feet hit the ground he sprinted as fast as he could to his rental car's driver's side door. The last image he saw of Andre, he was pulling himself off of his car's trunk. Jon shoved the key into the ignition and turned. As he shifted the car into drive, he saw Andre rushing to his own vehicle.

"Come on, just let me go," Jon said alone in his car as he revved its engine. Jon shifted the car into drive and burst out of his parking spot. He tore through the quiet neighborhood with only one thought in mind; he had to get out of Columbus.

He whipped the car around the corner and onto the neighborhood's main street. He wasn't sure how much rubber he was unintentionally coating on the older suburban neighborhood's streets, but he could smell the noxious fumes coming from his overheated tires. Passing cars on both his right and left as he weaved through the mild traffic, Jon began thinking he was home free. However, just as he passed a random side street, Andre and his orange Mustang burst out from his right and left a layer of fresh rubber as he spun onto the main street right behind Jon and his rental.

Immediately Andre started annoyingly honking and cursing at him from outside his rolled down window. "When I get my hands on you I'm going to rip out your throat," he yelled while shaking his free fist. Jon increased his car's speed, trying to put some distance between him and his maniacal friend.

Without warning the orange Mustang lurched forward and knocked into his car's rear bumper.

"You've got to be kidding me," Jon yelled as he was tossed around in his seat from the impact. He hoped Andre hadn't damaged his car too much, but for the moment that wasn't his greatest concern. Jon began to realize that Andre was really trying to hurt him. Jon pushed the accelerator to the floor and blew through a yellow light. Now traveling at close to sixty miles an hour with a forty five mile per hour posted speed limit, Jon was flying in between the light traffic and getting honks and angry glares for doing so.

Even though the next light turned red before Jon's rental had finished crossing the intersection, Andre had no issues following him. Andre also raced through the red lit intersection, having to swerve around a car coming towards him at the last second who now had a green light. As they raced through the street, Andre and his orange Mustang began regaining the ground he had lost serving to avoid the previous oncoming car. Jon's small subcompact import was simply no match for Andre's American muscle car.

Just before Jon watched in horror as Andre's Mustang came in for another rear ending, they passed a patrol car, stopped at a red light. Jon watched the officer's calm demeanor instantly morph into rage as their speeding cars passed his position. The officer didn't need the computerized help of his laser speed gun. He knew the two passing cars were well over the posted speed limit.

The patrol car's lights lit up as the officer mashed his accelerator to the floor and whirled onto the major roadway. Through his rear view mirror, Jon saw Andre's reaction to seeing the cop car pull in behind him. Fortunately for Jon, Andre eased off of the gas, increasing the distance between their two cars just before he would have hit him again.

Both Jon and Andre let their cars' top speeds begin to drop as the police officer quickly caught up. As the brightly lit police cruiser approached Andre's car, Jon knew this was probably his one chance to get away. Jon watched as Andre began pulling to the side of the road with the police cruiser matching his every move. Jon slowed his car down even further, to where he was only a couple of miles above the posted speed limit. He had no intention of pulling over now that the officer was preoccupied with Andre and hoped no additional cruisers had been dispatched to give him a speeding or reckless endangerment ticket too.

In his rear view mirror, Jon could see the officer now outside of his cruiser and staring at his car as he left both the officer and Andre behind. He knew he should have pulled over, but now just wasn't the time. Jon continued to the airport, taking side streets he'd learned over the past four years he'd lived in the city, trying to avoid any unwanted attention.

Eventually Jon made his way back to the airport, circumnavigating the major crossroads and thoroughfares just in case the police were still on the lookout for his tiny compact rental. He desperately wanted to call Andre and find out what had happened after the unnamed officer pulled him over, but he knew Andre wanted nothing to do with him.

After returning the rental car and having his insurance charged for the slight damage to the rear bumper and the mess Beth's bright pink nail polish had made, Jon brought his lone bag into the airport to book a flight home. What a mess, he thought to himself. What should have been a great day with his girlfriend had been the complete opposite. He wished he had thought of the time difference before flying a third of the way across the United States to surprise someone who currently wanted to see him dead or dying.

Through persistence and overly large smiles to his airline's customer service agent, Jon was finally able to find a hodgepodge of flights and layovers that would get him home later that night. What should have been two flights and one layover, turned into three flights and two layovers, but it was worth it in the end.

Jon unlocked his front door a little after 2:30 a.m. and tossed his unused bag on the floor. Without heading to the bathroom or grabbing a quick snack, he went straight to his bedroom. Jon flopped himself on his bed, remembering only briefly a mere twenty one hours had passed since he had left earlier that morning, before passing out from the day's exhausting events.

CHAPTER 9

SUSPECT

As the midday's sun fought its way through Jon's closed blinds he began to stir. Although the rest of his house was kept at a cool seventy-eight degrees, the afternoon's sun always brought his bedroom a few degrees higher. Still tucked under his sheets, Jon began growing uncomfortably warm and started to sweat. He rolled around in his bed, trying to kick off the sheets clinging to his skin, but was constantly thwarted as they stuck to him like glue.

With each kick Jon became more awake and the more awake he became the more he remembered the people closest to him wished he was dead. Finally with one thrusting motion Jon pushed the last remnant of the lightly woven fabric off his legs and onto the floor. He spread his legs and arms out against the width of the bed's mattress and felt the cool breeze from his ceiling fan, as it cooled his warm body.

Eventually Jon came to the realization that no matter how much he wanted, he wasn't going to go back to sleep. He rolled over to the end of the bed and lifted his head. His alarm clock brightly displayed 2:35 p.m. Normally Jon would have been up hours ago, but at this point in his life what did he have to get up for? His girlfriend hated him, his best friend had tried to run him off the road and of course he couldn't forget the worst of them all; his uncle who at times had been closer to him than his dad had tried to shoot him with a shotgun.

Jon groaned at the thought of it all. It was almost too much for him to handle. While sighing and hanging his head at the thought of being utterly alone, he reluctantly threw his feet off the bed so they were dangling towards the floor. Although his mounting depression was giving him little desire to eat, his stomach begged to disagree with a loud rumble.

With another sigh, Jon pushed himself off of the bed and lumbered out of his room. He passed the bathroom and the living room where his bag from the previous night was still resting in the corner, continuing on into the kitchen. After scouring through the pantry's contents and then searching the fridge, he came to the realization that there wasn't a solitary scrap of food in the house he felt like eating.

Although his mind was still telling him it didn't care if he ate or not, Jon shuffled to the refrigerator's left side and found a clipping with his favorite pizza place's number scrawled on its back. He wasn't stupid in the fact that regardless of what his emotions currently were, he knew he needed to eat.

After he called in an order for a large supreme pizza and a two liter bottle of Mountain Dew, Jon headed for the shower. The previous night's bad dreams, mixed with his room's warm afternoon sun had left him ripe and needing a good rinse. Within ten minutes he was done with his shower and shaving and was just finishing brushing his teeth when the doorbell rang.

Throwing his wet towel over his boxers, Jon sauntered to the front door and saw Detective Briggs. Seeing it was only the detective and not necessarily someone he should be more modest in front of, he opened the door.

"Detective Briggs, how's it going?" he asked in as cheery of a voice as he could muster.

"Fine thank you," the detective replied, more flatly than Jon had anticipated. "May I come inside? I have a few questions to ask you."

Jon opened the door further and ushered the detective through his front door, while gulping in anticipation of bad news. Everything else had turned to crap in his life, why would his parents' investigation be any different? With my luck I bet the police are now thinking I killed my parents, Jon joked inside.

"I'm going to be straight with you Jon. I've been discussing the case with Officer Ryan we both believe that you're hiding something about your parents' deaths."

Jon stared white-eyed at the detective while his newly washed skin began sweating all over again.

"What are you talking about? I've helped you in any way possible that I could think of. I even found out where my dad's brake line was punctured for God's sake!" Jon almost yelled at the detective. He was so mad and so flabbergasted at the complete dump his life had turned into over that past month he almost didn't know what to say. It was at that moment that Jon internally felt he had to make a decision. Was he going to lie down and take all of the terrible things that kept coming his way or was he going to fight? Jon knew he had to fight; giving up wasn't a phrase in his vocabulary.

"Yeah about that puncture," Detective Briggs replied, while Jon was still lost in thought. The detective looked the young man in the face and could tell his mind was elsewhere.

"Oh, I'm sorry am I boring you Mr. Coulter?" the detective said in a demanding voice.

"No, no, I'm listening," Jon quickly replied as the detective's cutting words brought him back to reality.

"Well, as I was saying, Officer Ryan and I feel it was almost too perfect the way you found that puncture in your dad's hose as fast as you did. We're trained professionals and neither one of us would have thought to look there." The detective paused for a second as he studiously watched Jon's facial expressions change to a more defensive nature. "Do you have something you want to tell me?" he asked.

Almost at a loss for words, Jon tried to form a reasonable rebuttal. "I just got lucky. I wish I could elaborate further, but there just isn't much more to say. You told me the brakes failed, so looked at what I thought was the most obvious place."

Detective Briggs furrowed his brow at Jon's answer and replied, "So, are you calling me stupid, that I don't know how to do my job? I'll have you know I looked at the line, but of course you *knew* what you were looking for, didn't you?"

Again, at a loss for words at being openly attacked Jon replied, "What? No. Of course not. I'm just saying I got lucky, that's all. Remember I wasn't even in Dallas when the accident happened." Detective Briggs watched Jon as he nervously paced back and forth across the living room floor, still in nothing but a towel and boxer shorts.

"Yes and about you being at school. I called both of the contacts *you* gave me and each of them said you weren't anywhere to be seen. Both of your friends, Beth and Andre just yesterday said they didn't know where you were. Now it's a little farfetched to believe you drove all the way back to Dallas, sabotaged your father's truck and then drove all the way back to Ohio, but if someone was really determined to have an alibi I guess it could be done."

Jon had stopped pacing after the detective mentioned Beth and Andre. Of course they were now conspiring against him; they hated his guts. Even worse, the way they were acting Jon wouldn't have been surprised if they were conspiring against him.

"What no comeback this time?" the detective taunted Jon after he had stood motionless for a few seconds. "I think it's time you and I have a frank discussion about what really happened to your parents."

Just before the detective was able to really start applying the heat; the doorbell rang. Thankful for any reason to have the detective's not so subtle interrogation paused for a moment, Jon double timed it to the door. Outside was the pizza delivery boy with his food and drink. Jon signed the bill and returned a few moments later with his late lunch in tow.

"This is a pretty cushy life you have going on here Mr. Coulter. Sleeping in until noon, pizza and mountain dew for lunch and not a care in the world. How much money did your parents leave you again?" Detective Briggs asked baiting Jon, hoping he would crack under the pressure.

Finally Jon snapped and threw his food at the floor. The pizza box's lid flew open, where two slices toppled out onto the floor, while the thickly molded plastic of the Mountain Dew bottle only bounced, saving the over carbonated drink within.

"How dare you imply that I had anything to do with my parents' deaths!" Jon yelled on the verge of tears. "I was in Columbus. Call my teachers. Call my fraternity. Check my receipts. I have been nothing but helpful in your investigation, so if you're going to charge me with something; do it. Otherwise get out of my house! If you want to talk to me again you can contact my parents' attorney." Jon finished yelling. He could feel his body shaking with rage. Due to his mental exhaustion and being public enemy number one in his life, he was done taking crap from the detective.

"If you're finished, I would advise you not to leave town. There's something fishy going on here and I'm going to find out what it is. It'll be better for you in the long run the sooner you come clean," Detective Briggs said upon standing. Jon stared the detective down with clenched fists, not saying a word.

Detective Briggs shrugged his shoulders, unfazed by Jon's intimidating demeanor and calmly strolled to the front door. This wasn't his first rodeo and Jon wasn't the first suspect to get into the detective's face and Detective Briggs knew he wouldn't be the last.

"Remember what I said and enjoy your lunch. I'd be careful opening your two liter though," the detective said, smirking at the spilt pizza and soda bottle that looked almost ready to explode lying on the floor. Once Detective Briggs was two steps outside of Jon's house Jon slammed the door behind the public servant, causing his mom's glass trinkets and expensive china to rattle in their wooden cases.

Jon took a deep breath and stooped down to pull the two pieces of his supreme pizza off the floor. Thankfully each piece had landed with the crust down and not on the gooey cheese. He carried the box of recovered pizza and Mountain Dew to one of the living room's end tables and turned on the T.V. He ate in slow silence as the television's broadcasting gradually numbed his aching soul.

Two hours later, Jon was still sitting in the same spot slowly eating his pizza like a cow chewing its cud and drinking Mountain Dew straight from the bottle. Only two slices were left from the monstrous pizza along with almost one liter of soda. Jon's belly ached from slowly gorging himself, while his bladder yearned to be relieved. Still in a melancholy mood, Jon was about to head to the toilet when a commercial came on the T.V. he'd seen probably over a hundred times before.

Hal Roberts' face appeared full centered on the T.V. screen as he was touting *Evergreen Resources* as the Dallas-Fort Worth area's pride and joy. Jon watched as the company's headquarters was plastered on the screen while appearing to rise majestically above the Dallas downtown's skyline. The longer Jon fixated on the minute long commercial, the more he began to think maybe there was a way out of the absolute hell his like had become.

What if his biological father was right? What if the device and its weird blue and white burst of light had changed everybody in the world, but only in how they saw him? He knew it was absolutely ridiculous and probably not even possible, but at least fixing the machine would give him something to do. What was the worst that could happen? And of course at the moment it appeared Hal was ironically the only friend he had.

By the time the commercial was over, Jon was dancing in front of the T.V. and holding himself, trying not to wet his pants. Even though the commercial had played hundreds, maybe even thousands of times over the past few years, this time Jon wanted to watch it in its entirety. Jon cursed himself for not taking a bathroom break earlier and once the commercial faded to black, he sprinted to the closest toilet.

Before resuming his place in front of the T.V. after emptying his bladder, Jon walked to his room and retrieved Hal's business card from his wallet. With his cell phone in hand, he resumed his half slumped over position in his dad's old recliner and dialed his new dad's number.

"This is Hal, what can I do for you," his biological father said sounding somewhat annoyed at having to answer his phone.

"Hal, it's Jon Coulter," Jon responded. He felt awkward calling his biological father by his first name, but felt equally awkward at calling him Mr. Roberts. In reality this was only going to be the third time he was going to be talking to his estranged father after they had both learned of their biological connection. Regardless of what name Jon used, how could the conversation not be somewhat uncomfortable?

"Jon, my boy!" Hal exclaimed. His voice almost sounded cheery at knowing it was Jon at the other end. "I was hoping you'd call, but I thought you were supposed to be in Ohio visiting your friends?" Hal paused for a second as his mind worked over the possible reasons Jon might have returned so soon. "They weren't the same were they?"

"No, nothing is the same," Jon said somewhat dejectedly. "Ever since Nebraska it's like the world has been turned upside down, but only in regards to me. My girlfriend and best friend want nothing to do with me. In fact I think they'd both like to see me dead. The detective working my parent's accident was just here and all but accused me of sabotaging my dad's truck. My uncle tried to kill me with his shotgun and then there's...," Jon trailed off, not sure if he should continue. He didn't want to unload all of his feelings on his estranged father, but with everyone else he loved despising him, what other choice did he have? There simply wasn't anyone else to talk to.

"And then there's me, right?" Hal said finishing Jon's sentence for him.

"Yeah," Jon sighed. He didn't want to open up to Hal. In fact he didn't want Hal to exist at all, he simply wanted everything back the way it had been a few months ago. Even though Jon constantly felt like he was waking up from a bad dream, he knew that however unfortunate this new reality of his was, it was here to stay. With all that had happened to him in the past forty-eight hours he desperately needed someone to talk to.

"I'm sorry for what you're having to go through, but we'll get through this together. Why don't you come down to *Evergreen Resources* first thing tomorrow morning and we'll work this out together. I know I told you this before, but from what you've told me I'm even more convinced that your dad's machine somehow caused this mess. Right now I don't feel there's anything to be gained by sloshing through the how's or the why's of what happened, but I do have an idea of what we could maybe try to revert everything back to the way it was before you accidentally turned that machine on."

"That sounds good. I'll be at your building around eight," Jon replied not even close to convinced Hal could make everything better no matter how much he wanted to believe him.

"Great! I can't wait to see you Jon," Hal said with exuberance before hanging up the phone.

Jon tossed the cell phone on the end table where the last two pieces of pizza and half drank bottle of Mountain Dew were resting. Although in a melancholy mood, Jon bounced his nervous leg, from all of the caffeine, up and down on the room's plush carpet, while resuming watching the monotony of daytime television.

As Jon lay in bed, he watched the morning sun's rays slowly travel up his bedroom's walls through a crack in his blinds. Although he'd set his alarm for seven, leaving him plenty of time to eat and be at his biological father's workplace around eight, he had woken up close to five thirty in the morning, unable to go back to sleep. He continued watching the sunlight move ever so slowly to previously darkened corners as he waited for his alarm to sound.

He wasn't sure what had caused him to wake so early. His blinds were tightly shut, there hadn't been any storms around the area and he didn't feel *all* that nervous about seeing his estranged biological father. Yet once he had stirred ever so slightly, his mind had switched on and was unable to find sleep again. He however found it humorous that his only friend at the moment was a father he'd never known.

BEEP! BEEP! BEEP!

Wide awake, Jon whirled over on his bed and slapped the top of the alarm clock, quieting its infernal racket. He let out a long yawn before hopping out of bed and readying himself for the day. After a quick shower and a bite to eat, Jon was on the road heading towards downtown.

Only a few minutes before eight in the morning, Jon walked through the massive skyscraper's double doors and into the lobby where *Evergreen Resources'* corporate offices were housed.

"Hi, I'm Jon Coulter, here for Hal Roberts," Jon informed the lobby's front desk. Almost on cue, just as the pretty receptionist handed him his badge, Hal appeared from around the corner where Jon knew the elevators were located. Although it had been years since he'd been to his father's place of work, it seemed like only yesterday he'd come with him, excited to see his father's new inventions he was always working on and talking about.

"Hey, Jon!" Hal yelled across the spacious lobby. Jon smiled and waved back before clipping his temporary I.D. badge to one of his belt loops on his khaki cargo pants.

"I was hoping I'd find you down here," Hal cheerfully said. "Why don't I give you a tour around the building before we talk? Does that sound okay to you?"

Jon looked into Hal's eyes and could see his genuine longing to spend some time with his son. "Sure, whatever you want is fine with me."

"Great, follow me then." Hal replied. He escorted Jon to the elevator, which sent them over twenty stories into the air before softly stopping at the intended floor. "I think you're going to get a kick out of this Jonny boy. This is our engineering floor where people like you dream up new projects for any type of electrical generation devices you can think of. Some of them are simply tweaking already known processes while others are on the cutting edge of technology."

Hal trotted in between the cluttered maze of desks and workstations, showing Jon the intricacies of each project being worked on. Jon found Hal's enthusiasm towards his company's work intoxicating. Out of his eye however, Jon saw coworker after coworker glaring in their direction. Initially, after the few days he'd had, Jon thought they were looking at him, but gradually he began to realize it was Hal who was getting the scornful glances. Although one of the most profitable businesses in the southern half of the United States, his employees hated their CEO.

Jon remembered his aunt and uncle's lack of trust for his unscrupulous biological father and Chet's cautionary warnings. However Jon found it hard to buy into their rhetoric as he sensed Hal's love and longing to be a part of his life was genuine. Of course if Hal's feelings were nothing but a manufactured lie because of his dad's prototype, then all of this was for nothing.

"Hey, come over here and look at this son," Hal excitedly said, grabbing Jon's arm and pulling him back to reality. "This is your dad's experimental solar cells I retrieved from your uncle's barn."

"Don't you mean stole?" Jon said, almost immediately wishing he hadn't.

"Jon, you're my son and I want you to work with me at my company, but don't think for a second that you can judge the relationship your dad and I had. Your father used my company's resources to engineer and then build these prototypes. That makes them my company's property, no one else's. So if you're going to throw around accusations of theft, you should look at your father before me." Hal looked Jon squarely in the eyes, making sure he understood his point. From his perspective he hadn't stolen anything.

Jon reluctantly nodded, knowing he shouldn't have opened that bag of worms to begin with. Interestingly, while Hal was lecturing him about his dad, he didn't seem to be mad at Jon's comment. Yes, Jon could clearly tell Hal didn't like his deceased father, but for a comment like that Hal probably should have yelled at him, but had instead tried to show his side of the story.

Hal smiled and patted Jon's shoulder trying to show there was no animosity between the two of them. He then continued showing

Jon around the large engineering portion of the skyscraper's office space. While Hal was giving Jon demonstrations of some of his company's most promising innovations, he was inwardly reflecting on how much he'd changed.

If one of his subordinates or even Jon's father had ever accused him of stealing, they'd be kicked to the curb so fast it would make their head spin. But for some reason when this kid, a kid he barely knew, made the same accusation he didn't feel anger. All he wanted to do was prove to his son that he wasn't the monster everyone thought he was. However, deep down Hal knew what he was a monster and that was probably too generous of a term. The people he'd hurt, those whose lives he'd ruined and even been the reason for their deaths; he was worse than a monster. What was even worse than what he'd done was that he felt almost no remorse for any of it and knew if necessary he'd do it again in the future.

Jon and his company were Hal's only saving graces. Just as he'd done most of those horrible acts to further the interests of *Evergreen Resources*, he'd also do whatever was necessary to bring happiness to his son as well. As soon as they were done with Jon's tour, his son's happiness was what Hal wanted to discuss.

"So, that's basically it," Hal said as they headed to the floors back stairs. Hal liked to stay as fit as possible and being the CEO of a fortune five hundred company he generally had little time to work out. The stairs however, were always there and begging to be used.

"If you can handle it we've got three flights of stairs up to the management floor," he said kiddingly.

"Yep, I think I can manage," Jon replied with a grin. Man it felt good to be around someone who actually wanted to be around you, Jon thought to himself.

Once on the management floor, Hal walked Jon through some of the vacant offices and even others that weren't; telling Jon to pick, that any one of them could be his for the taking.

"I'm going to get a coffee. Do you want one or a Coke? They're both free and in the break room," Hal offered, while showing him the way.

"Yeah, a coffee or Coke sounds good to me. Anything that's got caffeine in it would be nice," Jon replied while trying to stifle a yawn.

All of the walking and talking between him and Hal was starting to remind Jon's body of the hours of sleep it had missed.

After grabbing a cup of coffee and an ice cold can of Dr. Pepper, Hal ushered Jon to his office and shut his door. Hal wasn't dreading the conversation that was about to take place, but to say he'd lost sleep thinking about it was an understatement. He was about to lay out his plan to return Jon's life back to normal. But if he was right, would that return him back to normal too? Would his feelings for this young wonderful man sitting across from him disappear? Hal didn't know the answers to either question, but their possible outcomes scared the crap out of him.

Jon stared across his estranged dad's gigantic mahogany desk as Hal had his head turned, staring out of his favorite window in his corner office. Again Jon tried to stifle a yawn by taking a long drink of his cola hoping the surge of caffeine would wake up his tired body.

"So, what did you think of my little company?" Hal asked wanting to lighten the mood before getting serious.

"Well I wouldn't call it little for starters. I must have seen over two hundred workers just on the few floors we were on and I know you have offices all around the world. But I think you're company is awesome," Jon exclaimed, genuinely impressed. Although he'd been on a few of the floors before with his father, his dad had never given him such an exclusive tour as Hal had just done.

"I'm glad you feel that way Jon. I really do hope you'll consider working here with me in the future. Like I've said before I know you're a bright young man. If you wanted to start in the engineering department, I know you would fit right in from the get-go. But if you wanted to take the management track like me, any of the offices on this floor could be yours. Sure, you'd probably have to take a few econ and business classes, but with your book smarts I don't think that would be much of a problem." Hal gazed at his son across the desk, while taking a sip of his dark coffee. He hoped with all of his heart that Jon would want to work with him. There was no time like the present to start regaining all of the time he'd lost over the past twenty years with this kid, his son who was barely more than a stranger.

"Well, as you know you have caught me at a pretty opportune time, since I'm between jobs and all," Jon joked while fighting down a burp from the carbonated drink. "I'd be a fool to turn down a job here, with you being my biological father or not, so the answer is yes. I'd love to work for your company."

Hal's eyes lit up with excitement and admiration for his son at his decision. He reached across the table and gave Jon a solid robust handshake and welcomed him to his company.

"So what are you thinking? Management or engineering?" he asked, trying to hide his joy at Jon's decision, but finding it hard to do so. Hal couldn't remember the last time he'd had a real, honest to God friend. Throughout the years he had alienated anyone and everyone he had ever called friend. Although highly successful, he was one of the loneliest people on the planet, yet resistant to change his ways.

"Now that, I'm going to have to sleep on," Jon thoughtfully replied to his question. "I'm leaning towards engineering because that's what I've always wanted to do. Plus I'm a little burned out from studying the past four years in college. I'm not sure I would want to go back to school right away."

"I completely understand Jon. I'd love to have you up here with me, but in the short term I could really see you excelling with our engineers a couple floors down. With your biochemistry and electrical engineering background, you might just be able to knock the socks off the current stiffs I have working down there. Who knows maybe you can combine your two majors and focus on biochemical engineering, like organic light emitting diodes or organic solar cells. The sky's the limit."

"Yeah, that could be pretty cool," Jon agreed. As he let his mind wander to the hundreds of different scenarios that could play out while working for his biological father, he was growing rather hungry and needed to take a leak. Jon squirmed in his chair, trying to fight back the urge to relieve himself and burped from the Dr. Pepper again.

"Hey Jon, I need to make a few work phone calls. They'll only take a few minutes. Why don't you go across the street and get us a table for lunch. There's a great barbecue place a few buildings cattycorner from here. They've got some of the best barbecue throughout the city. It's normally a twenty minute wait or so. So why don't you get us on the list for a table and by the time we're ready to be seated I'll be finished with my phone calls and be over there to meet you."

Jon sprung out of his chair, not needing to be asked a second time. "That sounds great Hal. I'll see you there," he said already halfway out of the door and heading for the bathroom. As Hal watched Jon almost run down the wide carpeted hallway he smiled at how excited Jon appeared to be, not knowing Jon's bladder was crying to be emptied.

He leaned to the side of his desk to where he could see Jon exiting the maze of cubicles. Once Jon was out of sight, Hal reached for his throwaway cell phone, which was only used to call Mick, in the back of one of his mahogany desk drawers. At lunchtime he'd tell Jon his plan on what he intended to do to make his son's life right again. But first he needed to call Mick and catch him up to speed on the situation. If Hal was going to clear up the mess of Jon's life he'd created, then his unsavory partner's help would definitely be needed.

CHAPTER 10

THE PLAN

On his throwaway phone Hal brought up Mick's phone number, which was the only number stored on his secretive device. He pushed send and waited for an answer.

"Yeah," the cranky voice on the other end of the phone finally answered.

"Mick, it's Hal. Look I have another job for you."

"I'm listening," Mick gruffly responded. He'd be a fool not to listen to Hal's ridiculous request whatever it may be. Last time Hal had paid him thousands of dollars just to fly to Nebraska and take a few pictures. It was almost too good to be true.

"Remember the place you went in Nebraska?" Hal asked. "Well, I want you to go back there. When you were there last time you took a picture of a large fusion reactor. I want you to return and take a few more pictures for me. Precise pictures."

"Look, before you say anymore I'm not a rocket scientist. What picture I sent you was of a fusion reactor? I can barely say it let alone know what one looks like," Mick said feeling annoyed Hal expected him to understand his scientific mumbo jumbo.

"It's the largest object you sent me a picture of. It has wires running all over it and lots of stainless steel tubing."

"Oh yeah, right I remember that large hunk of machinery. So what shots of the machine do I need to get?"

"When you see it you'll understand. I went to the farm after you sent me the pictures and there was an altercation. All you need to know is that the machine was damaged and I need you to take detailed pictures of wherever you see anything broken on the machine. I don't care how small of a nick or scratch you see. Take a picture and send it to me. I'll pay the same rate as last time, but you're going to have to be very thorough because I need to know exactly what parts I need to fix."

"Consider it done," Mick responded with a little more pep in his voice. Another forty thousand dollars, how could he not be somewhat excited? It sure beat risking getting caught stealing three or four cars, chopping them down and hoping the return was at least half as good.

"Oh and one more thing."

"Yeah?"

"Watch out for the farmer that lives there. He's one crazy nut job. He barely missed blowing my head off with his shotgun last time I was there. If I were you I'd wait for him to be gone before I even thought about trespassing on his property."

"Good to know. I'll be prepared," Mick paused. Normally he didn't care one iota about anyone else's business, but he was starting to find Hal's fascination with this farm in the middle of Nebraska intriguing, maybe even a little suspicious.

"I know this isn't any of my business and normally I could care less about the whys of what you ask as long as I'm getting paid, but what is so special about this farm in Nebraska? This is twice you've now asked me to get some photos, but the amount of cash you're throwing my way says there's something more at stake. Plus now you're telling me to watch my back cuz there's some crazy farmer with a shotgun running around the property. I think it's time you tell me what's really going on, or regardless of how much you pay me; I'm going to have to walk on this one."

Mick hated the sound of the words coming from his mouth, but they were true. However, turning down money wasn't part of his personality. If this little escapade Hal wanted to send him on was as dangerous as he was letting on, then Mick had a right to know what he was getting himself into.

"Okay, I'm going to tell you the complete truth. You might think I'm crazy but just remember you asked for it," Hal said after strongly considering whether he should be honest with Mick or not.

"Spill it," Mick replied.

"So, you know the farm is owned by you know who's sister and brother-in-law right? I can't remember if I told you before, but the Coulters had a son. The day of the accident I found out that their son Jon wasn't John Coulter's biological son, he is mine."

"I'm listening," Mick replied, clearly intrigued by the situation's growing complexities. Again he thought to himself Hal's current predicament sure was more interesting than stealing and chopping cars.

"Anyway, after you sent the photos a few days ago, I took a trip there myself. No one was home when I got there so I followed your directions into the barn where Mr. Coulter had set up his little workshop. Unfortunately a few minutes later Jon and his uncle showed up and all hell broke loose. His crazy uncle stuck his shotgun in my face. I tried to wrestle it out of his hands and knocked Jon into the fusion reactor you saw.

When he hit the reactor, Jon accidentally turned it on and it blew. I mean pieces of metal and wires shot out of it in all directions. But here's the part you might not believe. When the reactor exploded there was this blue and white circular disc of light that burst out of it. I've been an engineer my entire life and I've never seen anything even close to this before. Jon was touching the reactor when this light escaped it, but the disc went through both his uncle and me and from what I can tell every person on the planet."

"I didn't feel anything," Mick said butting in. He wasn't a scientist or engineer, not that he really knew or cared about the difference between the two professions, but if Hal said he'd seen a weird light then he would at least take him for his word.

"Yeah, I wouldn't have expected you to Mick; I didn't either until I thought about it later. So this fusion reactor was set up using parts that I'd have never combined with each other in a million years, so I'm not sure what exactly caused the light, but let me tell you what happened next.

As soon as the blue and white disc passed through his uncle and me everything changed. Yeah his uncle still wanted to shoot me in the back, but I think he wanted to fill his nephew with lead even more. And for me, before that disc flashed through my body, I couldn't have cared less about my son.

Well, actually that's not true. If I'm going to be completely honest, I hated the fact that the kid was mine. Was he going to want money from me? Was I going to have to babysit him? Truthfully I didn't want any part of him in my life. A few days prior I had offered him a job, but that was just so I could keep my eyes on the punk. Sure, I was slightly interested about having a son, but in reality I was more concerned about the negatives and how I didn't want to have to think about anybody else.

But that was before the blast and now I can't think about anything else besides wanting to spend time with him and let me tell you Mick, those are not feelings that I normally have. Anyway, his uncle went from loving him to wanting to blow his head off. I went from despising him to loving this boy more than I can remember loving anyone, ever. And it's not just his uncle and I that have changed. Now his girlfriend and other friends hate him for no reason too. And the real reason I have to try and make this right, is that the detective on the case now thinks Jon tampered with his dad's brakes. Right now he's their prime suspect and I can't just sit here and do nothing," Hal finished. He stopped at that point and allowed his crazy story to percolate in Mick's unsavory skull. In reality Hal didn't care if Mick believed him or not; he simply needed his help.

After a few moments of silence Mick cleared his throat on the other end of the phone. He wasn't worried that Hal's new misgivings about their illegal actions would lead him to do something stupid, like turning him in to the cops, but he was intrigued.

"Alright I'll help you. I'm not sure if I believe the tall tale you just told me but if the cash is the same then I'm in. I just hope you're not going insane on me and going to get us both killed, because that would kind of suck."

"That's good to hear Mick. If you believe me or not, that's up to you but I do need your help. I need those pictures so I can find the parts to repair the device. Once I have the parts then you, Jon and I are going back to Nebraska together and we're going to fix the reactor and turn it on again. That's Jon's only way out of this mess."

Mick wasn't sure turning on some piece of junk that had just blown apart a few days ago was such a good idea, but he wasn't the boss. "It's gonna cost you double if I'm heading to the middle of nowhere twice. That's eighty thousand you're going to owe me. And this time I want it all up front."

"Agreed." Hal smiled on the other end of the phone knowing Mick was now on board. However what Mick didn't know is that he'd wasn't going to be around to spend any of his money. Once the reactor was taken care of, Mick would only be a loose end that needed to be purged from Hal's life, nothing more. Unfortunately for Mick, he was probably going to have an accident of his own.

After finding his way to the bathroom and not a moment too soon, Jon took the skyscraper's elevator back down to the building's expansive lobby. He waved to the cute receptionist, who reminded him of Beth and strode through the lobby's main doors and into the midday sun. He hadn't realized how cold the building had been until he felt the giant orange sun's rays of light hit his skin, warming his chilled flesh.

Looking across the busy downtown street and to the right, he saw the barbeque place Hal had mentioned. He quickly looked both ways and seeing no traffic jogged across to the other side. Just as he put his foot on the curb on the opposite side of the street, directly in front of him his dad's friend Chet exited the building across from *Evergreen Resources*.

"You," Chet seethed.

"Oh crap," Jon muttered under his breath. He had since giving up hope that anyone he knew and liked would still feel the same way. Immediately Jon wished he'd stayed on the other side of the street and walked down to the pedestrian crosswalk instead of jaywalking through traffic.

"You've got a lot of nerve showing your face around here," Chet said as he took a step closer. As usual the man's hair was unkempt and at close to three hundred pounds, Jon thought he might have gained weight since the funeral. Jon had never known Chet to be anything but a boisterous happy-go-lucky type of fellow and hoped his coming closer didn't mean another fight. His cheek still hurt from where Andre had smacked him.

Jon didn't want any trouble. He put his head down and tried to walk away, but Chet was faster than his overweight body led him to believe. Before Jon had taken two steps, Chet was right there in front of him.

"How could you do it Jon? I talked to Detective Briggs. I know that it was you that killed your parents."

Jon whipped his head up and stared Chet directly in the face. "That's a lie. I wasn't even there," he said through gritted teeth.

"I used to think you were a good kid, maybe even better than your old man, but then you go and do something like this. You should be ashamed of yourself. And now what, you're hanging around outside like nothing ever happened. Let me guess you were just up there?" Chet said pointing to the upper floors of *Evergreen Resources,* "with your new dad chumming it up. You make me sick. But I guess you and Hal Roberts probably deserve each other in the long run. I know how he screwed over your mom and I've heard how he treats people in general. I guess it's true what they say about the apple not falling far from the tree or like father like son. I just never thought you'd turn out to be like him. "

"It's not what you think," Jon said wanting to explain everything to his father's friend even though he knew doing so was futile.

"Just get out of my sight you little turd. Keep on enjoying life because one of these days you're going to get what's coming to you," Chet said taking a step backward. "You know if I wasn't in better shape and a few years younger I'd beat the crap out of you right here and now."

Jon nodded in acceptance not wanting to cause any trouble. He could see the doorway of the barbeque place only a few buildings down the street and wished more than anything that he was at its door.

"What, don't you have anything to say? I hope they fry you once you're convicted of what you've done. You're pathetic," Chet said after Jon refused to say anything back.

Jon put his head back down and started walking away from the usually jovial man that had been like an uncle to him. He didn't look back, but Jon could feel Chet's eyes burning through the back of his head as he walked away. Finally as Jon reached the restaurant's door he glanced behind him and saw Chet still glaring in his direction, not having moved a step.

Jon sighed at the loss of another friend and stepped inside the overly chilled restaurant's air. He didn't go up to the hostess right away, but sat down on one of the worn upholstered seat cushions for waiting patrons. He collected his thoughts and tried to regain a sense of composure before finally asking for a table of two.

By the time Hal finally made his way to the restaurant and found Jon's table, Jon was almost already done with a full pint of beer. He lifted his head to give Hal a fake smile as he approached and the table and then let his head fall back down again.

"What's wrong?" Hal asked with concern. He could tell by Jon's dejected composure, which was a huge change from only twenty minutes ago that something more was going on than just Jon feeling sorry for himself.

"Nothing… Everything…" Jon said not even sure where to start. "I just saw my dad's friend Chet outside."

"Oh," Hal said with immediate understanding. "I'm guessing he wasn't very happy to see you?"

"Yeah, you could say that. He accused me of killing my parents. He said he's been talking to Detective Briggs. I think I'm in real trouble Hal. I didn't cause my parent's accident, but with Chet and Beth and Andre all talking to the detective and telling him otherwise, I don't see how he's not going to pin their deaths on me."

"Jon, from everything I've heard from you, you can't deny that something changed for you that day in Nebraska. You can't just chalk it all up to random chance. Maybe you could argue the police department's investigation of your parents' death had turned Beth, Andre and Chet against you, but if that's the case how do you account for your what happened to your aunt and uncle? If we say that maybe a piece of shrapnel hit your Uncle Harold in the head and made him go crazy that still wouldn't explain why your aunt hates you too when she wasn't even there. Do you see what I'm getting at? There's just too much circumstantial evidence to say that everything that's changed in your life is just due to chance."

"Yeah, I know what you're saying. You're quoting Ockham's razor; the simplest answer is usually correct," Jon replied.

"Exactly. Everything in your life changed when your dad's fusion reaction exploded. That ring of light changed everyone who knew you, including me." Hal paused and sat down his drink. He stared Jon in the eyes and with the utmost sincerity continued.

"Jon I want to be completely truthful with you. When I first found out you were my son, I couldn't have cared less. Actually my first thought that crossed my mind was how having a kid was going negatively affect my life. When I saw you at your parent's funeral I gave you my card not to get to know you better, but to keep tabs on you."

"Why are you telling me this?" Jon asked, feeling a pit growing in the depths of his stomach.

"Because I want you to know how much that day in your uncle's barn changed me. And after you understand that, then you're going to know how much I'm willing to give up when I tell you my plan to set things right."

"I'm listening," Jon said. He could barely form a sentence as he could see the pain in his biological father's eyes. Sitting in front of him was the man everyone considered a monster, but at that moment in Jon's eyes he couldn't have been more human.

"You need to know how much that day changed *my* life son. As far back as I can remember, I've always been focused on me. Me. Me. Me. You can argue that's why I've been so successful in business, but at what cost? I have no friends, no family and no loved ones. That being said, these past few days have been some of the best of my life. Knowing that I have a son as awesome as you living in the world couldn't make me any prouder," Hal said. He sniffed and blinked away the water in his eyes.

"Your parents couldn't have raised you better and I find myself loving you more than my life itself. Building a company from the ground up has been my life's goal, but since that day on your uncle's farm I now realize how empty my life really was. So, if you take anything away from what I'm telling you, know this; I love you very much and I'm willing to risk everything I've gained from the explosion to help you."

"Thanks Hal, that really means a lot to me, especially after what's happened in my life lately," Jon seriously replied. "I'm lucky to have someone like you in my life right now."

"Ditto kid, but you're missing the point. I'm not a good person. And no matter how much I care for you right now at this moment, I'm afraid my feelings for you are going to disappear once we fix your dad's prototype. The light it produced changed me for the better, but if we reverse the polarity and run it again, I fear the opposite will happen. I hope I'm wrong, but I want you to know how much I love you and what I'm willing to risk to give you a better life," Hal said and paused to take a long drink of water.

"So what do you plan on doing?" Jon asked after a moment of silence.

"Ha, have you had enough of a retrospective into my lonely life?" Hal jokingly asked. He didn't wait for Jon to answer and began laying out his plan to return Jon's life back to normal.

"So here's what I propose. I have an acquaintance that I've already talked to and is currently heading back to Nebraska as we speak. I've charge him to find out what parts of your dad's prototype were destroyed in the explosion, so you and I can find their replacements and fix it. Now I don't have any definitive proof that switching the reactor's electrical charge is going to reverse its effects on everybody, but I think it's worth a shot."

"I guess you'd know better than I would," Jon said shrugging his shoulders. "Who's this associate of your though? Is this the same guy that found the prototype in the first place?"

"Yep, that's him. Once he returns with the pictures and we've finished compiling the replacement parts necessary to fix the reactor, then the three of us will head back to Nebraska. We'll repair the prototype and fire it up. Hopefully everything will work out."

Jon nodded in agreement. He hoped Hal's theory would pan out and his life would revert back to the way it had been before. At the same time however, he was enjoying getting to know his biological father. If what Hal had said was true, that he couldn't have cared less about Jon before the accident, Jon feared the bond between Hal and him that was forming would be severed and unrepairable based on who Hal really was at his core.

Hal took another long drink of his ice cold glass of water. He'd already laid himself bare in front of his son, but he still had so much more to tell him. Since Jon's dad had built his machine from parts borrowed from *Evergreen Resources*, Hal guessed he'd have maybe three or four days with Jon at the most before the fusion reactor was repaired. In the grand scheme of his life, that amount of time was nothing.

He had already told his son he loved him and he hoped Jon would understand that in the future if he changed back to his old self. But how could he be reverted into what he had been before, knowing what he knew now? Jon had done nothing to change his friends' opinions of him, but still they had changed. Although Hal's perception had changed from a negative to a positive view of the wonderful young man sitting across from him, would he again despise his son for no good reason, other than he wasn't part of his master plan?

Against his better judgment, Hal knew he had to get what he'd done off his chest, at least partially.

"Jon, there's something else I need to tell you. You know that I'm not a good person, right?"

"I've heard that, yes," Jon uncomfortably admitted. "But I'm not sure I believe them anymore."

"Well you should. I've done terrible, unspeakable things in my past that I'm not proud of. But I just want you to know that out of everything I've done, I never once meant to hurt you," Hal said and took another drink of water for his suddenly dry mouth. He wasn't lying. The death of Jon's mom and dad had been for his selfish lusting for Lisa. He hadn't even thought about Jon's existence at the time; so he was in a way telling the truth. Hal wanted to believe that if he'd known Jon was his son that he'd have never asked Mick to proceed with that unspeakable act, but deep down Hal knew Jon's existence wouldn't have mattered.

"What have you done?" Jon asked while Hal was fighting his demons. "Can you tell me?"

Hal looked into Jon's brown eyes. At that moment he wanted nothing more than to be truthful to his son, but being truthful wouldn't benefit either one of them. If he told Jon that he'd been responsible for the death of his parents and that his associate, whom Jon would meet in another day was the man who'd actually pulled the trigger in a matter of speaking, what good would that do? His son needed a friend right now and what's more, Jon needed Hal's expertise to fix the reactor.

"No, I'm sorry son I can't," Hal replied, gazing past Jon towards one of the restaurant's walls. "I just wanted you to know that what people say about me is true. Right here, right now I wish it wasn't, but the fact is I'm not a nice person. Anyway, I'm not sure why I told you because none of that really matters right now. All that matters is we get your life back on track and to do that we need to go back to my office and take a look at your dad's diagrams of his fusion reactor."

"Agreed," Jon said letting the subject drop. He desperately wanted to know what Hal was hiding. Hal wouldn't have said anything about him being such a horrible person if there wasn't something on his chest he wanted to tell him. Although Jon badly wanted to know his father's secrets, Hal was right that for the moment they didn't matter. Plus, it wasn't like he'd been the one responsible for his parent's death or anything as crazy as that.

CHAPTER 11

CORNERED

After lunch Hal had his overly well-endowed, but not too bright secretary, clear his schedule for the remainder of the day.

"Come over and have a look at this," he said to Jon, who was at the moment admiring his view across the Dallas landscape from his corner office's windows.

"Man, what a view," Jon replied, pulling his attention away from the window.

"Yep, she's a beaut," Hal replied. "So here's your dad's schematics of the fusion reactor he was building. I've looked these up and down over ten times and I tell you the more I study them I don't think he meant this to be a fusion reactor at all."

"I thought you were sure it was for generating energy?" Jon replied.

"Well, I did. But now I'm not really sure what it's for. If ten engineers took a quick glance at these schematics I'm pretty sure they'd all agree it was some sort of energy generation device, but the more I study them I can't tell you what they're for. I mean, in all my years of being in this industry I've never seen anything like it before."

"So what is it then?" Jon asked trying to make sense of the extremely detailed sheets of paper. Although he had graduated at the top of his class in electrical engineering, he hadn't had enough real world experience to be very useful at deciphering someone else's crude schematics, especially with something as complicated as his father's sketches were.

"I still think it's some sort of device to produce energy, but I'm just not sure how. If you look over here he has quite a large current being passed through the device holding the tritium, but there's nowhere for the excess energy to go. It just doesn't make any sense, but that being said, your dad was a great engineer. There's no way he was just slapping together this and that, hoping he'd stumble on something that could revolutionize the energy industry."

Hal sighed; annoyed he couldn't decipher his worker's coded schematics. "Who knows, maybe I'm just missing something and this really is supposed to be a fusion reactor. Scientists have been working on these for years and have never gotten one of them to work. Maybe, and I'm just speculating here, your dad stumbled onto something the rest of them had missed."

Hal scratched his head while still studying the maddening sheets of paper. Jon, who recognized only bits and pieces of his father's schematic, looked up at Hal knowing it was up to him figure out his dad's design.

Hal was about to begin another round of going through Jon's dad's drawings for the eleventh time when his office phone rang. Grateful for the distraction he jumped at the chance to give his aching mind a break.

"Yeah, what is it?" he said a little more rudely than he intended to his secretary.

"Sorry to bother you Mr. Roberts, but there's a detective and a couple officers that are here looking for Jon Coulter."

"Umm, what do they want?" Hal questioned, fearing the worst. If Jon was right and his used-to-be friends and Chet were lying to the police about his whereabouts the night before his parents were killed, then they were probably here to arrest him and Hal couldn't let that happen. If they suspected Jon of killing both his parents they'd lock him away for sure. Assuming the lawyer asked for remand, there would be no way Jon would ever be able to make it back to Nebraska.

"I can't tell you sir, but another two officers just entered the building behind them," she replied.

Hal quickly tried to think of what to do before answering, "Alright, stall them if you can then send them up." Hal hung up the phone and looked at Jon. Immediately Jon could tell something was up from Hal's furrowed brow.

"Was that about me?" he asked.

"Jon, you need to get out of here. Your detective friend has brought the police with him and I'm guessing he's here to arrest you for your parents' murders."

"But I didn't do anything!" Jon yelled.

Hal approached his son and placed a reassuring hand on his shoulder. "Son, I know you didn't have anything to do with their deaths, but you have to get out of here. If they arrest you, there's not going to be any bail, not for a crime like this. "

"What do I do?" Jon pleaded as he looked around to see if any of the officers were yet on the floor.

"Go find a place to hide inside the building. Wait a few hours and then come back here. I don't know if they actually know you're here or if they're just looking for you. Take the back stairs around the corner and go to the sixteenth floor."

"Why the sixteenth?"

"They're redoing that floor. Besides a few workers, the floor should be completely empty. Find a place to hide and just wait them out. Better yet, don't even come back up here. I'll find you on the sixteenth floor. Now go, hurry up before they get here or you're never going to get a chance to get back to Nebraska fix this."

Jon walked out of Hal's office as nervous as he could possibly be. He knew he was innocent. Why did he have to hide? If Hal hadn't instructed him otherwise, Jon would have gladly give himself up to the first officer he met; he was innocent after all. But deep down, Jon knew his biological father was right. Everyone was turning against him and there was no way he was going to get a fair shake with the police, especially after the lies they'd been fed.

Shaking from his frazzled nerves, Jon looked each way up and down the rows of cubicles as he headed for the back stairs. His paranoia made it feel like everyone on the office floor was watching his every move and that each of them were going to turn him in, in a moment's notice.

Jon took one last glance over his shoulder at the rows of offices and cubicles before ducking into the elongated stairwell, which stretched from the skyscraper's basement levels to forty-three stories into the air.

Almost as fast as he could without tripping over himself, Jon began flying down the beige colored, seldom used flight of stairs. He passed a door leading to the thirty-eight floor and then the thirty-seventh and so on and so on. Each time he rounded a landing with a door leading to an unknown floor of offices, he would slow down ever so slightly to read it's number, even though he knew the sixteenth floor was still a ways off.

Standing with his back to his office door, Hal nervously chewed on a piece of fingernail, hoping Jon was okay. He hated separating himself from his son, but Jon would have a better chance evading the police if he was alone and Hal was able to slow them down.

He wasn't sure if the police were actually in his building to arrest Jon or not, but why take the chance? Hal bit down hard on another fingernail, annoyed at how much he found himself caring for Jon. There were times during the day when he would try to take his mind off of him, but within seconds he'd realize he was yet again wondering what his son was up to or planning father and son events in his mind for the future.

KNOCK KNOCK KNOCK

Hal whirled around to see a detective in plain clothes with no less than four officers standing behind him.

"Hal Roberts?" the detective asked.

Hal looked at the detective and while sizing him up noticed the look of unimpeded determination on the man's face. This guy could be trouble, he thought.

"I'm Mr. Roberts," Hal responded with an emphasis on the mister.

"Um, yeah, sorry Mr. Roberts. I'm Detective Briggs and I've been working the case of your deceased employee John Coulter. Anyway, we're looking for his son also named Jon Coulter. We were led to believe that he is somewhere inside of the building." Although Detective Briggs did not appreciate the tone Mr. Roberts was using, he like everyone else in Dallas knew how powerful the man was. From his generous donations to the city's police funds, to his reputation of being a ruthless S.O.B., Detective Briggs wanted to stay on his good side if possible.

"Can I ask why you are looking for his son?" Hal asked in a rather demanding voice.

"We have reason to believe he was involved in his parents' deaths."

"Involved?" Hal questioned, already knowing what the detective's response would be. He was only interested in wasting the detective's time and that of his officers to allow Jon enough room to find a proper hiding spot.

"Yes, involved. As in he might have had a hand in tampering with the vehicle that malfunctioned and killed his mother and father," the detective replied a little annoyed at Mr. Roberts' lack of cooperation.

"Oh, I understand now," Hal replied playing stupid. "Nope, can't help you. I haven't seen him for a while now." Hal wasn't lying; it really had been a while since Jon had left his office depending on the detective's definition of a while.

"Look, let's cut the crap. I know he's here and we're here to arrest him. Are you going to help us or not?" the detective pressed his subject taking a step forwards. Hal simply folded his arms in defiance and stared the detective straight in the eyes. This wasn't his first rodeo standing in the way of the police trying to do their job. He'd been so nice lately with Jon around, Hal actually felt alive and a rush of excitement at standing up to Dallas' finest.

"Have it your way Mr. Roberts, but if you're hiding him then you're an accessory and I don't think your stock holders would be very happy about that," Detective Briggs threatened the CEO, taking his proverbial gloves off. One of the richest men in Dallas or not, there was no way this guy was going to stop him from making an arrest.

Detective Briggs turned to walk out of Hal's office and said over his shoulder before leaving, "By the way I know he's your son. You need to think about if you want to spend time getting to know him in prison with him or out here with the rest of us."

Hal kept his arms crossed and didn't move a muscle at the detective's threat. He wasn't surprised the news had started leaking that he had a son and he definitely wasn't expecting the detective to be the last person to use it against him. Once the tabloids and new stations found out he had a son out of wedlock and hadn't known about him for the past twenty years, they'd have a hay day.

Detective Briggs left the middle-aged tycoon's office and stared out into the cubicle farm laid out before him. Slowly and methodically he and his officers dispersed amongst the maze of plasterboard and computers showing Jon's picture to anyone they met.

Detective Briggs was about to pass an older man off to his left when the man reached out and tugged on the side of his jacket.

"Hey, is there a reward for that kid you're looking for?" he asked and licked his lips in anticipation.

"No, not yet, but you'd be doing us a favor if you know anything," Detective Briggs replied wishing he had a twenty or a one hundred dollar bill on him at the moment.

The man looked up at the detective from his rolling chair, thinking over whether or not to help him out. "Well, no cash kind of sucks for turning in the big boss's son, but in case you didn't notice Mr. Roberts is kind of a jerk."

"So did you see him or not?" Detective Briggs asked growing annoyed. He had plenty of other people to question and didn't appreciate this man wasting his time.

"Yeah, he went down the back stairs a few minutes ago. I don't know where he was going, but he looked like he was in a hurry that's for sure."

Without thanking the man, Detective Briggs whistled to the other officers roaming the cubicle farm, who at the shrill sound quickly returned to their superior.

"He went down the back stairs," Detective Briggs said already walking fast towards the closed door.

Once inside the stairwell he held up a hand for silence. Immediately he heard someone's footsteps many floors down. The noise and speed at which the individual was almost running gave the detective credence that it was the person they were seeking. Along with his fellow officers, they started jumping down the beige stairs as fast as they could go.

Jon paused for a quick second as he heard a door slam shut on one of the floors above him. Looking to his left he saw that he was on the twenty-seventh floor. Without hesitation he then lurched forward, continuing his descent to level sixteen. Only a few seconds after he had commenced descending the giant flight of stairs, he heard the echoing of many fast-paced footsteps above.

There was no question in Jon's mind that the footsteps above him were from the officers sent arrest him. He quickened his pace, in some instances jumping two or more stairs at a time, trying to get away from his pursuers. In between the twentieth and nineteenth floors, Jon attempted to jump down the last four stairs at once and onto the landing below. As soon as he hit, his right ankle gave out, dumping him to the ground.

Jon gritted his teeth in pain as he grabbed his sprained ankle. He cursed at himself for being too fast, especially with the head start he had on those following him. He could hear the officers' pounding steps growing closer and forced himself off the floor. Upon putting only a fraction of his weight on his swelling ankle, Jon was forced to grab the hand railing in pain.

Jon hopped around the landing and to the next set of descending stairs. He stretched out his long arm to where he had a firm grip on both sides of the hand railings and began carefully hopping down one stair at a time. The police officers were still growing closer, but at least he had started moving again.

Eventually Jon arrived at the sixteenth floor. By now his ankle's throbbing was on his mind almost as much as his pursuers. He tried to push the pain to the back of his thoughts, while throwing open the sixteenth floor's door.

Immediately inside the doorway, Jon saw plastic sheets hanging from the ceiling and canvas drop cloths littering the floor. In some places the beige carpet was trying to be saved, while in other spots it had been ripped up completely showing the bare cement underneath.

As Jon quickly hopped into the room, he could now hear the officers clearly behind him. With his injured ankle he didn't have the time to pull the door shut. Instead he started making his way through the maze of half painted walls and plastic dividers. He pushed himself as far into the floor's open area as he could, before he heard voices to his rear.

"We've got an open door on the sixteenth," Jon heard an officer yell behind him. He could hear the officers' boots clicking as they stepped onto the floor's naked cement.

The officers were getting closer. His heart started beating even faster than before as he whirled his head back and forth, looking for a place to hide. Seeing none, Jon hopped further into the floor's open area, still searching for a secluded space. Finally he saw what he had been searching for. In the corner a few yards away was a large pile of the canvas tarps not far from the floor's exit to the elevators.

Jon hopped a few more feet before catching his foot on one of the spread out tarps, sending his body onto the floor. He hit the ground with an "umph," as his knees took most of the blow. Regardless of his rug-burned knees and his throbbing ankle, Jon didn't waste any time and started crawling towards the pile of dirty canvas. He could hear one of the officers rounding the corner as he entered the pile of dirty sheets.

The amount of dust, dried paint and bits of sheet rock on the outside of the canvas sheets made him want to sneeze, but he held it back. He could hear the officer's footsteps were now almost to where he was hiding. Jon hoped the officer would simply think he was only a pile of used construction tarps and leave him be.

The officer took a few more steps closer, to where Jon could hear the leather on his shoes creaking with each step. He felt the officer jab the canvas sheets around him a couple of times with his baton, but luckily for him, each time the baton found an open area of air never coming in contact with Jon's body itself.

Eventually the officer gave up and started to walk away. Jon started breathing a sigh of relief before he heard another officer approaching.

"Find anything?" one of them asked the other.

"Naw, this kid's probably good as gone by now," the other officer replied.

"Maybe, but Briggs doesn't want us to give up looking so what else are we supposed to do?" the first one questioned. Jon didn't hear an answer to the first officer's question and assumed the other officer had simply shrugged his shoulders in reply.

"All I know is that we've been told not leave this floor. The captain said he's sending a canine unit to check this level just in case," one of them said to the other.

"How long till they get here?" the other questioned.

"Ten. Fifteen minutes," the other replied as Jon could tell his voice was turning away from where he lay.

The two officers continued talking as they walked away to another corner of the floor, where Jon could no longer hear their voices. He held his breath and listened. For the moment he was completely alone. He lifted one of the flaps of canvas an inch off his face. Scouring the area he didn't see a single soul. He could hear them searching throughout the floor, but no one was close to him for the moment.

Jon knew there was no way he was going to be able to hide from a dog in his pile of rags. He'd be sniffed out for sure and probably bit in the process. Since he was alone for the moment and now knowing that more officers and a dog were coming, Jon knew he had to make a run for it.

Quietly with his arms he pulled himself out of the filthy canvas tarps and to one of the floor's square pillars. With his muscular arms he pulled himself upright. Blood started flowing back to his rolled ankle causing it to throb uncontrollably. He gritted his teeth as the swelling continued to worsen and hopped to the far wall.

Again he stopped and listened, but there was no one around him. With a burst of adrenaline Jon hopped on his good leg as fast as he could go towards the elevators on the far end of the floor. For the briefest of seconds he lost his balance and kicked a bucket of nails that noisily scattered across the floor.

Instantly the floor grew quiet.

"Hey did you guys here that?" he heard one of the officers yelling in the background.

Without anywhere close to hide, there was only one way out. Jon hopped in between the three elevators and repeatedly pushed the down button.

"I think he's on the other end of the floor," another one of the officers yelled back.

Jon could hear them running around the hanging flaps of plastic and canvas closing in on his position. If not for the hanging pieces of opaque plastic sheeting the officers would have instantly been able to see him at the elevators. But for the moment they had to run around the makeshift walls, which were costing them time.

Almost simultaneously each of the three elevators arrived at his floor. With a sudden burst of ingenuity, Jon thrust his hand into the first elevator and hit a button. He did the same to the third before hopping into the second. He hit the button for the first floor and hid behind the closing door just before the first officer came running around the last sheet of plastic. The officer didn't see Jon, but Jon saw him.

"Did you see which one he was in?" he heard one of the officers asking as his elevator started its descent. The next officer's reply was too far away and muffled for Jon to hear what he said, but he knew he was in trouble. Yes, he was off of the floor they were searching, but now he had just cornered himself. Frantically Jon pushed the fourteenth floor's button, but the elevator wouldn't stop. They were overriding the controls.

He tried to pull open the elevator's doors, but while it was moving he couldn't budge them an inch. All out of options he looked up at the elevator's ceiling. Just like in the movies there was a small door, smaller than he had hoped, leading to the top of the elevator car. He knew what he had to do.

Ever so gingerly he increased his body's weight on his swollen right leg. His eyes watered at the excruciating pain as he completed the transfer of his body's full weight onto his damaged ankle. As fast as he could, he reached his left leg up to the safety hand-bar lining the elevator's circumference. As fast has he'd lifted his good leg he even faster began lifting himself up on his good leg to reduce the pressure on his bad one.

Jon's strong undamaged leg's muscles propelled his body straight up to the elevator's ceiling. Without a place to grab onto, Jon was forced to push against the ceiling with his hands while still pushing upwards with his good leg, creating enough force on the opposite ends of his body to keep him in place. Next to his left hand was the elevator's hatch. Luckily for him, the latch was nothing more than a divot for a large flat bladed screwdriver.

Although Jon didn't have any tools on him, he did have his car keys, which worked like a charm. In a couple of seconds the hatch fell open on its set of double hinges and was gently swinging back and forth. With his free hand, Jon shoved his keys back into his pocket and grabbed hold of the side of the newly opened hole. Now that he had a firm grip established with one hand he thrust the other into the hole, leaving himself precariously balancing on only his good leg.

Jon took a deep breath before pulling himself up and through the narrow opening. On top of the elevator he was instantly mesmerized by the giant metal cables and long concrete vertical shaft as the elevator slowly passed by each floor. Knowing if he were a cop he'd check the elevator shaft for his prey: Jon knew he had to get off the descending car.

After pulling the hatch shut and tightening the bolt with the tips of his fingers, Jon stepped off at the next set of doors the elevator passed by. As he straddled the closed doors on the skyscraper's third floor he realized how close he'd come to not making it out of the elevator before it came to a rest at the main lobby, where he would have been arrested for sure by the waiting officers.

Carefully, Jon let go of the shaft's side with his right hand and started to wedge open the closed double doors leading to the third floor. Initially he only opened them only an inch, peering through the crack to see if anyone was walking about. Seeing nobody, in one quick movement Jon let go with his other hand and shoved it into the small crevice with the right one. Then, as though he was performing some sort of World's Strongest Man competition, he pulled the doors apart wide enough to squeeze through. Even with the building's generous air conditioning, Jon was drenched with sweat as he fell through the opening and onto the third floor's cold tiling. As he hit the floor, the thick metal double doors automatically closed on his bad ankle.

Jon wanted to scream in agony, but only a small whimper escaped his lips. Unable to pull his foot out of the semi-closed doors, Jon twisted to the side, turning his leg so he could reach them. He again pried them open, this time from the hallway side and sitting on the floor, where he had just enough room to pull out his damaged leg.

He wanted nothing more than to take a break on the floor and regain his composure. However, lying on the floor in the middle of a wide open area was definitely not in his best interest. Jon scanned his surroundings and spotted a men's and women's bathroom along with a janitor's closet across the hall. He knew he needed to take a break and one of the three rooms would have to do. Since he didn't have to use the bathroom at the moment, Jon elected for the janitor's closet and made his way to the closed door.

Jon turned the handle expecting it to be locked and sighed with relief as it turned with ease. He quickly entered the darkened room and couldn't have been more grateful to find he had just entered the Cadillac of janitor closets. Two long shelving units lined the room's rectangular perimeter with another set of shelves running down its middle. Jon ignored all of that and hopped all of the way to the back of the enormous supply closet. In the back he found at least thirty large boxes of paper towels and toilet paper stacked neatly in the corner.

He was able to move some of the boxes off to the side to where he then created a small hidden alcove in the supply closet's furthest back corner. Once he was inside the hidden recess, he piled up additional boxes in front of its opening as a ground squirrel would build up their burrow's hole so an intruder couldn't enter.

Gently he slid his back against the cold concrete wall and landed with a light thump on the room's floor. For the moment he simply rested and cleared his mind. He didn't want to think. He didn't want to feel. All he wanted to do was rest and let his throbbing ankle lay still for a while.

"Find him. He has to be somewhere," Detective Briggs ordered his army of officers. He had already requested for additional backup and had been told another six officers were in the hotel's lobby below.

"Anything?" he questioned into his walkie talkie to an officer in the hotel's lobby.

"Nope, all three of the elevators are down here and he's not in any of them," came the unwanted response.

"Check the hatches, maybe he crawled onto one of their roofs," the detective ordered as he spat into the receiver. There was no way this kid was innocent. Why would he have run if he was? That, when coupled with all of the information that he'd received from the kid's acquaintances and family, this Jon Coulter was sounding more and more like a piece of work all of the time.

Detective Briggs headed to the back stairs and continued his stalled descent to the first floor. Once inside the lobby he found a group of officers inspecting the three empty elevators.

"Well?" he said wanting an update.

"Sorry Briggs, but there's nothing here. We've checked all three of the shafts and he's simply not there."

"So you're telling me he's vanished like a fart in the wind?" he chided the officer.

"Sir, shift change is in an hour and he's definitely not up there. Maybe he's still in the building or maybe he's not, but we just got called to an accident on the thirty-five so you're on your own."

Detective Briggs glared at the officer, but what was he to do. There were over forty floors in the skyscraper and Jon could be on any one of them. Or maybe the officer was right and he'd gotten out of the building without them knowing it. Either way for the moment he was out of luck and Jon was free.

CHAPTER 12

SAFE

Although Mick wasn't particularly thrilled to be going to back to Nebraska so soon, he was pleasantly surprised when he found a set of round trip tickets available to leave that very day. There was nothing more that Mick hated than having something hanging over his head. He had accepted Hal's job offer and even though Hal wanted it done as quickly as possible, Mick wanted it finished even faster.

Six hours and a seven hundred dollar plane ticket later Mick was once again in a rental car driving on a dirt road through miles and miles of cornfields. Whereas last time he'd gotten lucky with the family going out to eat before returning home, this time he had another plan all of his own. Not only did he think his plan was genius to get them out of the house, but it'd be a test to see if his crazy employer was telling the truth.

A few miles from the farmhouse Mick pulled off to the side of the road and retrieved his cell phone from the car's middle consol.

"Hello?" a lady answered after he had dialed Jon's aunt and uncle's number.

"Yes, this is Officer Smith with the Grand Island police department. Do you by any chance have nephew named Jon Coulter?"

Only silence met his question. Eventually the lady answered. "What did that good for nothing turd do now?"

"I'm not at liberty to say over the phone ma'am," he lied. "If you and your husband could come down to the station I'd be happy to talk about it with you."

"Let me check with my husband," she said. He then heard crackling as if something was being placed over the phone. "Harold, grab your shotgun. The Grand Island police have Jon in custody," he heard her muffled yell to her husband.

A second later she returned to the phone. "We'll be there as soon as possible. Don't you dare let him out until we're there," she almost commanded him.

Mick chuckled to himself at the absurdity of them actually trying to bring a shotgun into the police station. What were they going to do, shoot him as he sat in the cell and then get arrested right on the spot for attempted murder? Either Hal was right and something had changed their opinion of their nephew or else they were as crazy as all get out.

Ten minutes later Mick watched as the aunt and uncle's car sped out of their farm's entrance spraying gravel and dust as they left. He slightly cringed hoping he hadn't caused the two loons to go out of their minds and do something stupid, but the thought tugging on his conscience quickly disappeared from his mind.

As the dust from their car began to settle, Mick shifted his rental into gear and drove onto their property; thankful this time he knew right where to go. Instead of parking on their drive, where the dogs were lying in wait, he drove right onto the grass by the barn's huge wooden door.

He quickly tossed two pieces of rawhide, laced with a generous amount of sleeping pills hidden inside, on the dry ground. With the dogs occupied and hopefully eventually fast asleep, he grabbed his large black Olympus camera and proceeded into the barn.

Once inside he turned on the barn's lights and made his way to its middle. Without hesitation he snapped over a hundred pictures of the charred device. The reactor or whatever Hal had called it didn't seem to be in all of that bad of shape. Sure, there were some burnt wires here and there and some other parts that appeared to have been warped during the explosion, but overall Mick didn't think it looked all that bad. But then again what did he know about electronic doohickeys and whatchamacallits.

After taking a few more close-up pictures of where smaller portions of the device appeared to be damaged, Mick slung the camera over his back and returned to his car. Sure enough, both of the dogs were fast asleep and drooling almost exactly where he'd tossed their treats.

Since he'd taken so many pictures and used the camera's highest resolution setting, there was no way he could easily send them to Hal without first having a high speed internet connection. Mick drove away, letting the sleeping dogs lie, back towards Omaha where he'd already booked a hotel room for the night. Once at his night-time accommodations, he would upload the files and send them to Hal before flying home the next morning. It was the easiest eighty thousand he'd ever made.

Jon stretched his aching legs and stood. The swelling in his ankle was ever so slightly starting to ebb. Just having turned twenty-one a few months ago, Jon was thankful for his youthfulness at that moment. Gingerly he put a small amount of pressure on the now red and purple ankle. Although there was still some pain, he was at least able to limp, rather than being forced to hop around like a rabbit hours ago.

According to his watch it was eight in the evening. He had called Hal's phone a few hours earlier, where he had been advised to remain in his secluded hiding spot for a little while longer. Now that their agreed upon amount of time had lapsed, Jon was ready to get out of the elongated janitor's closet. Carefully he began moving the boxes to create an opening out of his makeshift fort.

After replacing the boxes to where he had originally found them, Jon limped to the closet's door. At the same moment he reached for the handle the door swung inward. He quickly hopped back, not wanting to get hit and came face to face with one of the night's janitors.

"Hey, what are you doing in my closet?" the large black janitor roughly demanded.

"I… Um… I was just looking for some toilet paper," Jon lied. He wanted to scoot past the janitor and disappear, but the thickly muscled man was standing directly in his path.

"I know you. You're that kid they were looking for a few hours ago aren't you?" the janitor asked, his demeanor somewhat softening.

"I don't know what you're talking about," Jon tried to say with a straight face.

"Don't worry kid; I'm not going to turn you in, even if you are the son of that piece of crap with the corner office upstairs."

The janitor scratched his head, wondering why he didn't want to turn the kid in. For years he'd hated Hal Roberts for the way he treated him and everyone else in the building, like they were his indentured servants. He might only be a janitor, but he'd pulled himself out of a gang and was now doing the best he could to provide for his family.

Jon looked at the man's uniform and found his name embroidered inside of a white oval patch just above his shirt's pocket.

"Thank you so much Darrel," he thankfully replied. "I didn't do what they say I did. I just need to get out of here so I can prove I'm innocent."

"Man, I can't tell you why, but I believe you. Now come on, get out of here before somebody who's not as awesome as me calls the cops." What was he doing? For so many years Darrel had sworn if Mr. Roberts was ever in trouble he'd laugh and walk away. That went ditto for the pompous blowhard's son he'd just been made aware of through the office grapevine. Now he was helping him?

Jon thanked the janitor again as he slid past him and to the elevators. As he pushed the button for Hal's office floor, he could still see the janitor scratching his head. Unbeknownst to him, for only the second time since the explosion of his dad's cold fusion generator, the mysterious blue and white ring had actually changed someone's opinion of him for the better.

Finally the doors opened with Hal waiting outside of the elevator for his son. He greeted Jon with a big smile and a quick hug, happy to have his son back by his side. Jon had already relayed to him how he hurt his ankle and he was happy to see Jon was at least able to put some of his weight on it.

Slowly, trying not to force Jon to walk any faster than necessary, Hal led him back to his office.

"So I called the police department and you're definitely the top suspect for your parent's murder. They have a warrant out for your arrest so we need to get the parts to fix your dad's device and get out of town as soon as possible. Unfortunately that means that flying is out of the question, but Mick will take care of that," Hal said.

"Do I want to know how?" Jon asked, not sure that he did.

"Let's just say that he's going to get us transportation that can't be linked to any of us," Hal coyly responded.

"Fine, whatever, just as long as we have a chance to fix that stupid machine and hopefully end this." Jon still wasn't completely sold on Hal's numerous explanations of why fixing the device would change how everyone felt about him, but what else did he have to do? He could either get sent to prison for the rest of his life, continue running from the cops forever or he could stay with the one, the only friend he had left in the world and give his plan a shot.

"Great, that's the attitude," Hal said slapping his son on the back.

Once inside Hal's office, he started going through the pictures Mick had sent *ad nauseum*. For the moment Jon couldn't have cared much less. His leg, now up and being used again, was starting to throb and the afternoon's running from the police had left him wickedly hungry. Still, he propped himself up and stayed as studious as possible, studying the diagrams and pictures just in case the information would be needed later.

"See, here, just like I was saying, this isn't as damaged as I thought it would be. Thankfully your dad was building this out of almost everything we have here in the building or in one of our warehouses. Actually, there isn't one item that was damaged that I don't think we can easily get ahold of," Hal said.

"What do you want me to do now?" Jon asked, curious what his role was for the moment.

"Right now I'm going to take you to Mick's place, while I gather everything we need to fix the reactor. You just take it easy and I'll do all of the heavy lifting for the moment."

Jon didn't argue as a yawn escaped his mouth at the exact moment his stomach rumbled.

"You've been through a lot today. When I drop you off, get a bite to eat and then get some rest. Mick will be flying back in tomorrow morning and then we're going to head right back out onto the road to Nebraska."

"Fine with me," Jon said, feeling the day's events beginning to wear him down. A hot meal and a cozy bed really did sound nice. If Hal was sure he could find all of the items he needed without help, who was Jon to argue with him.

An hour later Jon had convinced Hal to stop at a McDonald's drive-through for some well-deserved Big Macs and fries. Both of them were slightly paranoid about being followed, but as they had continued driving and were yet to be pulled over, they each assumed for the moment they were in the clear.

As the enticing aroma of Jon's dinner filled Hal's black Mercedes, Jon's mouth salivated wanting to devour his meal right then and there. However at seeing Hal's disapproving glances towards his bag of grease and empty carbohydrates he resigned himself to wait until he was alone inside Mick's house.

"Now nothing stupid okay," Hal fatherly advised his son, pulling up to the front of Mick's darkened house. "That means no loud parties or running through the streets naked," he joked.

"Don't worry I'll be fine," Jon smiled back.

"Good to hear, but seriously don't be stupid. Don't call anybody or answer the front door unless it's me standing there. Mick knows you're at his house, but he won't be home until tomorrow and I don't plan on coming back until then either. So if someone's at the door, it won't be either of us, which means you should stay hidden. Okay?"

"Yeah I got it," Jon replied feeling like a little kid being lectured by his father.

"Alright, get on in there, eat your meal and then get some sleep. We're going to have a busy next couple of days."

Jon nodded in agreement and opened the car's door. Before leaving he turned to Hal and said, "By the way I just wanted to thank you for everything you're doing for me."

"It's not a problem Jon. Plus, I'm not doing it just for you. I'm doing it for me too," Hal replied, smiling at his son.

Jon shut the door and walked up the house's front steps. Hal watched his son leave. His heart ached for the unsaid pain that Jon must still be feeling about the loss of his parents. He felt sick inside that he had been part of something so cruel to his one and only son. He still didn't necessarily feel remorse at his involvement in John and Lisa's deaths, only that he'd hurt his son.

Truth be told, he was actually quite pleased with the outcome from John's death. Never in a million years would have found out about his revolutionary solar cell technology if the accident hadn't occurred. Hal shook his head, trying to clear the thoughts away and focus on his task at hand. A very long night was in store for him as he had over fifteen various transistors, bits of wiring and other electrical devices that needed to be collected. As he drove away, after seeing Jon had safely entered the empty house, one of his favorite Alice In Chains songs started playing on the radio. He sang along to *No Excuses* thinking it was almost an eerily perfect song to be playing at the moment.

Inside the house, Jon quickly sat himself down at Mick's horridly messy dining room table and scarfed down his burger and fries. Jon was so hungry he barely took a sip of his soda or broke out the ketchup for the fries as he stuffed the fast food into his face. Within minutes after filling his empty stomach with food, his eyes began to grow droopy, exhausted from the day's events.

Feeling a little odd sleeping in another man's bed, Jon pulled his tired and achy body out of the worn dining room chair and retired to Mick's leather upholstered sofa. Briefly he thought about turning on the T.V., but before making a coherent decision one way or another he was sound asleep.

Beth sat on her bed brushing her hair after a quick shower. For days now she could think of nothing besides Jon Coulter. Jon Coulter this and Jon Coulter that seemed to preclude every waking thought in her head. Even at night she dreamed about him. Usually he was being killed in some extraordinarily gruesome way while she watched from the sidelines with delight.

After he had unexpectedly showed up on her doorstep, she had been pondering his words. What had Jon actually done to make her hate him so much? Truthfully, she couldn't pinpoint one single action to make her hate him. But that didn't change the fact that she loathed him more than anyone else in the world. What she wouldn't do to see him be charged in the murder of his parents, regardless of his innocence.

KNOCK KNOCK

"Honey are you busy?" her mom asked through the closed door.

"No, come on in," Beth sweetly replied.

"You have a telephone call from that Dallas detective you talked with a few days ago. I think he wants to ask you some more questions about Jon," her mother said, wrinkling her nose in disapproval at mentioning the name of the boy that had thrown her family into chaos the past week.

"Thanks," Beth said taking the phone. She waited to answer the detective's call until her mom left the room, shutting the door behind her.

"Tell me you caught that S.O.B.," she said through gritted teeth. She could hear the words filled with hate spewing out of her, but she didn't know how to stop it. Beth knew that normally she wasn't such a spiteful person, but something had changed in her even though she didn't know what it was.

"No, not yet. I do have a warrant for his arrest, but what I could really use is a face to face with you and your friend Andre. Last time we talked briefly about Jon's whereabouts the night before his parents' deaths, but I'd like to get you on record with a more in-depth interview if that's possible."

"You mean over the phone?" she questioned, almost salivating at the thought of being partially responsible for Jon being charged with murder.

"No, for an interview of this type and length I'd like to do it in person if you don't mind. And I'd really appreciate it if we could do this as soon as possible. I know it's extremely quick, but I would like to fly the both of you out here tomorrow morning if possible. This Jon kid is just driving me crazy for some reason and I want to get this case off my plate. Once I get all of my ducks in a row and we find out where he is so we can apprehend him then I'm taking a vacation," Detective Briggs replied on the other end of the phone. He felt exhausted from his failed attempt at Jon's arrest and knew he was calling Beth at her house at close to eleven o'clock at night, but he'd simply never had a case like this before in his life.

Detective Briggs was finding it hard to eat and sleep. Never in his life had he misjudged someone as badly as he had Jon Coulter. For the life of him he couldn't understand why, from the first moment he had met Jon, he had been utterly impressed with the young man's calm demeanor and clearly bright intellect, only to have been proven completely wrong. It was as if a veil had been covering his eyes in the beginning or maybe it was the other way around. Detective Brigg's questioning nature made him wonder if his newfound disdain for the lad was causing him to lose focus and let his emotions get in the way.

"No, it's absolutely not an inconvenience. I would be more than happy to fly to Dallas and give Jon what's coming to him," she said a little over enthusiastically.

Hearing Beth's almost giddy reply at wanting to help in building a case against the boy he knew she had been dating for over two years only furthered the detective's wonderings if he was off base. His instincts were almost always right, but what if this time they were wrong?

"Umm, okay that would be great," he replied trying not to lose his train of thought, while navigating through the airline's webpage. "In that case I have you booked on United for a departure of 7:30 a.m. your time. That's not too early is it?" he asked before hitting enter and locking in the ticket for good.

"I just want to help in any way I can and get this over with," she responded a little calmer than before.

"Great, I've booked the ticket for you and I'll be there personally to pick you up when you arrive."

"Okay, well I'll see you tomorrow sometime," Beth replied and hung up the phone. She looked at her bedroom clock which now read 11:15 p.m. and yawned. Brushing her hair was supposed to have been her last chore before bedtime, but now she found she had to pack. She could feel her excitement growing at being so close to giving Jon what he deserved. She yawned again, but knew it was going to be hard to sleep regardless of how tired she was.

After packing a small suitcase and letting her parents know she was flying to Dallas the next morning, Beth returned to her room. She wanted to call Andre and see if the detective had talked to him too, but now close to midnight she decided to wait. If Andre was going, she was sure she'd see him tomorrow morning at the airport. For now she needed to at least turn off the light and try to get some rest, however hard that might be.

After hanging up the phone with Andre, who seemed almost as focused on putting his best friend in jail, like Beth, Detective Briggs let out a deep yawn. Although the time in Texas wasn't as late as in Ohio, the time was still approaching eleven o'clock and he was beat.

He still couldn't believe how they'd missed Jon in the skyscraper. He wondered how Jon had gotten out of the elevator without being seen. Had the other officers been wrong about Jon even getting on the elevator on the sixteenth floor? Regardless, the detective's prey had slipped through his fingers and he hated failure.

However, tomorrow was a new day. With Beth and Andre each eager to provide their testimony towards Jon's guilt, he was fairly certain he could provide a reasonably airtight case to the District Attorney who'd be leading the prosecution.

But still, the detective couldn't shake the feeling that something was terribly off. Why would Beth, who some said was planning on marrying Jon, morph from being madly in love with him to wanting him locked away for murder? The same went for his friend Andre. If that had been the only curiosity of the case, Detective Briggs could have overlooked it, but it wasn't.

Then there was also Jon's Aunt Jenny and Uncle Harold he had to contend with. Again, many people reported to him that his aunt and uncle had always been like a second set of parents to the young man, but now they too were against him. None of it made sense. The detective reasoned that maybe Jon's friends and family had all changed their opinion of Jon Coulter because they each firmly believed he was guilty. Although that line of reasoning did make sense, Detective Briggs' inquisitive mind still wasn't convinced. Plus there was still his own irrational hatred of the kid to think of, which had basically materialized out of nowhere.

The detective looked up at the large clock on the wall, where his eyes grew wide at realizing how much time had elapsed. With the clock now past 12:30 in the morning, Detective Briggs realized he'd been sitting almost as rigid as a statue, thinking about the Coulter case for over an hour and a half. Almost as if seeing the time on the clock reminded his body how exhausted he was, the detective let out a long yawn before retiring for the night. Like everyone else, the detective had the feeling tomorrow was going to be a very long day.

CHAPTER 13

ON THE ROAD

The next morning Beth's parents dropped her off in front of the United Airlines check-in station at the Columbus International Airport. She waved goodbye as they sped off towards home and noticed the Thank You for Visiting the Columbus International Airport sign not far in front of their car. She snickered to herself at Columbus having the audacity to call itself an international airport just because of a few round trip flights to and from Canada. However, Canada was another country, even if it wasn't that different from the United States she reasoned.

Beth pulled in one more deep breath of the early morning fresh air she had always loved and proceeded through the extra wide double sliding doors into the airport. She barely had to look around before Andre waved to her, already standing in line, waiting for his ticket.

"I figured you'd be here," he said over the elastic band separating their two portions of the line into a giant snake-like "s". "I just didn't think I'd be there first one here," he joked.

Beth smiled her sweet normal smile and said, "Well unlike you I couldn't just roll out of bed. I had to make myself look present-able to the detective. I don't think either of us want to come off as a couple of slobs, now do we?"

"Sheesh, alright I was just giving you a hard time," Andre said with an uncertain smile, holding his hands into the air, giving up. Ever since they had formed a united front against Jon, Andre felt something had changed between the two friends and not for the better. He had a harder time reading her these days and she seemed to be a lot moodier. Even though he knew without a doubt that she absolutely despised he ex-boyfriend, he felt that deep down, unbeknownst to her, that she really did miss him.

"Sorry, I didn't mean to snap at you. I just didn't get all that much sleep last night," she said with a yawn.

Andre nodded his head in understanding and turned to face the airline representative waving him forward. Just as Detective Briggs had informed him, the nice lady in the dark blue vest handed him a ticket to Dallas-Fort Worth's international airport and sent him on his way with a generous smile. Andre didn't really want to wait for Beth after their semi-tense banter, but knew he'd be rude not to.

After another five minutes Beth was finally issued her ticket and met up with Andre just before entering the secured area.

"So, are you ready to do this?" he asked, trying to make simple conversation.

"Probably as ready as you are," she replied furrowing her brow. Last night she had been so hyped up about screwing over her ex, she had barely been able to sleep a wink. Now in the light of day, she was honestly a little too exhausted to care what happened to Jon at the moment. She still definitely wanted him to suffer, but for the time being that all-encompassing feeling she'd felt the last couple of days, was being pushed aside by her body's desire for sleep.

She yawned again as the security guard looked her up and down and then up and down again for no apparent reason. With her golden-blonde hair and her deep penetrating blue eyes, she knew the man was checking her out more than really considering her a possible terrorist. Where the TSA agent's actions would have normally warranted an eye roll or a quick glare, this time they barely registered on her sleepy attention.

Eventually they made their way through the moderately paced security line and to their plane's waiting gate. As Andre had suspect in the ticket line, he and Beth would be sitting next to each other for the flight to Dallas. He'd have to thank the detective for that when he saw him in a couple of hours, he thought sarcastically.

After sitting in silence during takeoff and up to their cruising altitude of thirty-three thousand feet, Beth felt she needed to ask Andre a few questions before inevitably falling asleep for the rest of the flight. Not sure how to begin, she just blurted out her question.

"Have we both gone crazy?" she asked in a quiet voice, staring at the tray table in front of her.

"What?" Andre returned, somewhat taken aback by the question and not absolutely sure he had heard her correctly.

"I said, have we both gone crazy?" she repeated this time a little louder than before. She turned to look Andre in the face, only to feel stupid at asking her ridiculous question and quickly resumed staring at the seat cushion on the seat in front of her.

"What are you talking about?" Andre asked, clearly not following her train of thought. "Oh," he said a second later, "you're talking about Jon aren't you. Why would you think we're crazy, I mean he killed his parents," he said as a matter of fact.

"Come on, we both know he probably didn't kill them. You said yourself you were in the room when he got the phone call that they'd died. Don't get me wrong, I probably hate him more than you ever will, but maybe there's a better way to give him what he deserves."

"And that would be?" Andre asked clearly not impressed with her wavering on their plan.

"I don't know. I've just been wondering ever since he showed up at my house why I hate him so much. It's kind of crazy. I know there's no one I'd rather see get hit by a bus or have their life ruined, but for the life of me I can't reason out why," she said. For the moment Beth was being completely honest with her friend. She knew she hated Jon, but why? And why so much? She'd gone over the last few weeks Jon and she had spent together numerous times and each time the conclusion was the same. She had loved him and been happy and now she was not.

Andre looked at her and shrugged his shoulders. He was a guy. His feelings and the reasons behind them were a little less important to him. For Andre, like Beth, he knew Jon had been his best friend, but now he hated him with a passion. But unlike Beth, that was all he needed to know and he was fine with that.

"Look let's just take this little trip of ours to Dallas and talk to Detective Briggs. If you still feel the same way then you don't have to tell him anything. As for me, I've made my decision. That jerk's going to get what's coming to him." Andre said his last sentence with such hate that Beth knew his mind had been made up for good.

She yawned again, not trying to stifle it in the least and laid her chair back. Although her mind was still racing about her odd feelings for Jon and what she was planning to do about it, her lack of sleep from the previous night quickly put her mind to rest. From then until when the plane landed on the hot and humid Dallas-Fort Worth tarmac, Beth was passed out in her seat from exhaustion.

With bloodshot eyes from catching the first flight back to Dallas, Mick lumbered off the plane and throughout the somewhat empty airport. The terminals, which were only now beginning to be populated with the day's travelers, were still slightly barren. With his red eyes and sour demeanor, Mick walked down the middle of the concourse, refusing to move to his left or right to avoid the oncoming traffic.

Finally, after passing kiosks full of knick-knacks and tabloid magazines, he came to the Starbucks he knew was waiting for him. Mick adjusted his cowboy hat and pulled up on his belt, hiking his dark blue jeans off of the floor. After ordering the largest, stiffest cup of black coffee the store had to offer, he resumed his trek towards his car waiting for him in the airport parking lot.

He regretted allowing Hal's son Jon to crash at his place while he was gone. Although it wasn't the first time someone wanted by the police was hiding out at his home, it was the first time he'd been the person responsible for the situation they were in. Now, not only had Mick been the one to basically murder Jon's parents, he was allowing the person, who if they were to learn the truth would undoubtedly try to kill him given the chance. Mick knew Jon staying at his house was a recipe for disaster, but what was done was done. Normally when Mick extinguished a life, he'd never have to come face to face with their family after the deed was done. This time was going to be different.

Before going to his occupied house, Mick needed to a make a quick stop. Outside of his chop shop, in a sketchy area of town where the cops preferred not to visit, was waiting a silver Jetta for him on the side of the road. Although the car clearly did not fit in with the other rusty dilapidated automobiles lining the street, everyone knew who the car belonged to. Had the shiny car been owned by anyone else it would have been on cinder blocks or stolen within the hour. However, everyone knew Mick's reputation and that the car was his, whether or not they'd seen it before. He could have left the keys in the ignition with the car running and the driver's side door wide open and not have been concerned.

After switching vehicles Mick proceeded to his house. He knew he was probably being overly cautious, but he wasn't willing to drive cross-country in a car that had almost certainly been filmed by the DFW's security cameras. Although Mick was fairly certain no one was looking for him at the moment, changing vehicle was simply smart business.

As he pulled into his carport from the house's back alley, he killed the engine, but did not immediately get out of his new car. He took one last drink of the strong brew and collected himself, knowing he was going to have to make nice with his house's occupant.

At his back door, Mick rapped against the window's loose glass before unlocking the dead bolt with his key. He wanted to give his temporary tenant a little warning before he went inside. When Mick finally opened the back door, there was Jon, standing in his kitchen waiting to meet him. Before Jon had a chance to speak, Mick walked straight past him towards the bathroom as if Jon didn't even exist. After the giant coffee, Mick's bladder was about to burst. As Mick quickly emptied his full bladder, he marveled at the facial similarities between Jon and his dad. This was most certainly Hal's son.

Upon opening the door to exit the bathroom, Jon was again right there to greet him. Mick sighed, knowing he wasn't going to have any peace until Jon made his introductions and relented to the young man's insatiable desire to introduce himself.

"Hi, I'm Jon. I just wanted to say thank you so much for letting me crash at your place. I slept on the couch and haven't touched a thing," Jon said while holding out his hand to the grumpy owner.

Although Mick had found Hal's explanation of what had happened at Jon's aunt and uncle's farm to be somewhat absurd, the moment he took the time to say hi to Jon he realized Hal was right after all. Something had changed; and in him as well. Mick, who didn't normally particularly like anybody, found Jon agreeable from the moment he spoke.

Mick actually found himself reaching for Jon's outstretched hand *wanting* to shake it, not just performing the customary obligation out of annoyance like he usually did.

Mick smiled at Jon and said, "Not a problem at all Jon. It's good to meet you. When Hal told me what you've been through lately it broke me up inside. I can't tell you how sorry I am at your parents' death and your trouble with the police."

"Yeah, thanks," Jon replied, happy the stranger whose house he was staying in was so cordial and sociable. He had been slightly apprehensive about crashing at Hal's associate's home from the vague description his biological father had provided of the man's professional endeavors.

"Have you heard from your father?" Mick asked in reference to the items Hal was supposed to be gathering. Jon's ears perked up. He hadn't known if Mick knew he was Hal's son or just some charity case that needed their help.

"No. When he dropped me off last night he said his night was going to be a long one and he probably wouldn't see me until today. I hope everything went okay."

"So do I," Mick replied. He found the young man in front of him a refreshing mix of honesty and integrity; qualities much different than those found in many of his usual business associates. Looking Jon in the face Mick thought he could see the sorrow about his parents, but wondered if it was just his emotions playing tricks on him.

Like Hal, now meeting Jon and instantly liking him, Mick was sorry for the pain he'd been responsible in Jon's life. Not that he'd killed two innocent people, but that his actions had hurt Jon. Deep down his mind was telling him to get away from this kid, that his emotions were going to get him in trouble, but his heart said otherwise. The kid needed help and since Mick had been partly responsible he would do what Hal asked.

"So, are you ready to drive across country with a couple of old dudes?" Mick said, trying to start some small talk to avoid the uncomfortable silence. Normally silence was what Mick desired, but for some reason with Jon he actually wanted to have a conversation. Again, he knew Hal was right, something had *definitely* changed.

Mick was having feelings for this kid he'd only met ten minutes ago. Feelings he hadn't felt in a long time. Feelings that at their core scared him, but at the same time helped him feel a little more human again.

Jon laughed at Mick's humor. "Naw, you guys aren't that old," he said trying to be polite.

Mick grinned, seeing right through Jon's lie. He made a living playing on the emotions of others and he could spot a false statement a mile away. Plus, he could tell Jon was about as honest of a person as they came, which made his lies even easier than most to catch.

KNOCK KNOCK KNOCK

"Stay here," Mick ordered Jon at hearing the sound at his front door. Jon followed Mick's hefty frame with his eyes and saw his hand drift to the back of his trousers. Since Jon had only been facing Mick's front, he had failed to see the revolver stuffed down the back of his pants. As Mick slid the curtain to the side on the door's upper window, his other hand grabbed the gun's hilt.

Jon's head began to perspire as he wondered if Mick had a reason to suspect his gun was going to be needed. As Mick peered through the smudged glass, Jon saw his arm relax and drop to his side. Mick opened the door and Jon saw Hal standing on the front porch with two giant black duffle bags in each hand, no doubt filled with the spare parts necessary to fix his dad's failed generator.

"About time, the boy and I were growing restless," Mick gruffly said at seeing his temporary employer. Jon instantly noticed the change in Mick's voice and attitude towards Hal when compared to his own conversation with the career criminal just minutes earlier.

"Nice to see you too," Hal said as he skirted past Mick's round belly without so much of a hello. In his mind, Jon wondered if what he was witnessing were Mick's and Hal's true personalities coming through. Was this the way they normally treated everyone in their lives?

"How'd you sleep Jon?" Hal asked caringly, setting the large bags gently on Mick's outdated dark brown carpet.

"Actually pretty good. I was pretty beat after yesterday and the swelling in my ankle is way down. It's not good enough for running, but overall it's a huge improvement."

"Good to hear," Hal said. "So, are we ready to get on the road?"

"I sure am. I don't like feeling like I'm being watched all of the time," Jon replied a little nervously. In truth during the previous night at Mick's house, he had woken numerous times to unknown and strange sounds. He could have sworn someone was walking around Mick's house, spying on him, but Jon knew it was all in his head. Even though this was his first time meeting Mick, Jon had been relieved just to have another soul in the house and to no longer be alone.

"Well, we're all together now, so hopefully that'll make you feel a little more comfortable," Hal said empathetically.

"If you two are done holding hands how about we get a move on," Mick butted in, ready to hit the road.

"Let's do it," Jon replied enthusiastically, just ready to get out of town. He didn't want to think about where he was heading after what happened last time. For now he was content to be with two people, who for the moment seemed to enjoy his company, which had been a rarity lately.

Hal reached down and retrieved the two black duffle bags off the floor and followed Mick and Jon out the back door. He carefully set them down in the Jetta's carpeted trunk and sat in the car's back seat.

"Mind driving Jon?" Mick questioned, tossing him the keys before he had a chance to say no.

"I've been up since the crack of dawn to get back here so we could go to Nebraska together and I'm guessing Hal was up most of the night retrieving the parts needed to fix that hunk of junk in your uncle's barn."

"Why didn't you just wait for us in Nebraska?" Jon asked as he opened the driver's side door.

"Well I couldn't let you guys take one of my cars without me in it. That and your father here thought the two of you might need my help along the way in case a *situation* arises," he said. Immediately Jon understood what the word situation meant and wondered if he had more than one gun hidden on his body.

Father. This was only the second or third time someone had directly called Hal is father. Although Jon had only spent a few days with his biological father, he was beginning to feel an attachment to him; an attachment that went deeper than Hal just being an older mentor. Jon was still so confused about everybody's feelings towards him along with his concerning them; he tried to push the thoughts out of his mind.

"Did you find all of the parts that you were looking for?" he asked Hal, trying to focus on something else.

Hal yawned and said, "Sure did. It took me the better part of the night but eventually I found everything that I think we're going to need. I even grabbed a few pieces that didn't appear to be damaged just in case Mick missed something."

"Missed something? You had me in the middle of nowhere taking pictures of some giant hunk of junk that I know nothing about and you think I might have missed something?" Mick shot back from the front seat indignantly.

"Alright guys, it's going to be a long car ride," Jon said, interceding between his older travel companions.

"Sorry Jon. I guess I'm just a little grumpy from being on the road and the early flight," Mick replied apologetically. He then turned and gave Jon a quick wink to further let him know he felt bad for his outburst.

Jon marveled at how Hal's and Mick's mental switches could turn on and off so easily. One moment they were at each other's throats, while the next; they were as gentle as doves to himself. He couldn't say for sure, but Jon was almost certain their changes in attitude toward him, but not everybody else, were a direct result of the mysterious disc of white and blue light.

"Don't worry Mick, I'm sure you did the best you could. And hey, I don't have much better of a clue to how that machine works either," Jon added, trying to smooth Mick's ruffled feathers.

"So, were all of the parts in your building like you thought?" Jon asked returning to Hal.

"Unfortunately no. I had to go to three different warehouses to scrounge up all of the pieces we're going to need. That's why I was up so late last night; driving to one place and rummaging through their inventory and then to the next place. It's too bad we're keeping this so hush-hush, otherwise I would have called in one of my employees and given him the shopping list," Hal replied, letting a long yawn escape.

Jon glanced over at Mick, who had fallen asleep and was snoring from Hal's overly detailed descriptions of the parts and where he had eventually found them. The conversation between Jon and Hal eventually died down and in the Jetta's rear view mirror, Jon could see that Hal too had fallen fast asleep; resting against the door's molded plastic. For the meantime it was only Jon and the empty desert-like interstate ahead of him.

Two hours later, just past the halfway point between Dallas and Oklahoma City, Jon decided to pull over and top off the small car's tank of gas. He pulled into a somewhat vacant gas station, which appeared to have sprouted out of the middle of nowhere. Jon opened his wallet and debated between using the last bit of his cash or opting for the quicker, but traceable credit card.

Since Jon reasoned the police weren't actively looking to arrest him in Oklahoma, hopefully just in Texas, he decided to save his cash in case it was needed for an emergency. Plus he was in another state. What were the chances a nationwide manhunt was underway to apprehend him? Jon pulled out his credit card and swiped it through the pump's reader as a burst of dry southwest wind whipped at his face.

As the plane gently touched down on the tarmac in the middle of Texas, Andre carefully nudged Beth to bring her out of her slumbering state. Between Andre bumping her and the plane roaming back and forth to find its gate, it didn't take her long to wake up. Somewhat still dazed from her deep sleep she noticed a slight pool of drool on her shoulder and quickly rubbed at it before anyone noticed.

"Don't worry dear, we all do it," said the lady on her left, who must have been in her early sixties.

Beth smiled at her somewhat embarrassed at being caught and turned to Andre. "Wow I feel so much better after that nap."

"Nap? You call that a nap? Man you were snoring and your head was falling all over the place, not to mention you were drooling on both of your shoulders. I wouldn't call that a nap, I'd say you passed out," he chided her.

Sure enough, when she looked at her other shoulder, there too was a small wet spot of escaped drool.

Eventually the plane wound its way through the maze of large aircraft and wandering vehicles and pulled up to its gate. After what seemed an eternity of waiting for everyone else ahead of them to exit the plane, Beth and Andre were finally free to move themselves. Since they had each only packed a carry-on bag and not large suitcases, they were at least spared waiting again for the spinning luggage carousel to spit out an additional bag like many of the plane's other passengers.

Almost as soon as they exited the restricted area there was a man standing off to their right that Beth could have sworn was Patrick Stewart's twin brother. The man was holding a piece of yellow lined legal paper with "Beth" and "Andre" crudely scrawled on its surface.

Beth and Andre slowed their pace as they saw the sign and approached the detective.

"Glad you could both make it," he said, introducing himself and shaking their hands. "Again I'm sorry for booking such an early flight for the two of you, but this case has been a real pain in my butt and I just want to get it over with as soon as possible. So besides the early time, how was the flight?" he asked making small talk.

"Not bad," Beth replied, almost fully awake. She felt so much more with it after her quick power nap and was again ready to proceed with their plan.

"Yeah, no bumps and no delays, so it was a good flight," Andre added.

Detective Briggs continued idly chit-chatting with his informants as he ushered them to his waiting unmarked car. After another twenty plus minutes on the city's busy roadways, the detective finally turned into his precinct. By now the Dallas' morning sun was beginning to beat down on those below it, causing each of them to lightly perspire from simply walking from the car to the building's front doors.

Once inside, the detective showed them to a private room and left to get his pad and paper and a few colas for his guests. As soon as the detective was out of earshot, Andre turned to Beth.

"Are you ready to do this? You're not still squeamish like you were before are you?" he asked hoping they were back on the same page.

"I'm ready," she solidly replied. "Don't mistake my not wanting to lie, to not hating Jon. Once we're done with this I'm sure I'll feel a lot better," she replied, hoping that what she said was true. When she and Jon were dating, Beth couldn't remember a time when he wasn't somewhere in the back of her mind in a positive way. Now, with her feelings somehow completely opposite than before, he was in her mind just as much, but in a hateful way that was close to driving her insane. Beth knew what she and Andres were about to do would eventually lead to perjury, but she couldn't continue living like this. She had to try something.

As the detective roamed the outside hallways looking for his, and two other detectives' shared secretary, he couldn't help but wonder if Beth and Andre were telling the truth about Jon's whereabouts. He had checked his credit card usage and had even gone so far as to call some of his teachers, all of which pointed to Jon having been in Columbus, not Dallas. Plus, Jon's bank accounts and phone records he'd been able to get ahold of hadn't lent credence to Beth's or Andre's account of Jon's whereabouts.

However, all of that seemed to be pushed aside in the detective's mind. He wanted to believe Beth and Andre because of his similar dislike for the Coulter kid. Finally he found his secretary lounging with a cup of freshly brewed coffee in the central break room.

"There you are Eileen. Get the news stations on the phone and have them plaster the arrest warrant for Jon Coulter for the murder of his parents on the noon broadcast. Now that I've got the two friends here, in my office signing the evidence as we speak, there's no reason not to push forward. Oh, and have them send it to the surrounding states too. No telling with this kid. With Hal Roberts as his pappy, Jon Coulter has enough money to go anywhere. So, get his profile to the news outlets and get his mug on the TV. Okay?" he said slightly annoyed as she was still sitting in her seat and not jumping at his command.

"Okay boss," Eileen replied as she slowly stood up with a sigh.

"Thanks, you're a doll," he added as a thank you to which he receives an annoyed arching of her eyebrow in return.

As Detective Briggs was returning with the two ice cold Cokes and his pad of legal paper to the interrogation room, he heard Beth and Andre talking. Like any good detective, he moved to the wall and inched his body closer to the door, where their muffled voices were a little clearer.

Although as close to the door's frame without being seen as he could be, Detective Briggs still had a difficult time hearing exactly what they were discussing. Through some of the louder words he thought they were trying to get their stories to gel together, but he couldn't be certain. He listened another minute, but still not able to hear anything worth his time, he entered the small room to begin finding out what the two colluding twenty year olds really knew.

CHAPTER 14

HUNTED

After letting the silver Jetta drink its fill of gasoline, Jon decided he might as well empty his bladder before hitting the road again. Entering through the small convenience store's single sliding door, Jon was greeted with aisles of salty and sugary snacks and walls lined with refrigerators filled with sodas, sports drinks and beers. For the moment Jon ignored the tempting foods and proceeded to the back of the store.

Once he was finished with his business and had washed his hands, Jon exited the less than clean bathroom and reentered the store's main room. At the opposite end of the aisles of food was the checkout counter where a young woman was ringing up and bagging the items of a burly individual with hairy arms and a worn out baseball cap, Jon assumed had to be a truck driver.

Jon looked just past the two individual's transaction and at the TV showing the noon's local newscast. It looked like the weather would be somewhat nice for the next few days around Texas and Oklahoma, but closer to Nebraska and Colorado the chance of thunderstorms was increasing.

He removed his gaze from the TV as they went to a commercial break and began hunting through the aisles of comfort foods for Corn Nuts and a bag of Combos. Eventually he found both and approached the counter. As he was paying for his not so healthy snack, his eyes widened in horror as the news resumed its telecast by plastering a photo of him and a list of the charges he was accused of.

Quickly he signed the receipt and tossed it towards the woman at the counter, never looking back. In a state of panic he tossed his munchies and a bottle of Mountain Dew on Mick's unsuspecting belly and slammed the car into drive. He laid down a fresh layer of rubber on the gas station's heavily stained pad of cement as the Jetta's tires squealed trying to find traction.

"What gives?" Mick said sitting up annoyed. He picked Jon's snacks off his large belly and uncaringly tossed them to the floor. He leaned over to Jon's side of the car and peaked at the speedometer.

"Jon, you better slow down or we're going to get pulled over," he said as calmly as he could.

"My picture was on the TV," Jon replied. "The police, they're looking for me, in Oklahoma!"

"Okay, just settle down. That's not ideal, but I'm not surprised. From what I've heard from Hal it was bound to happen at some point. Just slow down to the posted speed limit and we'll be fine," Mick said trying to calm Jon's nerves.

"What's going on?" Hal asked from the back seat, also waking up from his nap.

"Your boy's a fugitive," Mick replied, liking the chance to get a dig in at the world-famous millionaire CEO.

"Now listen, did any one see you that might have seen you're picture on the news?" Mick asked as he popped open Jon's bag of Corn Nuts.

"Maybe the clerk," he confessed. "I don't know, it all happened so fast. I was checking out when I looked up and saw my picture on the TV. I don't think I played it very cool though."

"Well, this car is unmarked so the only way they'll be tracking it is if the cops know you're in it. Did you pay with cash or credit?"

Instantly Jon felt stupid. He had thought about using his cash, but didn't think there was anything wrong with the credit card.

"Plastic," he dejectedly replied, knowing he was a fool.

"Don't beat yourself up over something you couldn't have known. You made the best decision with the knowledge you had at the time. What more could you ask for?" Hal responded from the backseat. He felt somewhat responsible for Jon's plunder, having advised his son that he probably only needed to be worried about law enforcement in Texas. Sometime between Hal talking to his inside guy and Jon filling up for gas, the detective's mind must have been changed, as he was now without a doubt expanding his search. Hal knew the warrant for Jon's arrest was stemming from the detective's feelings and not from hard evidence. Who else would know for certain Jon wasn't the killer, than the perpetrator himself?

"What do you think we should do Mick? You're the expert in this field," Hal subtly jabbed at the hefty individual sitting in the seat in front of him.

"Can't tell you Mr. Big Shot. I wasn't in the store so I don't know if we have a reason to be worried or not. You're guess is as good as mine, but I'll say this, we're heading due north on a fast interstate. We could probably get off on a side highway, but there are cops patrolling them too. If time is of the essence, which based on what we've just learned, I'd definitely say it is, then my vote is to continue on the road we're on," Mick replied, not appreciating Hal's cheap shot.

"Do you agree Hal?" Jon asked, turning back to his biological father for confirmation

"I don't think we have much of choice. Like Mick said, we need to get to your uncle's farm fast."

"Alright, then it's straight at head," Jon announced to the car's passengers. He was starting to feel a little more relaxed as both Hal and Mick didn't seem to be too upset with his stupidity. He should have used the cash regardless of what he thought he knew. No way would the cops have come at him with dogs at *Evergreen Resources* if he was just a suspect. He was acting just plain dumb.

Figuring he wasn't going to get anything useful out of eavesdropping on Beth and Andre, Detective Briggs pulled himself away from the wall and entered the bland grey-walled room. He set the two Cokes in front of his guests and placed his pad of legal paper directly in front of him.

"Alright, so let's get started," he began. "I want to know what both of you know or think you know. I hope I haven't gotten ahead of myself, but I just sent word to the TV stations to start showing Jon's picture on their telecasts."

The detective looked at Andre, who was smiling at Jon's predicament, while Beth had a scowl on her face and was gritting her teeth. Between the two completely different facial expressions, Detective Briggs was having a hard time figuring these two out. He had been performing his due diligence. Having talked to their friends and families, everyone had told him how close both of them had been to Jon a few weeks ago.

Although he found it curious how their feelings about Jon Coulter had changed so suddenly, he tried not to dwell on the fact as he knew his were no different. Now he was getting the chance to talk to Jon's onetime best friend and girlfriend face to face. It was time to find out if he was being played or not.

"So, Andre let's start with you. Why don't you tell me where you were the night before Jon's parents' deaths. Just the simple details, where, what, why, that kind of thing. For example I don't need to know what you were eating, just the basics. Then you can tell me what Jon was up to. Okay?"

"Sure, not a problem," Andre said while trying to reign in his enthusiasm at sticking one to his ex-buddy.

Just as Andre opened his mouth to spew forth his lies, Detective Briggs' secretary knocked at the door. She motioned with her eyes and a slight movement of her head that he needed to follow her outside of the room.

"Excuse me for a moment," he said to his guests and removed himself from their presence.

"What's going on?" he asked his secretary once in the hallway.

"The warrant issued for Jon Coulter's arrest made it onto the news at noon. Anyway, we just received a call from a gas station close to the border with Oklahoma that our suspect was there. Apparently he saw the warrant for his arrest on TV and freaked out. The clerk thought he looked suspicious and called it in."

"Fantastic!" Detective Briggs exclaimed. "That's got to be a record for finding someone that fast."

In his mind, Detective Briggs was already trying to figure out his next step. While he knew he needed to be nailing down Beth's and Andre's stories about Jon's whereabouts from the night in question, he desperately wanted to be there when Jon was arrested. Making up his mind, the detective returned to the sparsely decorated room.

"Sorry guys but I have to step out for a while. I've got your numbers so why don't the two of you go see the sights while I attend to some business," he said with a smile.

"Okay, we'll find something to do," Beth replied. Immediately after the detective left the room, she turned to Andre.

"Did you hear what they were saying in the hall?" she asked.

"Yep, they're going after him. Sounds like he's heading north, but where is he going?" Andre asked inquisitively.

"I'm surprised you don't know," she replied. "I'll bet he's headed to his aunt and uncle's farm."

"Are you sure?" Andre asked, not completely convinced Beth knew what she was talking about.

"I think it's as good as a guess as anywhere else. I say we rent a car and head there ourselves."

"Why? You heard the detective and the lady talking out there. They're going to find him and arrest him. It sounds like a waste of time to me," Andre replied, grabbing his can of Coke, now covered in moisture from the office's humidity.

"Just chalk it up to women's intuition. Look, the worst that will happen is we head north and then Detective Briggs calls us and wants to talk again. If that happens then we'll just drive back here, but in the case that I'm right, I want to be the one turning Jon over to the police. I want to be there when he's arrested so he knows it's me who turned him in," Beth said, laying her cards out on the table.

"I like the way you think," Andre agreed with a devilish grin.

Beth left her unopened Coke in the middle of the interrogation officeand left the police station with Andre following close behind. After calling a taxi and renting a car, they were heading north on Interstate 35. Again Beth reclined her seat, like on the airplane, still trying to recover some of her lost sleep from the night before. Although the time it took her to fall asleep was longer than on the plane, eventually she dozed off, dreaming of Jon dying in a hail of gunfire with a smile on her face.

Feeling fairly secure on their decision to continue on the interstate, Jon for the moment failed to see the single Oklahoma state trooper's cruiser closing in behind his flashy silver Jetta. Both Hal and Mick had again fallen asleep from their busy nights after reaching a car-wide consensus on continuing towards Nebraska on I-35.

Jon had since turned the music up loud and was humming to some of his favorite 90's alternative tunes, which easily covered the siren's ever-increasing sound. Finally, once *Black Hole Sun* by Soundgarden was finished, there was a slight lull in the radio's programming to where there was only silence in the car.

Now, Jon was able to hear the ever closing sound of the sheriff's waling siren. Looking into his review mirror, Jon saw the car's flashing red and blue lights as it pulled up directly behind them.

"Oh crap!" he yelled, instantly waking Mick and Hal. "There's a cop behind us, what do I do?" he said in exasperation.

Mick pulled his tired body more upright in his seat and turned to gaze at the car behind them. He didn't want to stop, but what else were they to do.

"Were you speeding?" he asked.

"I wasn't trying to, but I might have been going a little fast here and there," Jon admitted. How could he be that stupid to have two blunders of this magnitude on the same day?

"Well either he's after you for speeding or you were spotted at the gas station. Either way we've got to pull over," Mick reasoned.

As Jon slowed the car and pulled over to the interstate's median, Mick brought out his loaded pistol from the back of his pants. He moved the gun to his right side and let it hang down between his seat and the passenger door, where the highway patrolman would not be able to see it.

Jon watched through the car's side mirror as the sheriff left his vehicle and began walking towards them. With a gulp and a growing pit in the middle of his stomach, Jon pressed the button, lowering the car's window.

"Good morning officer," Mick said smiling as he looked over Jon and through the open window. "How can we help you?" He hated being fake, like some cheerleader pretending she and someone she hated were friends, but if they could get out of here with only a ticket, Mick would be ecstatic.

"License and registration please," the officer said to Jon, ignoring Mick's pleasantries for the moment.

Jon pulled out his wallet and withdrew his Texas driver's license, while Mick fished through the car's glove compartment for its new registration. Mick wasn't worried in the slightest about the car checking out. He'd been in this game for years and knew all of the tricks of the trade. The only way this would end badly would be if the sheriff was pulling them over for Jon and if that was the case he felt badly for the sheriff as he probably wasn't going to survive their encounter.

"Stay in the car. I'll be right back," the trooper said and proceeded back to his patrol car.

"What's the plan Mick?" Hal finally asked from the rear seat. As much as his persona wanted to take charge, he knew Mick was much better suited for the situation with his extensive criminal background.

"Hopefully we won't need a plan, but in case we do I'm not letting him take us." Mick turned in his seat to face Hal. "I've been doing a lot of thinking about our phone conversation yesterday and I've come to the conclusion that you're right, something has changed in both of us. And since you seem to know that it was from the machine, I have to take your word for it. But it's because of that change and I can't stop hating myself for what we've done and I'm going to make it up to this kid here no matter what I have to do or how long it takes and I'm pretty sure you feel the same way. That's why we're both here trying to set things right in the first place."

Mick could see the horror on Hal's face at him bringing up topics that shouldn't be discussed in front of Jon, but he didn't care. He would have kept going, wanting to come clean, but the sound of another siren in the distance caught his attention.

A second state trooper's car pulled in behind the first one with its lights flashing. Jon and his passengers watched as the newly arrived state trooper left his car and approached the first trooper currently on his radio. After a brief conversation between the two officers, the first officer exited his car and they both began walking forward.

"Just be cool guys," Mick said, gripping his gun tightly.

Jon sat stoically in the car's front seat as the two officers approached. He searched the hands of the first trooper on the scene for his documents, but found none. He didn't have to be in Mick's shoes to know that was a bad sign.

"Jon Coulter please step out of the car," one of the officers commanded.

Without hesitation, but as nervous as he'd ever been, Jon complied, opening the door and stepping onto the hot pavement. As he stood outside with the midday sun beating down overhead, he watched the other cars with no care in the world zip by him on the busy interstate. Why couldn't his day have been like theirs?

"Jon Coulter, you're under arrest for the murder of John and Lisa Coulter. Anything you say can be used against you in a court of law. You have the…" the officer was saying in the middle of giving Jon his Miranda rights when Mick stepped out of the passenger side of the compact car.

"You get him to that farm and fix that machine," Mick said to Hal through the open window before turning his attention to the two officers. "Hey, what's going on here," he said as if he didn't already know.

"Sir, I'm going to have to ask you to return to you seat," the closest officer said, moving his hand from his cuffs to his gun.

"I know my rights and I don't have to sit down if I don't want to," Mick defiantly said. In fact Mick did know his rights and knew his last words were complete crap. He just needed more time to think.

"Sir, this young man is under arrest and you need to sit back down," the officer repeated and unsnapped his holster. The second state trooper behind the first then stepped out of his shadow and to the side.

"Are we going to have trouble here?" the second officer questioned Mick as he too lowered his hand towards his gun. He glared at Mick for his interference and from what Jon could tell, appeared ready to draw his weapon at a moment's notice.

"I can't let you do that," Mick said with such straightforwardness and protective ferocity that it sent a chill down Jon's spine. Before either of the officers had a chance to react, Mick already had his gun drawn on them and was rounding the hood of the car.

"Don't either of you move. I'm sorry I have to do this, but this kid's innocent and I'm not letting you take him."

Jon looked over at Mick, barely recognizing the man he'd known for the past few hours. Mick's face had distorted itself into the look of a stone-faced killer. The friendship Jon had seen in his eyes was now replaced with pure focus.

"Jon get back in the car," Mick ordered.

Jon hesitated for a moment to which Mick almost growled, "Don't make me shoot you in the kneecap." There was no way on earth he would ever shoot Jon, he and Hal had done enough, but he needed Jon back in the car and for the troopers to believe it wasn't Jon's decision flee.

"You on the side, handcuff your buddy here," Mick then ordered the second officer to arrive.

Obeying the command, the second trooper moved in behind his friend and pulled the handcuffs out of his belt. As he wrapped the first officer's cuffs around his wrists, Mick listened for the clicking of the internal ratchet as they were tightened. The second officer then whispered something to the one in front of him.

"Hey! No talking!" Mick yelled in response to the unpermitted whispers. He glared at both officers and threateningly waved his gun. From that instant everything happened so fast from Jon's seated vantage point he was barely certain of who shot first.

Almost at the same time Mick was yelling at the troopers for talking, the one in front said, "Yes." At hearing his response, the officer not handcuffed and in the rear pushed the other officer forward and into Mick, while at the same time drawing his gun. With the officer being pushed into him, Mick had no choice but to use both hands to stop the man's body. In doing so his gun was no longer aimed at either of the officers.

As Mick threw the first handcuffed officer to the ground, the second officer fired off two shots, both of them hitting Mick in the chest. Two small round pools of blood appeared on his shirt as he fell to the ground next to the first officer. While the second officer who had fired the shots moved his gun towards Jon and Hal, thinking Mick was as good as dead; with a heavy hand Mick fired a shot of his own.

As Mick was initially being shot, Jon was yelling no in his head, but was too shocked to realize he wasn't saying it out loud. As though it was in slow motion Jon now saw the second officer being hit square in his chest and falling dead to the ground. Jon burst out of the car and to Mick's dying side.

"Why?" Jon asked, wishing there was a way to reverse the last few minute's events.

"I'm so sorry Jon," Mick hoarsely said.

"You killed him," Jon lamented in disbelief at the dead police officer.

"Not about that, he had it coming," Mick replied unapologetically. "I'm sorry about your parents," he said and then broke into a fit of coughing. Bright red drops of blood made their way onto his chapped lips as he struggled to breathe.

"I know, you said so before," Jon said a little perplexed. Was this the end stage of Mick's life that was causing his mind to wander?

"No, I'm sorry about what I did to them," he said looking Jon directly in the eyes and then down at the ground. He tried to roll from his side to his back, but lacked the strength to do so.

From inside the car, Hal climbed over the middle console into the driver's seat. "Jon, come on we have to get out of here. He just killed a cop." Hal couldn't hear what Mick was saying to Jon, but he had a pretty good idea. Although he longed to tell Jon his demons too and ask for his forgiveness, Hal knew in the grand scheme of things it would only hurt his son.

"Just wait a second," Jon said, shooing Hal's request away. "What did you do to them?" he said turning his attention back to the dying man at his side. For a brief second Jon locked eyes with the handcuffed officer on the ground who was listening to everything. However, the trooper was still in restraints and was a non-issue at the moment.

"I'm the one who tampered with their brakes. I'm so sorry and I know you won't ever be able to forgive me, but I want you to know that if I was ever given the chance I'd take back that day in a heartbeat," he confided in Jon beginning to slur his speech and taking more time in between words. Mick's once heaving chest barely lifted half as high as it used to as his internal bleeding was slowly killing his body.

"Why... I don't understand," Jon replied unable to grasp what Mick was telling him.

COUGH COUGH COUGH

Mick spit up more blood and gagged on the upcoming fluids. He heaved for breath, but was unable to find as much oxygen as he required. Eventually his body relaxed its spasms and he was able to speak again.

"It was just a job," he said reaching for Jon's arm, but his hand never made it. As Mick's outstretched arm was in midair, his chest gave one final heave. He died there on the spot, with his arm dropping to the pavement with a thud.

Jon stared at the dead man in disbelief and then to the officer to his right. The world seemed as though it was in a haze. He could hear the officer saying something to him, while Hal was yelling at him to get in to the car. Like he was stuck in slow motion, Jon turned towards the officer lying on the ground.

"He just confessed to murdering your parents. Uncuff me so we can get this straightened out." Jon looked at the officer and then to Hal, who was sadly shaking his head no. If Hal was right and fixing the machine and then running the current in reverse could put his life back together he didn't have a choice. Just like the first explosion, he would have to be touching the device to not be affected by its force. If Hal was able to fix the fusion reactor and run it while Jon was in jail somewhere, then everyone would once again love him. But he might hate all of them.

"I'm so sorry about your friend, but I have to do something first," Jon said apologetically to the restrained officer and stood up. He looked down the interstate, back towards Oklahoma City. Although the traffic had started to slow to see what the two state patrol cars were up to, no one had yet stopped.

Without saying another word, Jon walked around their car and sat in the passenger seat. Normally a stickler for wearing his seatbelt, Hal had to tell him twice to put it on, with Jon barely registering either of his comments.

At the first interchange, speeding over ninety miles an hour, Hal pulled off the interstate and onto a more desolate highway. He continued speeding the car at least ten miles over the posted speed limit, trying to make up for any time they would lose not on the interstate. He wanted to put as much distance between them and the dead trooper as possible. As Hal drove, Jon sat in silence searching for where everything went wrong.

CHAPTER 15

NEBRASKA REVISITED

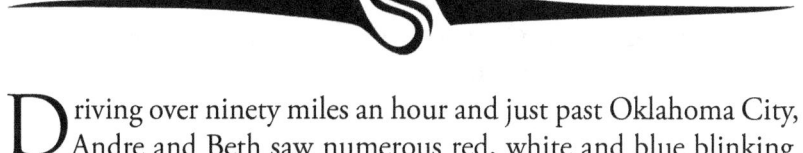

Driving over ninety miles an hour and just past Oklahoma City, Andre and Beth saw numerous red, white and blue blinking lights up ahead. As if Oklahoma's entire highway patrol division had decided to congregate at one specific location; their cars lined the side of the road as Andre slowly made his way through the congestion in the one open lane of traffic.

"Do you think that has anything to do with Jon?" Beth asked mesmerized by the buzz of activity.

"That goodie too shoos, I highly doubt it unless they're arresting him, but there's no way they'd need that many cops for that."

Andre continued through the maze of orange cones, now with the windows down and the music muted at less than fifteen miles an hour. With this much commotion on the side of the road, none of the drivers on the interstate wanted to go too fast in fear of missing what was going on. As their rental car entered the thick of the throngs of police officers, Beth pointed to a black body bag lying at the foot of an ambulance. Another officer was being interviewed by two of his peers only a few feet further down.

Andre glanced in the rear view mirror to see if there were any cars behind them. For the moment the interstate was clear. He slowed down to almost a complete stop in front of a group of officers discussing the day's event.

Beth stuck her head out of the window, trying to hear what they were saying. Even though the traffic was sporadic on the other side of the wide interstate she was still only able to hear bits and pieces of the officers' conversation.

"Like I said... backup... I had pulled over... Coulter... his arrest and then...," was all Beth could hear from the troopers' voices before one of them angrily waved them on.

"You can't stop here!" the officer yelled. Beth waved to the angry patrolman, embarrassed at getting yelled at before Andre sped them through the one lane of traffic.

"Wow, well I guess I couldn't have been more wrong on that one," Andre exclaimed, more shocked at knowing all of the fuss was because of Jon than him being wrong. Even though Beth hadn't been able to hear an entire sentence, just hearing Jon's last name was enough for them to know they were headed in the right direction.

"See I told you I knew where he was going. There's no doubt he's going to his aunt and uncle's house. You saw that back there. There wasn't another car, only those from the highway patrol. If Jon was there, we'd have seen him in the back of one of their patrol cars and we'd definitely have seen his ride."

Andre didn't say anything, but nodded his head in agreement. Now completely through the mess, he rolled up their windows and turned the car's music back on. What he wanted to know was what had just happened on the side of the interstate and what was Jon's involvement in it? Andre didn't know why, but the thought of the cops possibly wanting Jon even more after whatever had happened made him almost giddy.

"We should tell that detective what we just heard," Andre mentioned to Beth further down the road.

"Yep, I was thinking the same thing. It would be the right thing to do after all," Beth innocently replied.

As Andre returned the car to its ninety miles per hour cruising along the interstate, Beth retrieved her phone from her purse and called Detective Briggs.

"This is Detective Briggs," he answered sounding a little rushed.

"Mr. Briggs, this is Beth and Andre..." she started before getting cut off.

"Hey, tell me I just didn't see you and your friend drive through my crime scene," he said sounding annoyed that they weren't back in Dallas, let alone in a completely different state.

"Yeah, I'm really sorry about that," Beth replied, telling the truth. Even though John Coulter's machine had altered her feelings about Jon, it had not affected her overall personality. Deep down, Beth was still the sweet, loving person she'd always been and she felt ashamed disobeying the detective, regardless of her reasons. "But we overheard you talking in the hallway about Jon. He isn't there with you is he?" she asked.

"No he's not, but someone he was traveling with shot and killed a highway patrolman. Why do you ask?"

"I was just wondering," she said, for some reason growing hesitant to lay her cards on the table. She wanted to ask the detective who shot and killed the other policeman, but didn't want to sound too heartless.

"Just tell him," Andre pushily said from the driver's seat.

"I think I know where he's going. He's got an aunt and uncle that live on a farm in Nebraska and I think he's headed there," she finally admitted.

"Well that kind of sounds like an odd place to travel to, considering the last time I talked to his aunt and uncle they didn't want anything to do with him. Actually their story is pretty much similar to you and your friends. One minute all of their friends say they loved Jon and then the next they can't stand him, just like you and Andre," the detective said. The moment the words left his lips he knew he was talking about himself too. Again, he had a sneaky suspicion that there was something he was missing in the case.

"Regardless if they like him or not, I think that's where he's going," she nicely argued.

"Okay, I guess it won't hurt to have a patrol car checking the property every so often. I'm feeling like I can't talk you out of going there yourselves so just be careful and if something happens stay out of the way, alright?" Detective Briggs said, almost sounding like her father.

"Sure, we absolutely don't want to do anything that would allow him to escape," Beth said. She felt a slight pit in her stomach at the very thought of her life continuing like it had been for any further extended amount of time. Knowing that the detective had more pressing matters to attend to, Beth cordially said goodbye and hung up the phone. She stared straight ahead at the quiet and rather desolate interstate as Andre continued pushing them north.

After ending the phone call with Beth, who Detective Briggs was not happy to find out had left Dallas before giving her statement, he returned to the two dead bodies on the ground. Although no longer in Texas, the local law enforcement was being overly gracious by letting him take an active part in the early phase of their investigation.

As Detective Briggs zipped shut the black body bag of the slain trooper, probably for the last time before the dead man's autopsy, he felt ashamed for feeling lucky it wasn't someone he personally knew. It didn't take a detective to see the ring on the dead trooper's finger to know that there was at least one person out there that was going to be devastated at hearing he was dead. The only consoling aspect of the shooting was that the slain officer had killed the man who shot him.

The detective left the body bag and moved towards Mick's lifeless body. The large Texan was dressed in a plaid button down shirt with dark blue jeans and a larger than life belt buckle. Although he had never been arrested, Detective Briggs knew who Mick was right away as he'd been under limited surveillance by his department for some time now. The detective hadn't ever been directly involved in the building of Mick's case, but during their precinct wide meetings he had heard and seen enough to know who the man was.

Even though the scumbag sprawled out before him had gotten what he deserved, the detective still wanted to kick Mick's lifeless body in the gut. He knew it was wrong, but Detective Briggs was happy the man lying with two bullets lodged in his chest was dead. A few feet even further down, the clearly shaken first officer on the scene, who was now unhandcuffed, was recounting the early afternoon's horrific events for probably the fifth time.

"Man I can't stop shaking," the first trooper said to one of the EMTs standing next to him. He held out his hands so they could see that even with considerable effort he was not able to hold them steady.

"Don't worry about it. Just keep taking deep breaths and try to relax. You're still in shock, but it'll pass," the technician advised using a calm demeanor.

One of the officer's friends placed a hand on his shoulder. "Finish telling the captain what happened and I'll take you out for a drink. After what you've been through today I think you probably need one," his friend said, although alcohol might not have been the best choice at the moment.

"Alright," the officer said taking a deep breath. "Zack asked me if I was wearing a vest. The guy with the gun lying on the ground over there yelled at us to stop talking and then Zack pushed me towards the gunman and at the ground. I'm sure he asked about the vest to make sure I'd be alright, but I guess he should have been worrying about himself. Did I say the guy had his gun pointed at us?" the officer asked as his state of shock was slightly garbling his memory.

"Yeah you did buddy, but you're doing fine, just keep going and then we'll get out of here," his friend again said trying to help keep him on track.

"So Zack shoots him twice in the chest and then the gunman falls to the ground and from there he fires one shot hitting Zack in the chest and from what I could tell, it killed him instantly. But if the whole shooting wasn't horrible enough, this is where it got really weird. As the gunman is lying, bleeding to death on the pavement, the Coulter kid gets out of the car and kneels down at his side. So right now I'm still handcuffed, but I'm less than three feet from the two of them and I can hear every word they're saying. The guy Zack shot then starts apologizing to this kid about killing his parents."

The officer paused for a second and looked over at Detective Briggs who was standing a few feet away, but clearly listening in on their conversation.

"I know there's an A.P.B. on Jon Coulter for killing his parents, but I'm telling you, I was there and this kid had nothing to do with it. This was an honest-to-God confession if I'd ever heard one before. The gunman was dying and he knew it from the amount of blood he was coughing up. I'm positive he was trying to come clean before he was going where we all know he's going to end up," the officer said clenching his fists in anger.

"I appreciate your candor," Detective Briggs replied. He knew he had some real soul searching to do, because as much as he wanted to call Jon a murderer the facts simply weren't backing up his feelings and that rarely happened.

The officer could tell Detective Briggs was for some reason not necessarily buying into his account of the events and added, "And I'll testify to that if I'm ever called."

The officer's friend lightly squeezed his shoulder and began leading him away from the day's carnage and to a more quiet less busy area until they were told he could leave.

The detective watched the offices leave the scene and eventually returned to his own unmarked car. Maybe Beth was right and Jon was driving to his aunt and uncle's farm. Either way, Jon was no longer in Texas. Detective Briggs sat for over twenty minutes in his idling government car before finally deciding that if there was ever a case he needed to see through, it was this one.

Without turning around, the detective steered his car into the still only one lane of moving traffic and to the north. Not far after the violent scene of death and police cars had disappeared from his rear view mirror, Detective Briggs called his superior and notified him of his whereabouts. He briefly thought of requesting the use of some accrued personal days, but in the end he didn't want this case to be marred by a technicality or anything else that wasn't done exactly by the book. He needed to get to Nebraska.

"He killed my parents!" Jon was almost screaming at Hal from the passenger seat next to him. "That, that man you work with killed them? Why? What reason on earth could he have to kill them?" Jon asked somewhat to Hal, while also venting at the day's shocking news. He couldn't understand what connection Mick could have to his parents and then it hit him.

Jon sat motionless; trying to disprove in his head what he knew was true. His parents both knew and hated Hal; Hal knew what type of man Mick was and worked with him, how could his biological father have not been in on their deaths too? Jon wanted to ask Hal for the truth, but was scared to hear his answer.

Across from Jon, Hal continued driving and staring straight ahead. Although Jon was oblivious to the fact, Hal's pulse had been racing ever since Mike's dying confession and apology. He had wanted to shut Mike up, to stop him from revealing everything to Jon, but what could he have done? The man was dying and to make matters worse there was the officer that had pulled them over lying next to him; watching and listening to everything happening around him.

Hal continued sitting nervously, knowing that eventually Jon was going to ask him about Mick. Jon was a smart kid; there wasn't any way he wasn't going to put two and two together. What Hal truly worried about was his deep underlying desire to come clean to his son about what he'd done. Although he knew there was nothing to be gained, except a clean conscience, but everything to lose, his soul begged him to tell the truth.

Finally, after almost an hour of silence, Jon asked the question he didn't want to know the answer to.

"Did you have something to do with my parent's deaths?"

Acting as though he was shocked Jon could ever think he'd be capable of something that reprehensible, Hal replied, "Of course not Jon. How could you ever think such a thing?"

"It's true that you're my father, but I don't really know you. Have I been wrong this entire time thinking that you cared for me?" he questioned hoping for a truthful answer but only if it was the one he wanted. If this man sitting next to him had been involved in his parents' deaths, could he really continue driving with him the entire way to Nebraska like nothing had ever happened? Almost instantly Jon felt like he was going to be sick. Even though the car's air conditioning was on at full blast, he rolled down his window needing immediate fresh air.

"Are you alright Jon? Do you want me to pull over?" Hal asked, hardly able to fathom the emotions his son must be going through.

"No, I'm fine. Just keep driving," Jon said waving him away. With his head sticking out of the car's open window, the fresh air rushing by almost made Jon feel as though we wasn't in the car at all, which was exactly what he needed.

"Jon," Hal yelled against the deafening wind blowing into the car. "You have to believe me. I had nothing to do with your parents' deaths. What would I have gained? I didn't know about your father's prototypes until after his death. And if you're thinking it was about your mom, well, yeah I liked her, but that was over twenty years ago. If she hadn't been with your father I'd liked to have thought maybe she'd have given me a chance, but that was so long ago."

Slowly Jon pulled his head back into the car without rolling up the window. "But what about Mick? You and he worked together. Why else would he have killed them if not for you?" Jon asked. He stared Hal in the face, trying to discern if he was telling the truth or just an incredible liar.

"Mick doesn't work for me. He helps me with certain things from time to time. To tell you the truth, I hadn't talked to him for years before I learned about John's solar cells. There's nothing between us besides business, that's all." Hal briefly took his eyes off of the road and looked at his distraught son, trying to convey his honesty. Someday in the future, he would tell Jon the truth. His son deserved that much, but now definitely wasn't the time. However, Mick's death had made Hal's life easier. Now there was one less loose thread from the Coulters' deaths that Hal would have to take care of.

After another few minutes of accompanying silence, Jon pushed the small black button and rolled the window up. Almost instantly the warm summer air began to be replaced by the super cooled breeze flowing through the car's ventilation. By now both Hal and Jon were sweaty from the outside humidity and each was glad to have the window closed.

Jon didn't bring up the question of who killed his parents again. He wanted to believe his biological father's statements of innocence, but deep in the pit of his stomach he couldn't see how that could be true.

After another five hours of driving, Hal and Jon finally made it onto Interstate 80, which cut east and west along the state of Nebraska. Another hour later and they'd be just outside his aunt and uncle's farm. The entire length of the drive, after Jon brought up Hal's supposed involvement in his parents' murders, they never once discussed what happened to Mick. Neither one of them wanted to rehash the day's events, especially not Mick gunning down the state trooper in broad daylight.

Only a few minutes before they pulled onto the road passing his uncle's farm, Jon couldn't hold in his questions any longer.

"Did Mick have a family?" Jon blurted out into the car's silence. His words seemed to echo in the car after over an hour of silence.

"No, not that I have heard about," Hal responded. "He's got a bunch of unsavory characters that he worked with that he would probably call family, but actual blood relatives, none that I know of." Hal replied kindly to Jon's question; in truth he had been pondering the same question not long before Jon had asked.

Jon wanted to talk more about Mick now that he had finally broken the invisible barrier of silence, but now they were on the dusty road, he could start to see the top of his uncle's grain silo approaching in the distance. Just as they came to a four way intersection, a county sheriff's car turned in front of them on the same path towards his aunt and uncle's house. Hal slowed their vehicle to allow the patrol car to further the distance between the two of their vehicles.

"Do you think they're going to the farm?" Jon asked.

"We'll see, but after what happened in Oklahoma I wouldn't bet against it." Hal slowed their car even more to where they were barely moving above a crawl. Jon's relatives' farm was now clearly visible. They watched as the patrol car entered the farmstead. Once the police cruiser was out of view, Hal increased their speed. Without slowing down as they passed, Jon and Hal both stared out of the car's window observing two officers entering his uncle's house.

"Well, I was thinking we'd probably have to do our repairs at night anyway; this just confirms it," Hal said. "Let's head into town and get some food and maybe try to grab a few winks before we try again later tonight."

Jon shook his head in agreement as Hal turned the car, heading towards the closest town of Grand Island, Nebraska. Although it definitely wasn't Columbus, Ohio or Dallas, Texas, Grand Island wasn't that bad. With a population of over forty thousand there were plenty of restaurants to choose from. After eating they made a few quick stops at a couple of hardware stores. Even though Hal had done a fantastic job getting the parts needed to repair the fusion reactor, in his haste to collect everything before morning he had forgotten to pack any of the actual tools they might need to actually fix the device.

Once they bought the necessary tools, they found a cheap motel where Hal fell asleep almost as soon as he hit the pillow. Still sleep deprived from being up the entire night before, he was exhausted. Jon sat on the opposite twin bed and surfed the fuzzy channels on the out dated hotel's television. Even if he was as tired as Hal, there was virtually no chance of Jon falling asleep.

Earlier that day he'd witnessed a murder and watched someone die in front of him. Now, in a few hours, he was going to sneak back onto his aunt and uncle's farm, which was now apparently being watched by the police who suspected him of murdering his parents. There were simply too many thoughts running around in his head for his mind to slow down enough for sleep to take hold.

A little after 8:00 in the evening, Beth and Andre pulled into Jon's aunt and uncle's farm. The police had since left for the time being, but had said they would continue making random drive-bys throughout the night just in case Jon did indeed show up.

As Andre pulled the car into an open spot on the one pad of grey cement surrounded by yellow gravel, Jon's uncle's dogs came tearing out and barking at the unknown vehicle. Only a few minutes later Uncle Harold came out of the house with a shotgun in his hands.

"Shut up you mangy mongrels," he yelled. Almost instantly the dogs quieted their yapping and went to his side. "It's okay, you can get out, they won't hurt you," he said to the car's passengers.

Andre hated dogs with a passion after getting bit once when he was younger and was still hesitant to get out of the car regardless of Uncle Harold's promise of safety. Unlike Andres, Beth loved almost every animal in nature and barely skipped a beat before exiting the vehicle. Even before she shook Uncle Harold's hand, who recognized her from his sister-in-law's funeral, she was down on one knee petting both of the dogs at the same time.

The dogs were almost attacking Beth with slobbery kisses, but froze when Andre exited the car's other side. Like most animals, they could tell who enjoyed their company and those who didn't.

"Down," Uncle Harold said with authority. Again, immediately the dogs settled down at his voice. "What are the two of you doing here?" he asked out of curiosity.

"I think Jon is heading here and if he is I want to be here when he's arrested," Beth blurted out.

"I assume that goes for you too?" Uncle Harold asked Andre who nodded in agreement. "If that's the case why don't you two come on inside. Jenny just made a fresh peach pie and I've been looking for an excuse to cut into it. We'd be happy to have the both of you."

Beth eagerly followed Uncle Harold inside his old farmhouse, with Andre following behind, almost walking backwards not wanting to keep his eyes off of the dogs as they nipped at his heels. He finally felt relief when he was able to shut the screen door, locking the vile beasts outside where they belonged.

"Well, hi you two. I thought I heard Harry talking to someone out there," Aunt Jenny gushed at seeing Jon's two friends. She quickly walked to each of them and gave them a big hug. Although her feelings had changed about her nephew, she still adored his two friends.

"They think Jon's coming here to cause more trouble," Uncle Harold said as he reached for some plates and cups for milk. Aunt Jenny smiled at him, knowing he had been itching for a piece of her famous pie and arched an eyebrow.

"That's what those county sheriff's deputies were saying too. They said that Jon was involved in some sort of shootout in Oklahoma. But they also said they had heard through the grapevine that there was new evidence pointing to him not being involved in my sister's death," Aunt Jenny said, completing her husband's thought.

"Really?" Beth and Andre replied simultaneously. Under normal circumstances they would have yelled jinx at each other, but now they were worried Jon wouldn't be arrested after all. All of their hard work and scheming might have been for nothing if there was concrete evidence he wasn't involved in his parents' deaths. Luckily for each of them they had left Dallas before giving any statements on paper to the police calling Jon a murderer.

"Did they say if there was another suspect?" Beth asked hoping the answer was no.

"Yep, sure did. They said some guy from the car Jon was driving confessed after killing a deputy in Oklahoma," Uncle Harold replied right before shoving a piece of pie into his face.

"He was involved in a shootout? Really? Jon? That guy's as straight as an arrow. The only guns he ever sees is when I'm coming back from the gym," Andre said with a sly smirk.

"Yeah, I think we'd all like to believe that little twerp killed his parents, but in reality he's as harmless as a housefly," Uncle Harold added. All of them were thinking the same thing, Jon was no killer. As much as they hated his very existence; he didn't have an evil bone in his body.

"Well I for one, guilty or not, want that higher than thou, pompous jerk to show his face here tonight so I can give him the pummeling he deserves. Last time he was in Columbus he cost me a ticket for speeding. Now it's time for payback," Andre said gritting his teeth at the thought of having to shell out two hundred bucks for that stupid ticket.

"You're not the only one that hopes he shows up son," Uncle Harold butted in with a mouthful of pie. "The last time he was here with that good-for-nothing father of his, they blew up a hunk of junk in my barn and it still smells like burnt rubber."

"Whoa wait, I thought his dad was dead?" Andre said interrupting Uncle Harold's tirade.

"His dad is dead, but his biological father isn't," Uncle Harold said as he scraped his plate, not wanting to leave a smidgen of pie or its sugary goodness behind.

"Mr. Coulter wasn't his real dad?" Beth asked amazed Jon had never told her.

"Nope, Hal Roberts, CEO of *Evergreen Resources* is his real dad. He had a one-night stand with Jon's mom and well, the rest as they say is history," Uncle Harold said as he filled Beth and Andre in on Jon's true lineage.

"Man, this guy has everything," Andre said, his hate for Jon clouding his judgment. "So Mr. Coulter dies and then Jon's dad is instantly replaced by one of the richest people in the United States. I mean, what gives. No wonder I hate him so much; he seems to have everything!"

Beth clenched her fists in rage at finding out Jon had kept his secret from her. He was the heir to *Evergreen Resources* and he had never trusted her enough to tell her. She hated him more and more each second that ticked by.

"He never said anything to me," Beth seethed.

"We don't think he actually knew, but who knows with that kid," Aunt Jenny said with a scowl.

As the night progressed they moved from the kitchen to the farmhouse's living room. Even though the night was still warm and humid, they opened the windows all the way so they would be able to hear if anyone was approaching their property. As they waited to see if Jon would come, they continued discussing their most favorite topic without skipping a beat; how each of them hated Jon to the core of their being.

A little after midnight, when Jon and Hal assumed everyone at his aunt and uncle's farm was asleep, they left the hotel for the night. Hal felt reinvigorated after his lengthy powernap and was ready to see their mission carried through to the end.

Once they were out of town and beginning the approach to the darkened farmstead, Hal turned off the car's headlights, only using its smaller fog lights to illuminate their way. After seeing the authorities at the farm during their first drive by, this time they searched for somewhere to hide their car. Maybe if it weren't for his uncle's dogs they'd drive a little closer, but under the circumstances they each thought stashing the car was the best approach.

About a quarter of a mile before the farm, they found a dirt road leading into a neighboring cornfield. Hal turned off the gravel road and onto the uneven dirt surface. After he felt they had driven far enough from the road not to be noticed, he killed the engine.

"Are you ready for this?" Hal asked in the pitch black night. As much as he and Mick had virtually nothing in common in life, Hal deeply wished Mick was still around for the night's mission. Although Hal knew deep down he was a piece of crap, he was still a CEO of a fortune five hundred company, not a burglar and a burglar was exactly what they needed.

"As ready as I'm ever going to be," Jon responded noticeably nervous.

Hal smiled at his son, trying to reassure him that everything was going to be okay. He opened the car door, which triggered the cabin's light. Almost instantly gnats and mosquitoes living in the growing corn started to swarm as the glowing bulb lulled them towards it. Almost as quickly as the bulb turned on, it blinked off as both Jon and Hal shut their doors and moved to the open trunk. Inside were two large black duffle bags filled with the various parts Hal thought they might need along with a cordless drill set and another box set of tools.

"Whoa, this is heavy," Jon remarked as he lifted his duffle bag up and over his shoulder.

"Save your belly-aching. I've got the heavier of the two," Hal returned with a smile and an umph as he raised his up over his head.

Hal handed Jon the cordless drill in its black zippered bag while he took the toolset for himself. Quietly he shut the trunk and began walking. Without a flashlight to guide their way, the night's moon provided all of the light they required. They retraced the car's path along the dusty trail to where it joined with the gravel road, which was glowing an eerie pale yellow from the moon's soft light.

Silently, with only the sound of gravel crunching under their feet, they trekked the quarter mile to Jon's aunt and uncle's farm. The house's lights in what Jon knew was the living room were still on. He wondered what his relatives were still doing up at this late hour. As they made their way further into the middle of the farm, Hal grabbed Jon's arm. He motioned to the house and panted like a dog, worriedly communicating that at any minute their canine friends might make an appearance.

Jon waved away Hal's worry and pointed to the house and then to his watch. Immediately Hal understood Jon's limited charades that this late in the night they were probably inside. As they passed the last tree in front of his relative's house, Jon noticed a car in the driveway he'd never seen before.

Leaving Hal in the middle of the driveway, Jon slinked closer to the car. Hal shot him a look that Jon knew meant, "What in the world do you think you're doing?" Jon continued up to the rear of the unknown car and saw the plates were from Texas. With two fingers, Jon motioned for Hal to come see the car.

Unlike Jon who was curious about whom the plates belonged to, Hal shrugged his shoulders knowing that whoever was inside the house didn't change their plans. He tugged on Jon's arm towards the barn. They left the visitor's car and the occupied house alone and stopped dead in front of the barn's massive wooden door.

Jon stared at the massive slab of wood, knowing this was his one chance to set his life back in order, while Hal feared that when they fixed the machine and turned it on the only decent part of him would disappear into nothingness.

CHAPTER 16

END GAME

Gingerly they each set down their bags of spare parts off to the side of the massive door in a patch of tall uncut grass. Together they grabbed hold of the bottom of the wooden door and lifted while they pushed it to the side. With the door's wheels a few millimeters above the track, the door moved silently to the side, devoid of the shrill squeaking normally accompanied by its movement.

Once the door was open enough for them to squeeze through, they retrieved their duffle bags and proceeded into the barn. Still not wanting to risk attracting any unwanted attention, they slowly walked into the barn's middle without turning on the newly replaced overhead lights. With only a pair of mini flashlights, Hal began pouring over the beat-up machine. Almost instantly he came across a section of wires that were charred black from the previous explosion.

He directed Jon which bag he needed to dive into to find the replacement wires. For over an hour and a half they continued with the same process over and over again. While Hal was meticulously scanning each piece of John Coulter's fusion reactor, Jon acted as his assistant rummaging in between the two duffle bags for the necessary replacement pieces.

Finally after just under two hours, Hal stepped back from the machine and crossed his arms. With the small flashlight he panned over the maze of chrome tubing and brightly colored wires giving it a quick once over.

"I think that's everything," he advised Jon in a hushed tone. "Why don't you grab your light and we'll start at opposite ends to make sure neither one of us has missed anything.

Jon nodded in agreement and started on the machine's left, while Hal started at the right. Slowly and scrupulously they covered every nook and cranny of the giant refrigerator sized device until they were both certain anything that had been damaged in the previous explosion had been replaced.

"So what's next?" Jon asked after Hal was sure there weren't any more repairs that needed to be performed.

"I need to rewire which way the electricity flows through the cell holding the tritium and then I think we're good to go to turn it on," he said almost like he was thinking through the schematic's designs one more time in his head.

"I'm guessing I won't be much of a help with that," Jon stated.

"Unfortunately no, but if you'd help hold the light so I don't accidentally electrocute myself that'd be *very* helpful," Hal returned with a smile.

"Sure, I think I can manage that much," Jon replied and followed his biological father to the middle of the device where it seemed all of the bright silver tubing and colored wires flowed into.

"Man I'm getting tired," Andre yawned. He looked over at Uncle Harold who had fallen asleep over an hour ago in his recliner, tired and stuffed full of Aunt Jenny's peach pie. Andre felt his flat stomach and thought about going back for thirds. However, he didn't want any excess sugar sitting in his belly overnight. That would lead to a few more ounces of fat and he'd worked too hard to get his body into the shape it currently was in.

"I think I'm going to go for a walk," he said through another yawn. "It's safe to go outside around here at night, right?" he asked Aunt Jenny who was busy crocheting something that he still couldn't yet tell what it would end up being.

"Of course. What do you think is out there?" she said, curious at his fear of nature.

"I don't know. We're in the middle of nowhere, maybe there are coyotes and stuff like that," he said feeling stupid for having asked the question.

"Ha ha ha," she laughed. "There are coyotes all right and possums and raccoons and foxes, but unless they're rabid they won't come within a hundred feet of you," Aunt Jenny said trying to comfort Andre's irrational fears of the open country.

"Rabid?" Beth asked, pulling her head up from the couch's comfortable armrest. She was only seconds away from falling asleep herself in the quiet farmhouse, but Andre sparking up a new conversation was bringing her senses back. Being a city kid all of her life, like Andre, she knew relatively little about farming in the Midwest. She knew there were animals all over the place, but she hadn't a clue what being rabid meant.

"Don't tell me you haven't ever heard of rabies before," Aunt Jenny said in disbelief.

"Oh, rabies. Yeah, of course I've heard of them before. I guess I'm just tired," Beth said, a little embarrassed at her question. Now that Aunt Jenny had spelled out what it meant, Beth figured if she'd been a little more awake she would have made the connection.

"You do have to worry about rabies when you're out here. We've had two instances with rabid animals and both of them were skunks. Once one tried to get in the front door while Harry was out. The neighbor came over and shot it dead with his rifle that time though. The second one was worse. It was a skunk too and it got under our front porch where the dogs and cats like to keep cool. Well, our dog killed that critter, which was good, but then Harry had to take the dog and all of the cats out south of the farm and shoot them just in case they had been scratched by the skunk."

"That's so sad," Beth lamented.

"Yep, not such a good reward for a dog who was just doing his job. But rabies is a nasty little beast and back then the treatment wasn't as readily available as it is today. Even today if you take too long to find out if you're infected, you might not live."

"Sheesh, that's kind of creepy," Andre said once Aunt Jenny was done telling the sad story. "Well, against my better judgment after hearing all of that, I still think I'm going to take a walk. Beth do you want to come with?" he asked.

"Sure, why not. But I think I'm going to bed after we get back," she said. The time was close to one in the morning. If Jon was going to come, she thought he would have been here by now. Plus, if there were police occasionally checking on the property, maybe they had scared him off?

Since it was the middle of summer, the night was still plenty warm. The clouds beginning to form overhead and the incoming higher humidity were only adding to the night's already stuffy warm air.

"I wonder if we're going to get some storms tonight?" Andre remarked at the building clouds. Just outside of the house's door, they watched as one of the giant forming thunderheads swallowed the moon's light, covering the entire farm in darkness. Each of them whipped out their cell phones and turned on their flashlight apps. Sure it drained the phones battery faster than almost anything else, but they could let their phones charge overnight if need be.

For a few minutes they walked towards the road and listened to the night's sounds. In one direction they heard an owl hoot while in the opposite direction a coyote howled. The mournful cry of the dog-like creature sent a shiver up Andre's spine making him want to retreat into the safety of the house. However, he stood his ground and shifted slightly closer to Beth. If they wanted a meal, she would have to do.

Eventually they turned around and decided to take one loop around the barn, repair shop and Aunt Jenny's vegetable garden. As they walked along the farm's gravel drive, the rustling of the trees died down to where their footsteps were the only sound they heard. Andre was almost positive it would be raining by morning.

As they neared the barn, they began noticing an ever so slight amount of weak light escaping through some of the structure's old slats of wood. Wide-eyed they looked at each other in the hope that Jon was inside the barn. Quietly they crept to the open door and peered inside. To their delight at the far end of the barn was Jon holding a flashlight for a man they recognized from his parents' funeral.

"That must be his new daddy," Andre taunted after pulling his head out of the opening.

Beth snickered and nodded her head. "What should we do?"

"I think we should call the cops and then go inside with them. I don't want to be kept off to the side when he's taken down, but if we're with him we'll get front row seats," Andre surmised.

Andre turned off the light on his phone and dialed 911.

"911, what is your emergency?" the lady asked.

"Yeah, I'm at…" Andre held his hand over the phone's receiver. "What's their last name?" he asked Beth.

She shrugged her shoulders in return. "Your guess is as good as mine. The police already know about his place, just tell them who it is and I'm sure the message will get through," Beth advised.

"Yeah, um I don't know their last names, but we're at Jenny and Harold's whatever their last name is farm and Jon Coulter is hiding out in their barn."

"Don't get them in trouble," Beth chided Andre as he had made it sound like his aunt and uncle were complicit in his hiding.

"Oh, sorry, I know for a fact that the owners don't know he's here," Andre added.

"Okay, he's a wanted in two homicides so do not approach him. Just stay where you are and we'll send the police right away," she said. The 911 operator asked Andre if he wanted her to stay on the phone, but he declined and hung up soon after. Itching to rub it in Jon's face that they had alerted the police of his whereabouts and that they would be the reason for his arrest, Beth and Andre stepped into the barn to confront him.

Just crossing the Kansas border into Nebraska, Detective Briggs' cell phone rang. Normally someone who was more than happy to be alone and have his quiet time to reflect on life and his caseload, the detective gladly answered the phone. A little past one thirty in the morning, he was growing groggy and his eyelids were starting to feel heavier than he would have liked.

"This is Briggs," he said.

"Sir, this is Natalie Yost with the Grand Island dispatch service. I was told to alert you that there's been a sighting of Jon Coulter at his aunt and uncle's house."

Detective Briggs sat straight up rigid in his seat. The blonde beauty had been right; Jon was going to his relative's house. After what he had heard happened at the farmstead the last time Jon was there, the detective feared for the lad's safety. The reality of the detective once liking Jon and now not, didn't play on his mind one iota. For ten long hours he'd driven in silence, pouring over the facts of the Coulter case.

Somewhere around the eighth hour he'd come to the conclusion that Jon Coulter was most definitely innocent. A fact he lamented only for the reason he would have liked to see the pompous kid crap his pants at being sentenced life. But facts where facts and the kid was innocent.

Detective Briggs thanked the dispatcher for the update and floored his unmarked car. He pulled a small red siren out from underneath the dash and with its thick magnet stuck it to the top of his car. He pushed the cabled attachment into the car's cigarette lighter. Immediately, though without any sound, he could see flashes of red light blurring against the hood of his car as the red strobe light whirled in its glass ball overhead. With close to one hundred miles left to the relative's farm, Detective Briggs knew he was racing against time to save Jon's life.

Jon wasn't sure why, but for some reason he felt like someone was watching him. Still holding the flashlight where Hal was directing, Jon peered over his shoulder towards the open door. He froze as a small light illuminated two hazy figures.

"Hey, I think we've got company," Jon said, not moving the flashlight an inch.

Hal looked up from his meticulous attempt at rewiring the reactor's electricity flow, following Jon's eyes to the barn's open doors. Although he couldn't make out exactly who the figures were, he was instantly worried at the size of the larger one. From the hazy outline he could see the larger of the two's muscular arms and broad shoulders as he lumbered into the dimly lit set of stalls.

"I knew you'd be here," Beth said through gritted teeth as she entered the main area of the barn.

"Yeah, and we called the cops on the both of you just so we could be here when you get arrested," Andre taunted right behind her. He turned back to the barn's entrance and turned on the overhead lights, washing away Jon and Hal's secrecy.

Jon wanted to say he was glad to see them. He wanted to ask them why they hated him so much and why they wanted to see him in handcuffs, but he didn't. He knew the answer. The only thing that mattered now was buying Hal enough time to fix the device before the police or even worse, his uncle arrived.

"Stall them," Hal said quietly so only Jon could hear. He looked up at the bright yellow-orange bulbs overhead and was relieved his small flashlight was no longer needed. "I just need a little bit longer to finish this," he added as though he was reading Jon's mind.

"I just want both of you to know, regardless of what happens that I love you both," Jon said taking a step forward, distancing himself from the machine and Hal. "Andre, you've been my best friend for four years now and I've never known somebody more loyal and likable than you."

Andre folded his arms in protest at Jon calling them friends and spat on the floor.

"And you Beth," Jon said taking a step closer. "I've loved you more than any person ever in my life; more than my parents, more than my aunt and uncle and even more than myself. I'd do anything for you," he said, growing emotional just at thinking of his feelings toward the beautiful blonde.

"Would you drop dead?" she said with as much hate and ferocity as her normally good-natured mind could muster.

Jon smiled to himself and shook his head back and forth knowing she didn't mean what she was saying.

"Enough talk," Andre said, roughly pushing Beth to the side. "You cost me two hundred bucks for that little stunt you pulled in Columbus and now I'm going to beat it out of you," Andre said menacingly, taking two steps forward. Andre didn't intend Beth any harm, but his mind was clouded by rage from being in such close vicinity with someone he loathed as much as Jon.

"Hey, don't push her," Jon said protectively and stepped towards Andre. The two well-built males were only feet apart. Although Andre was thicker than Jon, Jon was taller by a little over two inches. If they ever seriously fought, one would be hard-pressed to pick the winner.

"Don't defend me," Beth spat and slapped Jon across his face, leaving a bright red handprint. "Don't you *ever* defend me! I can take care of myself!" she yelled, blinded by rage and hate.

In a moment their heated tempers exploded. Andre shoved Jon backwards, while Jon cursed at his old friend. Jon knew he needed to buy more time for Hal, but for the moment he was just trying to protect himself. Beth was yelling at them both, wanting to see Andre beat Jon unconscious.

Soon Jon and Andre were rolling on the hay-covered floor throwing punches, each trying to knock out the other. Beth continued yelling every vile phrase and hateful word she could think of at her ex-boyfriend, even delivering a few kicks when the opportunity presented itself.

Out of nowhere a loud blast, like an explosion sounded at the barn's entrance. In mid punch, both Andre and Jon paused, looking at the door. As a bolt of lightning flashed in the distance, they saw Uncle Harold holding his beloved shotgun with both of his dogs by his side. A light sprinkle was now falling and a small trail of steam was flowing off of the gun's barrel as the small drops sizzled from its heat.

"Now that's enough!" Uncle Harold yelled. "Knock that crap off Andre. This is my property and I'm going to deal with these trespassers my way," Uncle Harold snarled. He wiped away the rain from his forehead and entered the barn. The two wet and mangy looking dogs trailed close behind, followed by Aunt Jenny.

Andre smirked at Jon. "Now you're going to get it," he said before giving Jon one final shove back onto the ground.

Both Beth and Andre stepped back as Uncle Harold approached. They gave him, his gun and his wet dogs a wide berth, hoping he was going to make Jon suffer. Hal looked over his shoulder at the growing crowd, but continued diligently rewiring the device. He was almost done and it appeared he hadn't a second to spare before the situation turned really ugly.

As Jon started to push himself off the dusty hay-covered floor, Uncle Harold, quicker than Jon had ever seen him move before, smacked the end of the barrel of the shotgun across his face, sending him back to the floor. For a few brief seconds Jon saw stars from the thick metal making contact with his skull. He rolled over, groaning at the aching side of his face.

"You'd stay down if you knew what was good for you," Uncle Harold growled.

"All of you stay where you are," someone with a clear voice ordered from the barn's entrance. Of the five people, all of them looked at the four newly arrived policemen except Hal. He only had two more wires to reattach and then he was ready to turn on the device. He hoped with everything he had that his theory would work.

"This is private property and this man is trespassing. I have the right to defend myself against intruders," Uncle Harold yelled at the police officers. He refused to lower his gun, keeping it pointed at Jon's face.

"I said lower your weapon," the officer repeated. He, along with the other three policemen, walked into the large open room with their guns drawn. The rain was now falling much harder than before. The barn's old wood slatted roof was dripping, where cracks had formed throughout the years, while the sound of thousands of raindrops hitting above was almost deafening.

"Arrest him then!" Andre yelled. The police glared at Andre as he took a step closer to Uncle Harold. Immediately upon approach the old farmer's dogs began growling.

"Don't tell us our job young man. Now all of you back away. And you with the shotgun, nothing is going to get resolved until you lower your weapon," the head peacekeeper ordered.

"Do what he says, no one needs to get hurt here," Detective Briggs added, stepping into barn from the torrential downpour outside.

"Sheesh, how many people can this barn hold?" Andre scoffed at another person now entering the fray. At least Detective Briggs was on their side and the police would have to listen to him.

"Guys, lower your weapons," the detective advised his brothers-in-arms.

"We don't report to you," one of them returned with a glare.

"Just put your weapons down. Everything will be okay. I know all of these people, just let me try and talk to them. The last thing we need is people dying for nothing," Detective Briggs added.

Reluctantly the police that had been dispatched to the scene lowered their weapons. Not one of them holstered their guns, but lowering them to their sides was at least a start. While Detective Briggs passed the officers, approaching Uncle Harold and Aunt Jenny, Hal affixed the final wire into place.

"There, all done," he said to himself. All that needed to happen now was for the device to be turned on. Hal carefully stepped down the small ladder he had been standing on and walked to Jon's side. He looked at Uncle Harold who still had his gun pointed at Jon and felt an odd feeling of déjà vu, like he'd been here before some time not long ago.

"We're all set," Hal said to Jon as he reached down to help him off the hard floor. Uncle Harold shook his shotgun menacingly at Jon as he slowly got up, but did nothing more. As Jon stood, his Uncle didn't raise the gun, but stayed rigid like a mannequin, with the gun's jet-black barrel pointing at the floor.

"Lower your gun Harold," Detective Briggs ordered now ten feet away from him. He was holding both of his hands in the air, trying to prove he wasn't a threat. Beads of rain still sat atop his bald head and his tan light jacket was soaked from the night's storm.

"Aren't you going to arrest him?" Andre yelled taking a step closer to which Harold, who was standing in between him and the detective. Andre didn't notice the two dogs going rigid and growling with anger at him approaching their master.

"Son, just settle down. This doesn't concern you right now. I know you and your friend here," he said glancing at Beth, "were lying about Jon's involvement in his parents' murder. I blame myself for wanting to listen to your lies. I don't believe this man has done anything wrong, so back up and let me do my job."

"That's not fair," Andre yelled and took another step closer. For each of the rain soaked dogs, Andre crossed an invisible barrier that he shouldn't have at that moment. As if their brains were united as one, they lunged at the same time towards Andre. One dog ran behind Uncle Harold to get at Andre, while the other ran in front of his master, throwing him off balance.

As if it were in slow motion, Hal saw Uncle Harold unintentionally jerk the gun into the damp air with his hand still on the trigger. Hal threw Jon behind him harder than he intended to and into the repaired fusion reactor. While Jon was being thrown back, Uncle Harold's shotgun discharged into Hal's exposed chest from five feet away.

No one had a chance to react as Jon, half a second later, smashed with his back into the bright green ON switch in the middle of the machine. The barn's lights dimmed as the reactor turned on and began sucking away at the farm's available electricity. For a brief second a bright golden-yellow burst of energy formed in the reactor's tritium chamber just before the machine exploded like before, in five places at once.

Each of the barn's overhanging light bulbs burst as an enormous amount of electricity was returned through their wires from the reactor's explosion, showering the dilapidated structure's floor in sparks and shards of broken glass. Immediately the barn's dry hay started smoldering and then burst into flame.

However none of them initially gave much care to the growing embers around them. They were each mesmerized by a growing ball of brilliant blue light surrounded by the purest white they had ever seen inside of the tritium chamber. Initially, for a few seconds, the ball of pure blue seemed to grow larger until it filled the entire clear glass chamber. With one gigantic pulse the chamber ruptured and the brilliant blue ball flattened into a giant disc before shooting out in all directions.

Jon pulled himself off the smoldering floor and was holding onto the device as the spectacular disc of light burst forth and passed through him as though he was made of air. He watched it continue as it flowed through everyone around him as it began picking up speed, eventually disappearing through the barn's wooden walls outside. Jon looked to his right through the barn's open door and watched the blue and white disc of light spread out across the landscape, finally disappearing against the horizon.

Beth and Andre were touching their chests, trying to ascertain if they were okay. The four police officers were looking each other over as well, seemingly relieved that the strange light that had coursed through their bodies hadn't caused any damage.

COUGH, COUGH, COUGH

Jon was pulled out of his foggy haze by Hal coughing on the barn's floor. The fire was beginning to grow stronger around the barn; strong enough that smoke was filling its insides even with the main door wide open.

Jon dropped to his knees and grabbed his biological father in his arms. His chest was a mess of blood and singed fabric. Knowing he was dying, Hal looked up at his son, lovingly holding him in his arms. Although Hal's love for him had quickly faded after the machine's explosion, for some reason he still had the uncontrollable urge to come clean. Regardless if his desire was stemming from his conscience or simply the dormant humanity buried deep inside of him, he coughed and weakly looked Jon in the eyes.

"Jon I'm sorry for the man that I am; you deserve better. I paid Mick to kill your dad so I could have another chance with your mom," Hal admitted. Hearing the words come out of his mouth, his plan couldn't at the moment have sounded more insane. If he hadn't been shot, Hal would have found the nearest bar, grabbed a drink and tried to put the moves on the drunkest chic, not caring about his son at all.

However, he was shot and what was worse both of his legs were starting to grow numb. He was a thief, a scoundrel, a murder, but regardless of what he was, this was his one chance to do something out of his nature.

He looked up at Jon's hurt, but all-knowing eyes. Jon had been fairly certain Hal had played a role in his parents' deaths and wasn't shocked by his biological father's admittance of guilt.

"You don't deserve to die," Jon said with a tear in his eye. Even though the man lying in his arms had destroyed his life, he was still holding his dying father.

Jon glanced up and saw everyone standing around him. Not one of the officers were holding their guns anymore. His uncle's shotgun lay further behind them on the barn's floor. He could once again see Beth's love for him in her eyes as tears poured down her face at the sad scene. Uncle Harold's arm was coiled around his wife as she too was crying.

"Don't hate me," Hal whispered, unable to speak with his usually strong voice. "Everything that I have is yours," he said. In that brief moment, Hal came to the understanding that everything in his life that he'd accomplished up to this point was worthless. He now knew Jon was by far his best creation, not *Evergreen Resources* and all of the battles he'd won. He deserved to die alone, but even after telling his son he'd been responsible for the deaths of his mom and adopted father, Jon was still lovingly cradling him in his arms. He deserved so much worse. Hal took one more look at his son before closing his eyes and breathing his last.

A tear fell from Jon's eye and splashed on the forehead of his father the monster.

"Jon, we need to go," Detective Briggs said without hate, but with a sense of urgency. The fire was quickly spreading across the floor and into the lofts above. There wasn't much time before the entire barn was going to be set ablaze.

"Men, get the body," the detective ordered the four officers. Without question or hesitation they pulled Hal's lifeless body off of the floor and hurried him outside into the warm rain.

Jon stood up alone and followed the officers with Detective Briggs at his side. Uncle Harold and Aunt Jenny along with Beth and Andre followed behind. Neither of the four knew what to say to Jon, they had each treated him so horrible they were ashamed beyond words. Neither of them could understand why they had treated him as the vilest human in the world, but the fact was they had.

Outside in the rain, everyone turned and watched the entire barn be consumed by the brilliant orange and yellow fire. For an instant Jon turned his eyes from the fire and looked at Beth, who was staring back at him. At seeing him look at her, she burst into tears thinking there was no way possible to make amends for her actions. She'd treated the person she loved most in life like a vile disease, which she would regret the rest of her existence.

Although hardened by the experience of those he loved most turning against him, Jon's heart melted at seeing Beth's tears. He ran to her and embraced her with all of his muscles in the pouring rain.

He pulled her face off his shoulders with his hands and stared into those beautiful blue eyes dancing with images of the fire in the background.

"I love you so much," he said and the rain continued washing her tears away.

"I love you too," she sobbed. "Please forgive me. I don't hate you. I don't know…"

Jon stopped her mid-sentence, "I know, you don't have to say it. Everything is okay now. Just tell me you'll marry me and we'll forget this ever happened."

Beth's eyes opened wide, unable to fathom how this wonderful person she'd treated so poorly still wanted her. His love for her drove her into inconsolable sobs, as tears mixed with rainwater streamed down her beautiful face. In between bouts of sobbing and sniffing, she was able to get out the word, "yes".

Jon pulled her back in, letting her cry on his shoulder as everyone else continued watching the barn slowly burn to the ground. Regardless of the heavy rain, the amount of leftover hay and decades of old dry wood the barn had been made of provided ample fuel. An hour after the sparks from the lights above had fallen on the hay; the barn was nothing but a pile of smoldering rubble. Everything inside of it, including Jon's father's fusion reactor, had been burnt to a crisp. And Jon was glad.

Epilogue

After the police had finished their investigation only a few hours after the sun had risen, Jon and the others watched as the police examiner's van was the last to drive off the property with Hal's body tightly wrapped inside.

"I still don't understand what the hell happened," Uncle Harold said scratching his head. "I mean I hated you so much. If you would have died I don't think I would have cared a bit, but it doesn't make any sense." Everyone but Jon nodded at his uncle's comment, feeling the same way.

"Why don't we go inside and I'll tell you guys all about it," Jon said. After Aunt Jenny had finished providing the detective, Jon, his fiancé and Andre and Uncle Harold with a large piece of her famous peach pie with ice cream, they moved into the living room where Jon spent over two hours filling them in on the past two weeks of his life.

Through bouts of tears and laughter he recounted the trials and tribulations each of them had put him through. From Uncle Harold trying to blast him with his shotgun, to hiding on top of the elevator at *Evergreen Resources*; Jon laid everything out on the table.

"Wow, that's one whopper of a tale," Detective Briggs said after Jon finished his story. "If I hadn't been part of all of this I'd have never believed it. No way any of this is going in my report though. They'd throw me into the looney bin for sure."

"I acted like such an idiot," Andre said. "I still don't understand how I could end up hating you for nothing," he said turning to Jon.

"It's not a big deal. Everybody sucks from time to time, you guys just happened to be in a really bad mood for two weeks," he joked.

"Well I need to get back on the road back towards Dallas. I want to see how far I can get before I have to grab a nap," the detective said standing. "Jon, you take your time. As far as I'm concerned the case concerning your parents is closed. Mick and Hal are dead and I promise you won't have any more trouble from me," he said with a smile.

Jon rose from his seat and shook the detective's hand, wishing him well as he left the farmhouse's quaint insides. As Jon sat back down, Beth wanted to make a joke about her finger not having a ring on it, but still being too ashamed of her actions she decided against it.

She scooted closer to Jon as he resumed his seat on the couch and intertwined her arm inside of his. She loved him so much and she vowed that for the rest of her life she would try to make up for that past few weeks' happenings.

"Sorry again about trying to blow your head off," Uncle Harold apologized. "After that first explosion, when I saw your face I couldn't think of anything except how much I hated you. You know, the whole blinded by rage thing? That's the only way I can explain it."

"Hey, none of you guys need to keep apologizing for any of this. It was all that stupid reactor's fault and now that it has been reduced to ashes, nobody'll have to ever go through this again. I'm just lucky Hal figured out how to reverse the wiring and get everything back to normal," Jon replied to everyone, to which they all agreed.

Like Detective Briggs, even though they had gone without much sleep the previous night, they were all still too wired to sleep. Eventually Uncle Harold turned on the TV, which was on the national news channel.

Ironically, Hal's picture was plastered on the front of the screen as the reporter droned on about one of the richest men in America dying earlier that day.

"Turn it up Harry," Aunt Jenny ordered.

The reporter continued giving his spiel, "...and with the death of Hal Roberts we have learned that *Evergreen Resources* has been turned over to his son Jon Coulter. As of now that means he has inherited just north of five hundred million dollars..."

The reporter continued talking, but none of them heard a word. From all of the tragedy and heartache, Jon was finally getting some fantastic news. He had his family and friends back, he had helped change his father's soul in the last moments of his life and now he was a millionaire.

"Fantastic! Now you've got enough money to pay for the barn you burned down!" Uncle Harold joked with a smile.

Jon laughed as he knew he could afford to buy his uncle five thousand barns and barely bat an eye based on *Evergreen Resources'* net worth. Jon, Beth and Andre stayed at his aunt and uncle's farm for the next few days, rehashing the previous weeks' events over and over again. Not one of them could fathom how a random piece of machinery could warp their opinions of one of their favorite people. But the fact was that it did.

Jon thought of Hal and Mick from time to time, but as the days progressed, the little time he had spent with each of them seemed to fade. He wished he had gotten to know Hal better before his death, but he wished the same for his parents too.

Eventually they went their separate ways for a few months until they were all brought back together again for Jon and Beth's wedding, which they jointly decided should be had in the middle of Aunt Jenny and Uncle Harold's new barn. With wood still glowing with golden youthfulness, the barn was the perfect place for their wedding.

With Jon's ownership of the Fortune 500 Company, money wasn't a problem, which allowed them to fly in guests from around the United States, especially Beth's somewhat irritated family who couldn't understand why the wedding wasn't taking place in her hometown of Columbus, Ohio.

In the end their special day was completely perfect. The smell of the freshly cut cedar barn mixed with the country corn and alfalfa created a destination wedding no one would soon forget. Even the evening's cloudless sky, where every single star was easily visible due to the sparely populated countryside was magical.

During the past three months with Jon being fully consumed with his and Beth's wedding plans and following honeymoon, Jon was rarely seen at his company's corporate office. He wasn't worried though, as the company had a board of directors who knew what they were doing and would keep the company headed in the right direction. In fact, he figured they were probably happy that the new majority owner, a kid barely out of college was keeping his distance.

However, none of that really mattered to Jon. His only item of business when he would eventually make it back to Dallas was to see if his dad had any more of his crazy hidden ideas...

Thanks for reading. If you enjoyed this book please take a moment to leave a review and let others know what you think.

Below is the first chapter of Lightning, the first book in the World's Divide set of novellas. It can be downloaded for free from all major ebook suppliers.

Please visit my website at www.ryanhartung.com. I'd love to hear from you!

WORLD'S DIVIDE
BOOK 1

1

B OOM!
   Dust filled the chamber, clouding Colt Andrews's view. Coughing, he waved his hands, trying with little success to shoo the floating
dust particles away. The other two members of his tiny archeological
search team took a few steps backward as the dust slowly dissipated.

   Colt slapped his worn blue jeans and tan button-down shirt
with his red and yellowed-white baseball cap, causing miniature
dust clouds to explode off his clothes. As the dust continued settling, Colt grimaced as the damage to the ancient stone temple door
became more apparent.

   "I said push the door. Not break it down," Colt said scolding his
assistant Dominic Barboa; who was still lying on the temple's sandy
floor. Dominic had tried to budge the solid rock door by running
and hitting it at full speed, only to bounce off its solid surface and
onto the ground. However, the momentum built by his sprinting
start had nevertheless done the trick. But instead of pushing the
heavy stone slab inward, Dominic's rushing attack had hit the upper
half of the door, knocking it off its center of gravity and causing the

massive slab to crash to the floor.

"Sorry boss, guess I screwed up huh?" Dominic sullenly replied as he stood.

"Naw, we needed that door opened one way or another. The way I see it, you just saved us over a week's time by not having to get a team in here to move it the right way," Colt replied half joking while half serious. Colt paused before entering the newly unsealed room and fingered the Greek name for Zeus etched into the temple wall. "What I want to know is what are ancient Greek and Roman symbols and text doing in a temple in the middle of the Amazon? Can either of you tell me that?"

Colt Andrews—or Sir Colt Andrews as the Queen of England had just knighted him three months ago, was one of the finest archeologists in the world. His attention to detail and immeasurable knowledge of ancient civilizations, coupled with an almost prophetic knack of discovering lost treasures left him with no equals.

Three weeks ago, deep in the Peruvian portion of the Amazon rainforest, a group three American hikers had trekked to a remote citadel of the ancient Chachapoyas people. Unlike Peru's other darker-skinned ancient tribes, this particular race had been called the Warriors of the Clouds, as they were white skinned and had blonde hair.

While traveling through the ruins of the ancient city, the trio had accidentally stumbled upon a hidden underground passageway leading to a richly decorated temple after one of their party fell through a weakened tile slab outside of the citadel. The Peruvian government had then called the most respected archeologist in the world to come make sense of their newfound labyrinth.

"I don't know, maybe those other Americans carved it into the rock to screw with us," Colt's other assistant and girlfriend Hillary Chapman joked.

"Do you guys see that?" Colt asked, not paying attention to the joke. He pointed to a thin sliver of light emanating from a crack at the base of a far wall in the adjacent room.

"See what Colt?" Dominic asked. He squinted, but still didn't see anything. From Dominic's position the sun's bright light was still seeping into the ancient carved tunnel too much and was thus washing out any weaker sources of illumination.

"Follow me guys and watch your step," Colt ordered. He stepped through the threshold of the fallen door and into the next even more dimly lit room. After their eyes had adjusted to the room's darkness, Colt asked them again. "You two see it now?" He crouched low to the ground and waved his hand along the rocky crevice. For a few seconds his hand glowed a pale yellow. As he moved his hand away from the wall the yellow light again dissipated into the dark room.

"What do you make of it?" Hillary asked.

"I'm not exactly sure Hill. None of this makes any sense. What was a tribe of Caucasians doing in the Amazon? And why are these Roman and Greek symbols carved in only these underground rooms; not up above? I don't know why yet, but they must be interconnected somehow. Let's get out our flashlights and see what this next wall has to say."

Although the first two rooms had contained adequate lighting from the sun's afternoon rays as they shone through the American's accidental hole, the new more secluded chamber was beyond their reaches.

As the explores entered the new chamber, three sources of unnatural pure white light switched on, bathing the room's far wall in their eerie glow. The team's flashlights, although powerful, were not a match for the sun's brilliant rays, causing the explorers to venture even closer to the far wall. The wall appeared to be one massive continuous slab of dark brown stone with another similar doorway cut into its middle. Colt shifted his attention from the wall and to the singular door. Etched into the giant stone slab was more of the ancient Greek writing.

"What's it say?" Dominic quizzically asked. This being only his fourth trip with the world-renowned archeologist, Dominic had yet to pick up on the subtle differences between the ancient languages. When he had first agreed to join the team, Colt had left what Dominic considered a laughably huge stack of language and history books in his beaten up truck for some *light* nighttime reading. Dominic now wished he had at least opened a few of thick dusty books instead of scattering them around his messy apartment.

Colt studied the stone door. Carved lightning bolts surrounded the door's edges. The bottom half of the stone slab featured another singular lightning bolt, which was ten times the size of the smaller ones adorning the door's edges. The top half of the stone slab however, was covered in ancient Greek.

"It says. HERE LIES ZEUS, THE GOD OF LIGHTNING'S FINAL RESTING PLACE. THERE CAN BE ONLY ONE ZEUS." Colt read and scratched his head.

"What the heck does that mean?" Dominic asked.

"Not a clue. Only one way to find out though," Colt replied with a wry smile. He reached into his backpack and pulled out a long black iron crow bar.

Concerned, Hillary rested a soft hand on his arm. "What are you thinking? You can't just pry the door open. What if you damage it? Whatever's behind that piece of rock could be the find of the century."

"I know," Colt replied and patted her hand with his, trying to ease her worry. "Dom already busted down the first door and I *need* to see where that light is coming from."

Hillary saw the determination in Colt's eyes and reluctantly released her grasp and took a step back. Colt grabbed the iron tool and jabbed it into the door's sealed side with all his might. Chips of splintered rock sprayed his sweat-soaked shirt.

"No turning back now," Hillary muttered, unconvinced Colt's idea was a good one. Colt put his back into the crow bar and pushed with all of his might. The door didn't budge. He took a step back, leaving the crow bar precariously hanging out of the wall. Colt spit into his hands and rubbed them together.

"Here's looking at you Dom," he said and took a running start towards the iron tool. An "umph," escaped Colt's lungs and mouth as his impact with the rigid metal bar forced out any excess air. Undeterred by the brief loss of stale unused air, he continued prying against the door and dug his shoes into the hard ground. Finally, the rough sound of rock grating on rock began to hum throughout the room. The door opened an inch and stopped. Although barely ajar, the unmistakable odd pale yellow light was now showing through the entire side of the partially opened stone door.

"Hey, wanna give me a hand here?" Colt asked Dominic optimistically.

"Sure. I've already broken one priceless artifact, what's another," he dryly replied. Dominic's two hundred pound Hispanic frame, when added to Colt's thickly muscled core, made quick work of the rocky doorway. With two coordinated pushes, using the crowbar as leverage, they opened the door enough to where they were able to wrap their fingers along the back of the door's side and begin pulling. Hillary then helped the two burley men scrape the massive slap of rock along the floor's smoothed stone tiles.

Once the stone door was fully opened, they each stared in awe. The pale white light from the inner room bathed them and their surroundings. It almost seemed brighter than the sun. Initially the light was too bright to look at directly, but as time passed their retinas adjusted to where brief glances at the object stopped initiating immediate watering of the eyes.

"I'm going in," Colt determinedly announced. With a hand he shielded his eyes and took a small step forward.

"Are you loco?" Dominic gasped. "You don't know what the heck that thing is. It's not natural, that's for sure. Maybe it's alien, maybe it really is from Zeus. I don't give a crap. Seriously, you shouldn't go in there."

"He's right," Hillary said. "That light's not natural. You better be careful." Hillary knew when it came to Colt's work the only person he ever listened to was himself. His belief in himself was what had made him so successful. Ever since she'd known Colt, he'd marched to his own tune. Maybe that was one of the reasons she was so attracted to him. What woman didn't want an overly confident man, whose sole purpose in life was to travel for adventure and fun?

Dominic and Hillary nervously watched as Colt disappeared into the room filled with light. Once inside the chamber, Colt was barely able to open his eyes more than the tiniest of slits. The light inside was pure and blinding. He wasn't sure how big the room was, maybe twelve feet by twelve feet? All Colt knew, was that the unknown object emitting the freakishly bright light was growing closer with each step.

As he continued, carefully footing his steps forward, he felt the room's temperature increasing the closer the light became. After a couple more steps, Colt's foot kicked something solid. He'd been in enough temples and seen enough Indiana Jones movies to guess the solid object was resting on a pedestal or some type of alter.

Nervously and with shaking fingers, he reached out. His breathing quickened while sweat beaded from every pore on his body. He touched the object.

ZZZIIIIIIINNNNNNNNGGGGGG!

Electricity pulsed through Colt's body. Pain. The only sensation he felt was pain. The electrical force of the shock blew him out of his shoes and against the room's far wall. His senses went dead.

Please visit my website at www.ryanhartung.com. I'd love to hear from you!

Links to the full novella, Lightning!
http://www.barnesandnoble.com/w/lightning-ryan-hartung/1120206288?ean=2940046125559

http://www.amazon.com/Lightning-Book-1-Worlds-Divide-ebook/dp/B00MVHZEEM/ref=sr_1_1?ie=UTF8&qid=1411052980&sr=8-1&keywords=ryan+hartung

https://www.smashwords.com/books/view/469341

Acknowledgments

I am extremely grateful for my loving wife Elizabeth, for without her love and support this book would not have been possible.

I would also like to thank Nick Proudlove for his proofreading and always being anxious for the next few chapters.

Finally I would like to thank Zackary Capewell. of Raven Tree Designs for his exquisite covers and unwavering support throughout the publication process.

ABOUT THE AUTHOR

Dr. Ryan E. Hartung spent most of his life growing up in rural Nebraska. After earning his Ph. D. in organic chemistry from the Ohio State University he then made a quick stop with his family in the garden state before finally settling in Tucson, Arizona. Ryan continues to live in Tucson with his wife Elizabeth, his two daughters Amber and Keira, their dog Ginger and currently untamed hamster Brave.

CONTACT RYAN

Ryanhartung1953@gmail.com
www.facebook.com/ryanhartungauthor

To find out about Ryan's other books and projects visit www.ryan-hartung.com, and be sure to sign up to the mailing.list.
You will get updates on new relases and exciting news.

www.ingramcontent.com/pod-product-compliance
Lightning Source LLC
Chambersburg PA
CBHW061615170626
46811CB00001B/439